Fantastic Four

DOOMED IF YOU DON'T

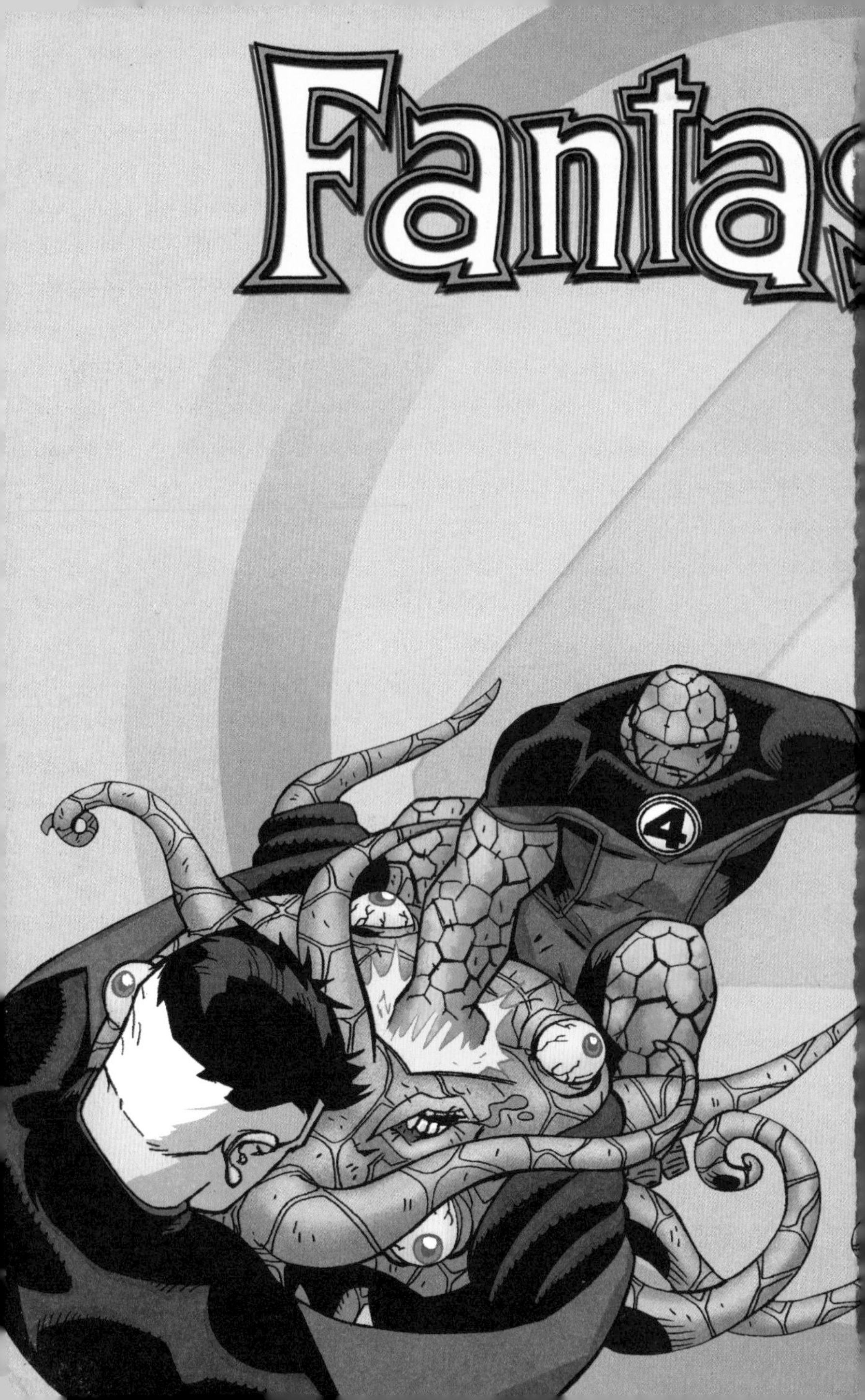
Fantas
4

tic Four

DOOMED IF YOU DON'T

Writer:
Paul Tobin
Artist:
David Hahn
Colors: **Sotocolor's Andrew Dalhouse**
Letterer: **Blambot's Nate Piekos**

Cover Artists: **Clayton Henry with Guru eFX,
Salva Espin with Wil Quintana
and Tom Grummet with Chris Sotomayor**

Consulting Editor: **Ralph Macchio**
Editor: **Nate Cosby**

Collection Editor: **Cory Levine**
Editorial Assistant: **Alex Starbuck**
Assistant Editor: **John Denning**
Editors, Special Projects: **Jennifer Grünwald
& Mark D. Beazley**
Senior Editor, Special Projects: **Jeff Youngquist**
Senior Vice President of Sales: **David Gabriel**
Vice President of Creative: **Tom Marvelli**
Production: **Jerron Quality Color & Jerry Kalinowski**

Editor in Chief: **Joe Quesada**
Publisher: **Dan Buckley**
Executive Producer: **Alan Fine**

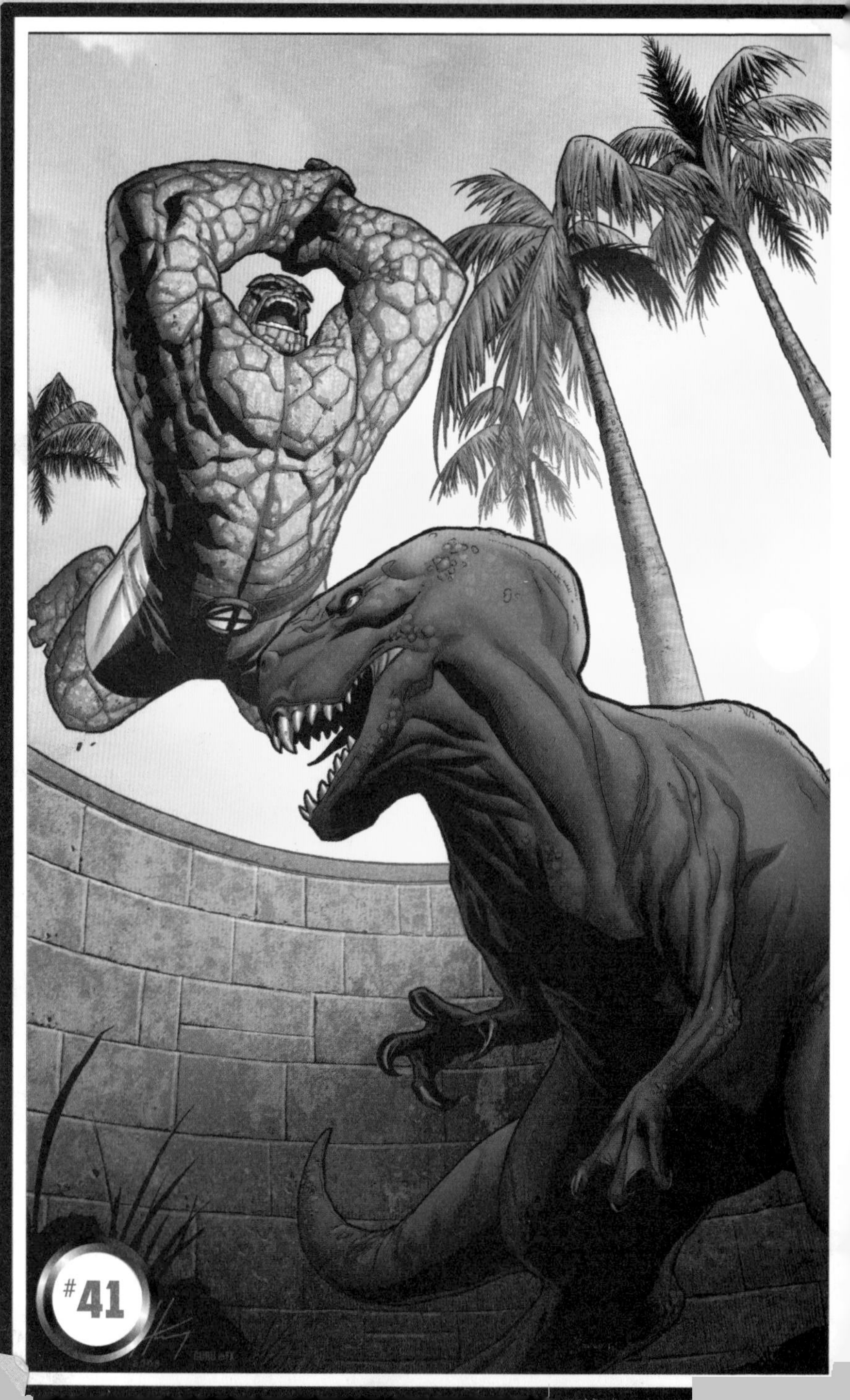
#41

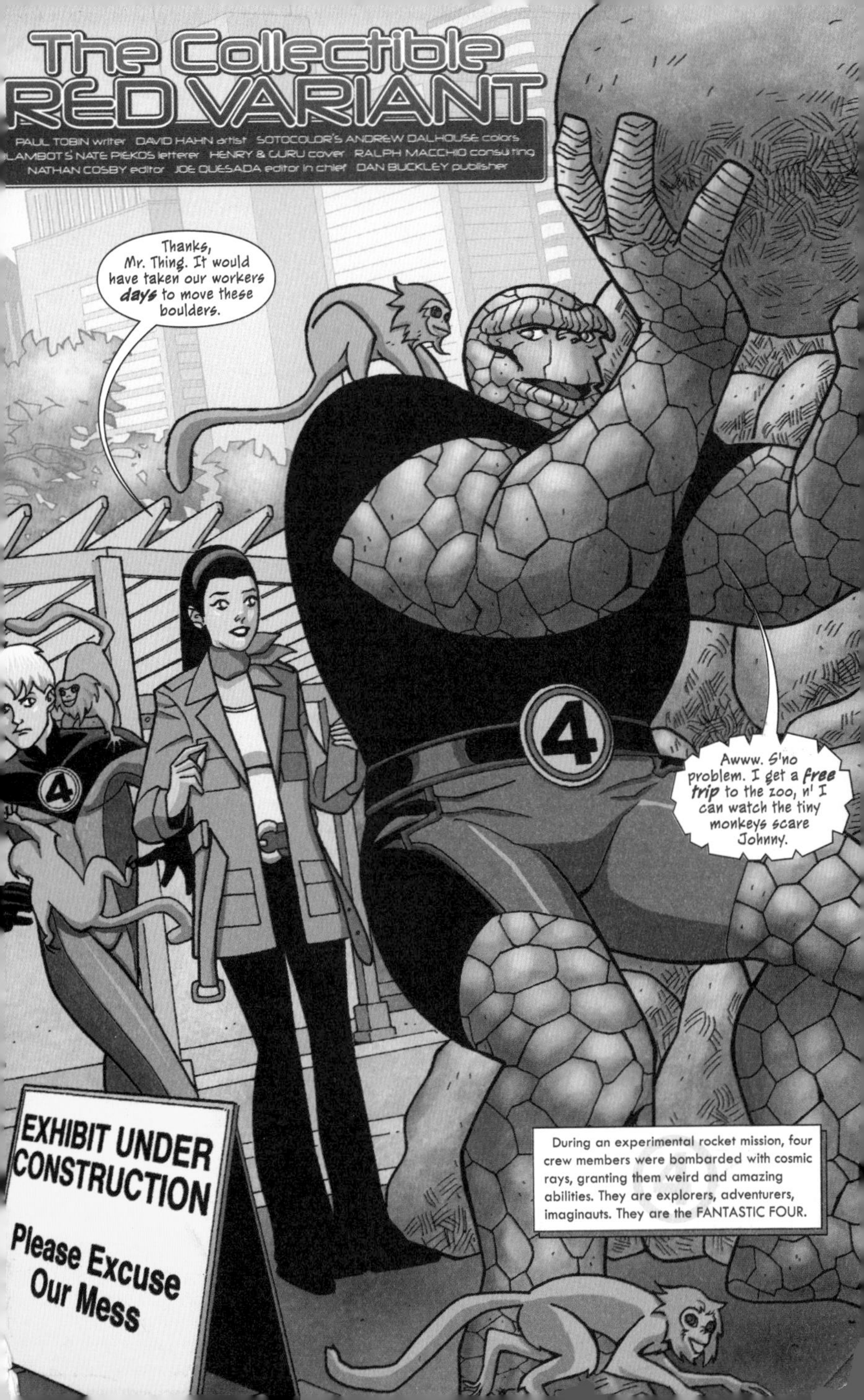
The Collectible RED VARIANT
PAUL TOBIN writer DAVID HAHN artist SOTOCOLOR'S ANDREW DALHOUSE colors
BLAMBOT'S NATE PIEKOS letterer HENRY & GURU cover RALPH MACCHIO consulting
NATHAN COSBY editor JOE QUESADA editor in chief DAN BUCKLEY publisher
Thanks, Mr. Thing. It would have taken our workers days to move these boulders.
Awww. S'no problem. I get a free trip to the zoo, n' I can watch the tiny monkeys scare Johnny.
EXHIBIT UNDER CONSTRUCTION
Please Excuse Our Mess
During an experimental rocket mission, four crew members were bombarded with cosmic rays, granting them weird and amazing abilities. They are explorers, adventurers, imaginauts. They are the FANTASTIC FOUR.

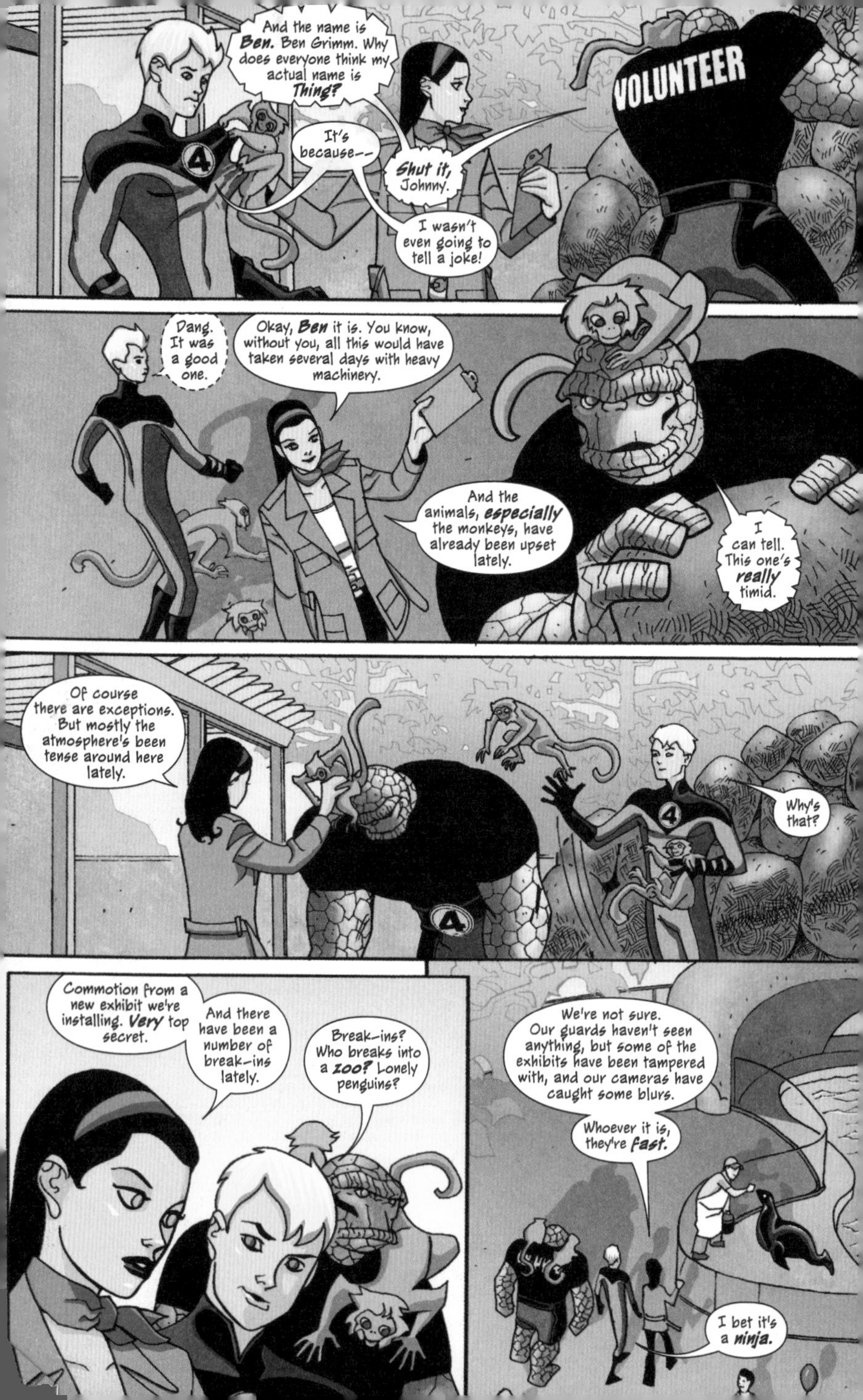

VOLUNTEER
And the name is Ben. Ben Grimm. Why does everyone think my actual name is Thing?
It's because--
Shut it, Johnny.
I wasn't even going to tell a joke!
Dang. It was a good one.
Okay, Ben it is. You know, without you, all this would have taken several days with heavy machinery.
And the animals, especially the monkeys, have already been upset lately.
I can tell. This one's really timid.
Of course there are exceptions. But mostly the atmosphere's been tense around here lately.
Why's that?
Commotion from a new exhibit we're installing. Very top secret.
And there have been a number of break-ins lately.
Break-ins? Who breaks into a zoo? Lonely penguins?
We're not sure. Our guards haven't seen anything, but some of the exhibits have been tampered with, and our cameras have caught some blurs.
Whoever it is, they're fast.
I bet it's a ninja.

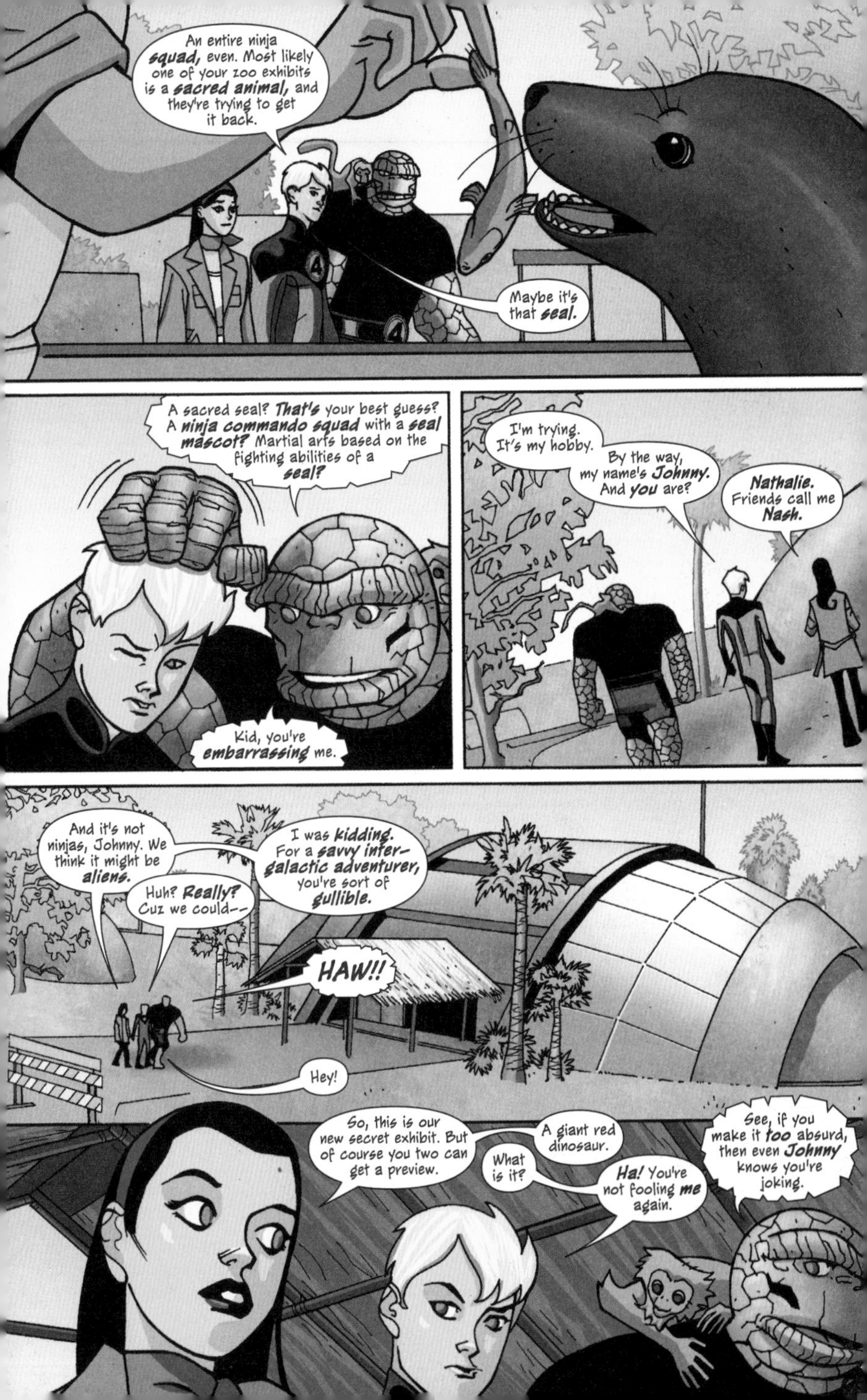
An entire ninja squad, even. Most likely one of your zoo exhibits is a sacred animal, and they're trying to get it back.
Maybe it's that seal.
A sacred seal? That's your best guess? A ninja commando squad with a seal mascot? Martial arts based on the fighting abilities of a seal?
Kid, you're embarrassing me.
I'm trying. It's my hobby.
By the way, my name's Johnny. And you are?
Nathalie. Friends call me Nash.
And it's not ninjas, Johnny. We think it might be aliens.
Huh? Really? Cuz we could--
I was kidding. For a savvy inter-galactic adventurer, you're sort of gullible.
HAW!!
Hey!
So, this is our new secret exhibit. But of course you two can get a preview.
What is it?
A giant red dinosaur.
Ha! You're not fooling me again.
See, if you make it too absurd, then even Johnny knows you're joking.

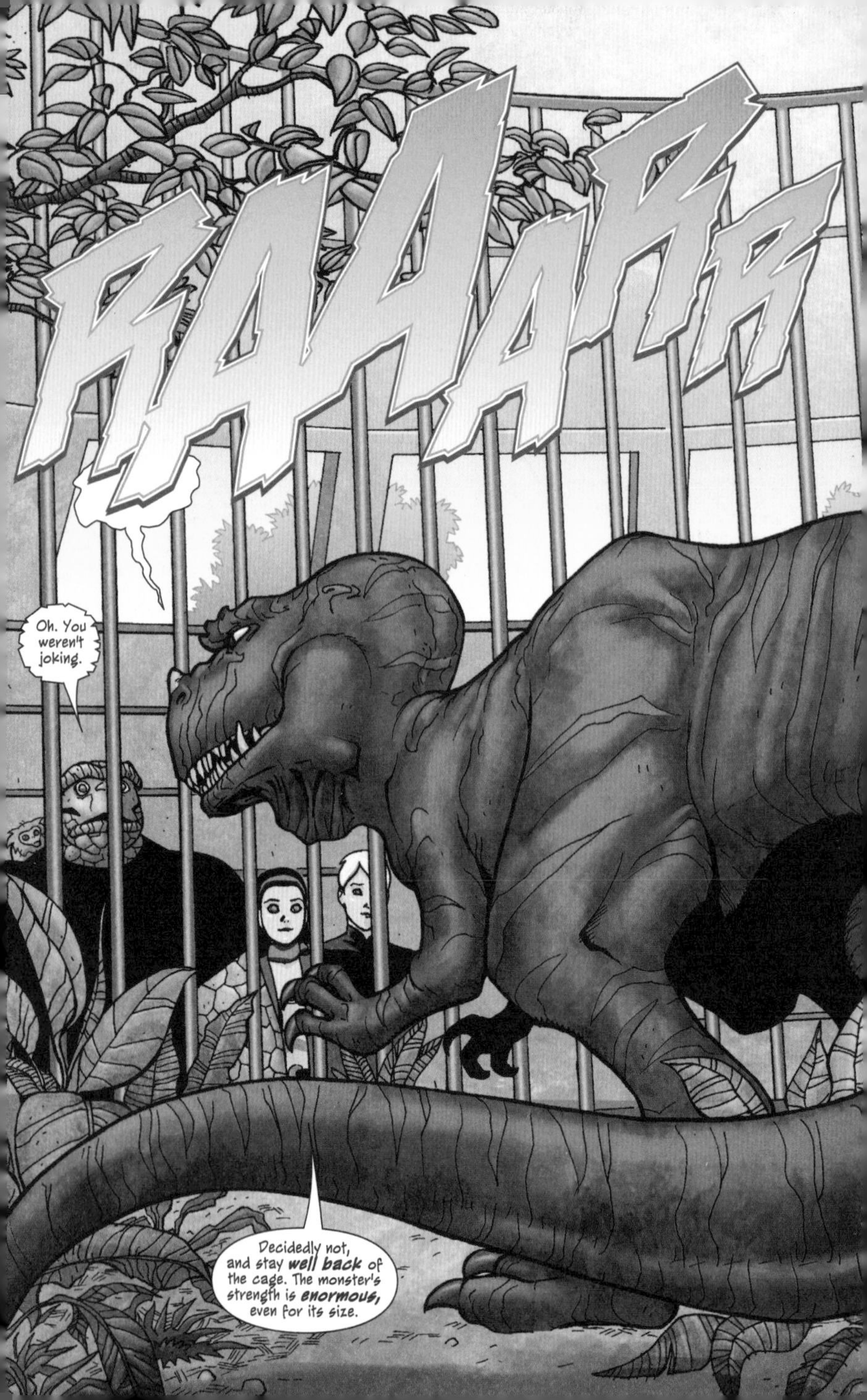
RAAARR
Oh. You weren't joking.
Decidedly not, and stay **well back** of the cage. The monster's strength is **enormous,** even for its size.

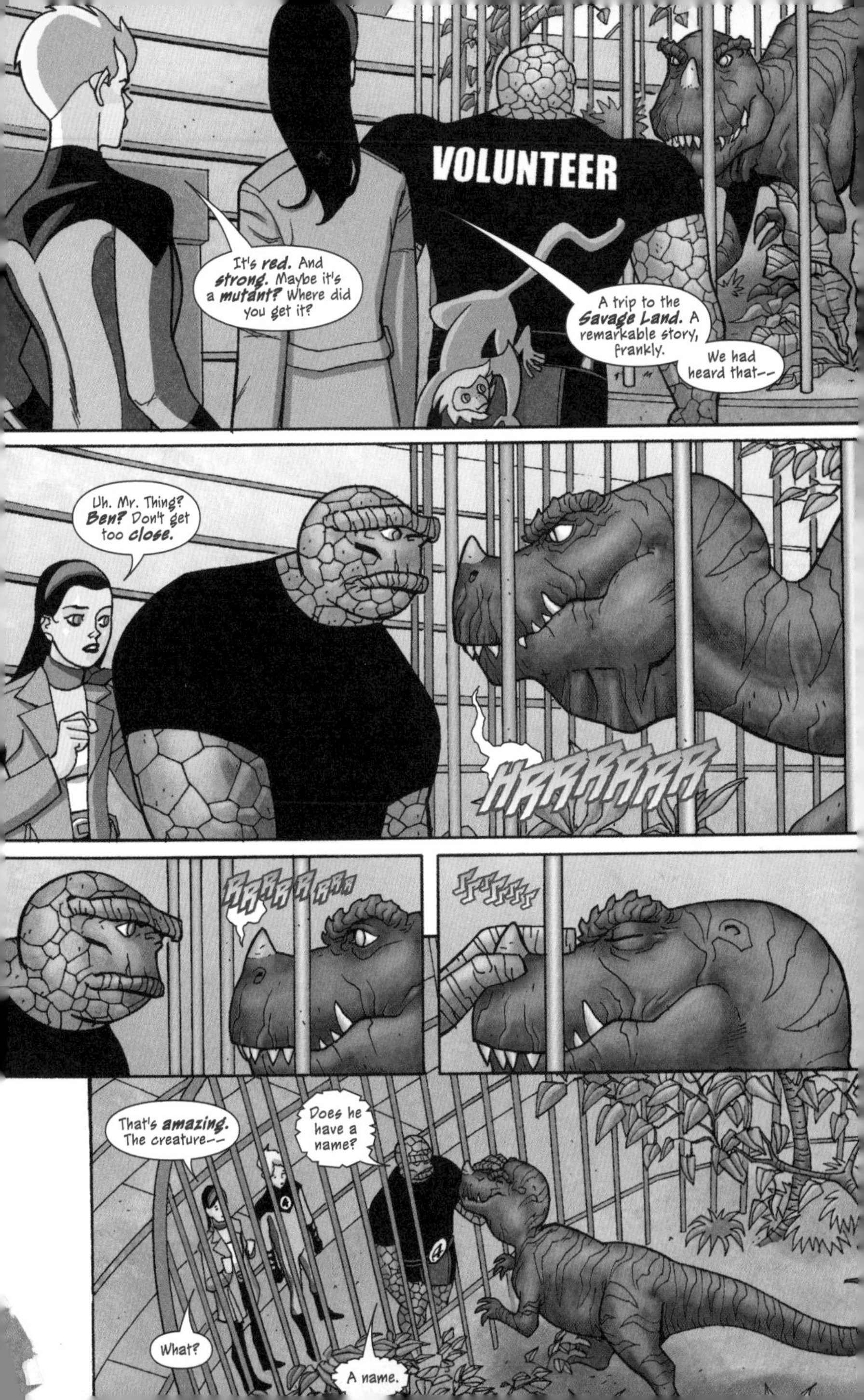
VOLUNTEER
It's red. And strong. Maybe it's a mutant? Where did you get it?
A trip to the Savage Land. A remarkable story, frankly.
We had heard that--
Uh. Mr. Thing? Ben? Don't get too close.
HRRRRRR
RRRRRRRR
That's amazing. The creature--
Does he have a name?
What?
A name.

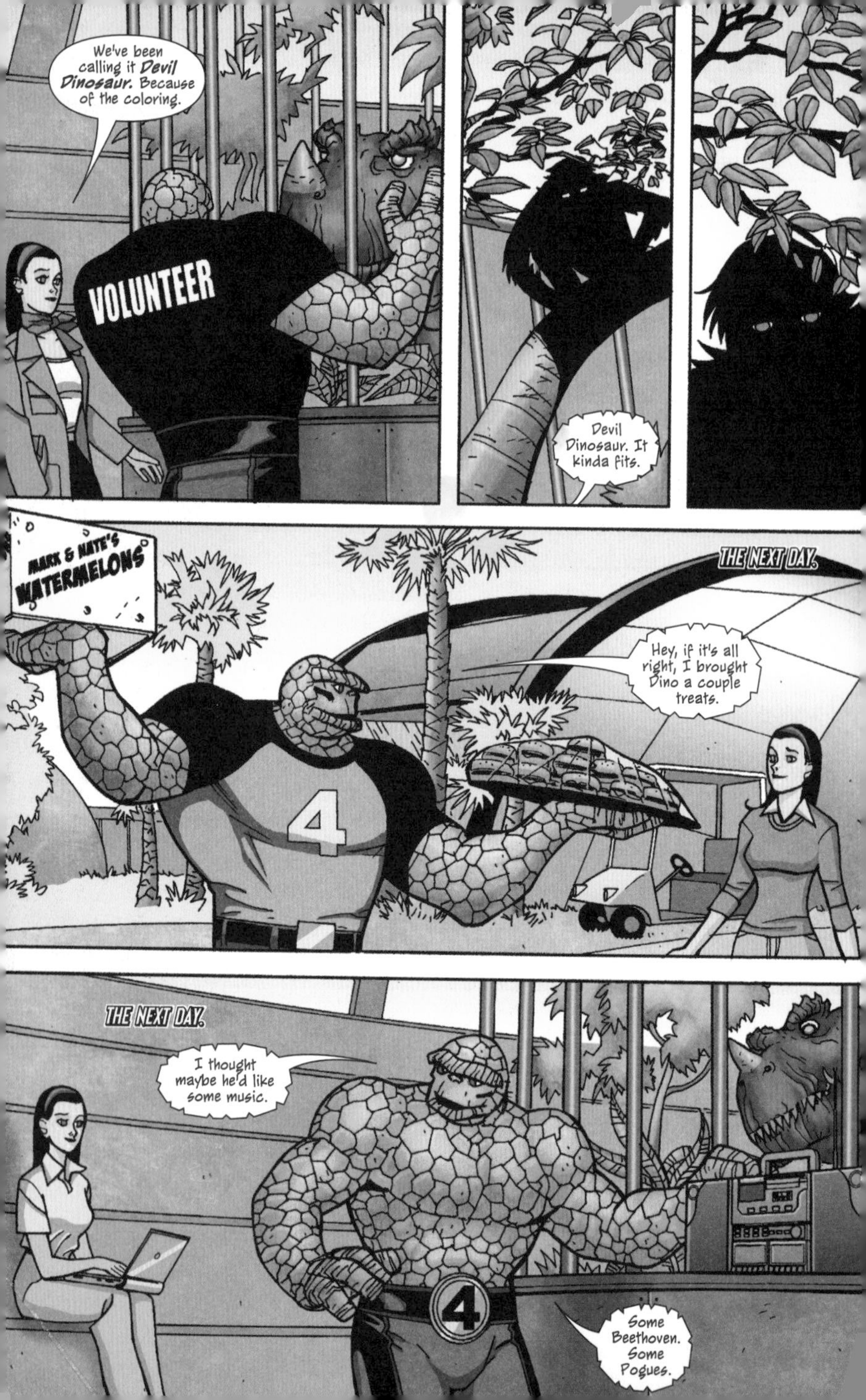
We've been calling it Devil Dinosaur. Because of the coloring.
VOLUNTEER
Devil Dinosaur. It kinda fits.
MARK & NATE'S WATERMELONS
THE NEXT DAY.
Hey, if it's all right, I brought Dino a couple treats.
4
THE NEXT DAY.
I thought maybe he'd like some music.
4
Some Beethoven. Some Pogues.

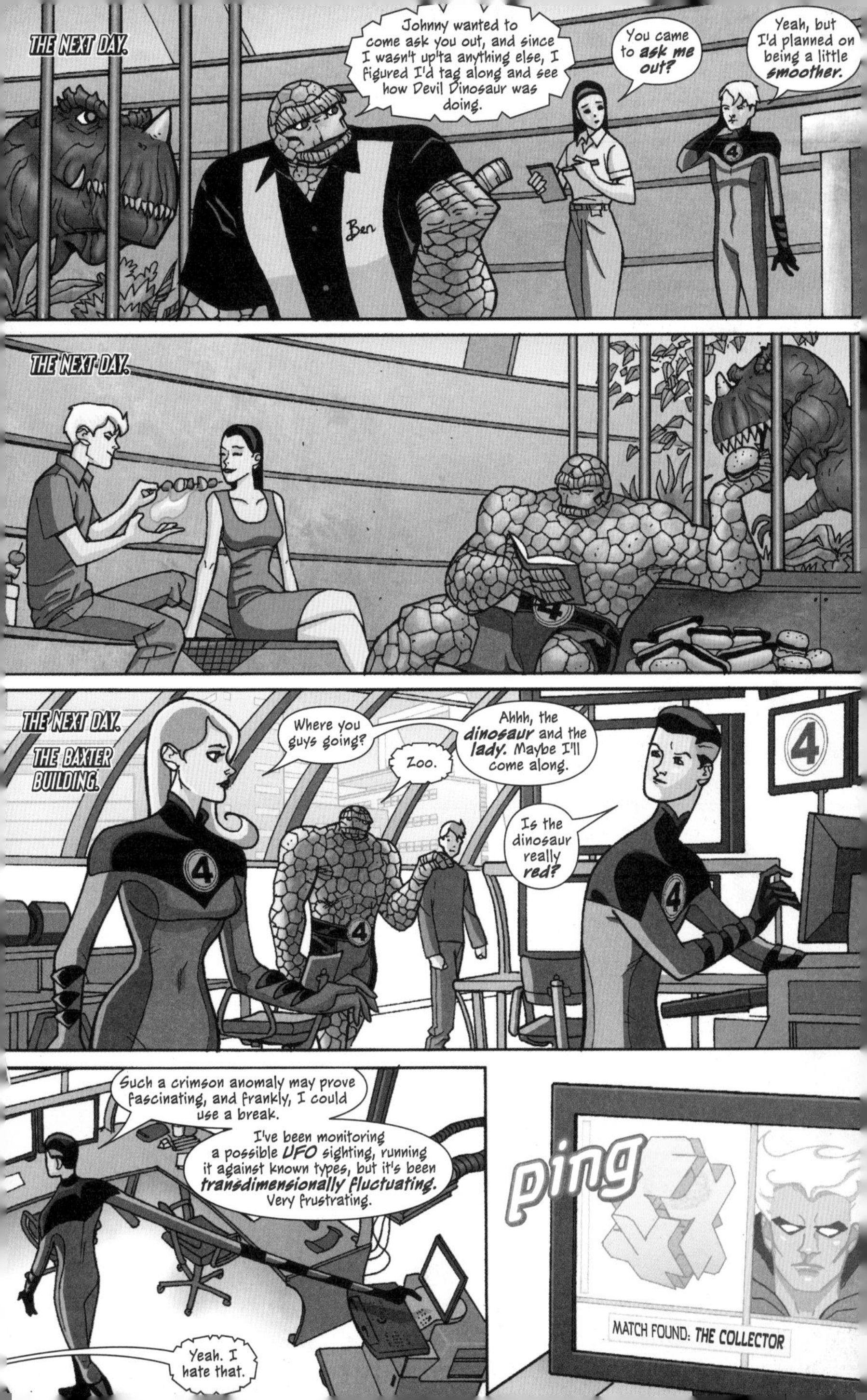
THE NEXT DAY.
Johnny wanted to come ask you out, and since I wasn't up'ta anything else, I figured I'd tag along and see how Devil Dinosaur was doing.
You came to **ask me out?**
Yeah, but I'd planned on being a little **smoother.**
Ben
THE NEXT DAY.
THE NEXT DAY.
THE BAXTER BUILDING.
Where you guys going?
Zoo.
Ahhh, the **dinosaur** and the **lady.** Maybe I'll come along.
Is the dinosaur really **red?**
Such a crimson anomaly may prove fascinating, and frankly, I could use a break.
I've been monitoring a possible *UFO* sighting, running it against known types, but it's been ***transdimensionally fluctuating.*** Very frustrating.
Yeah. I hate that.
ping
MATCH FOUND: THE COLLECTOR

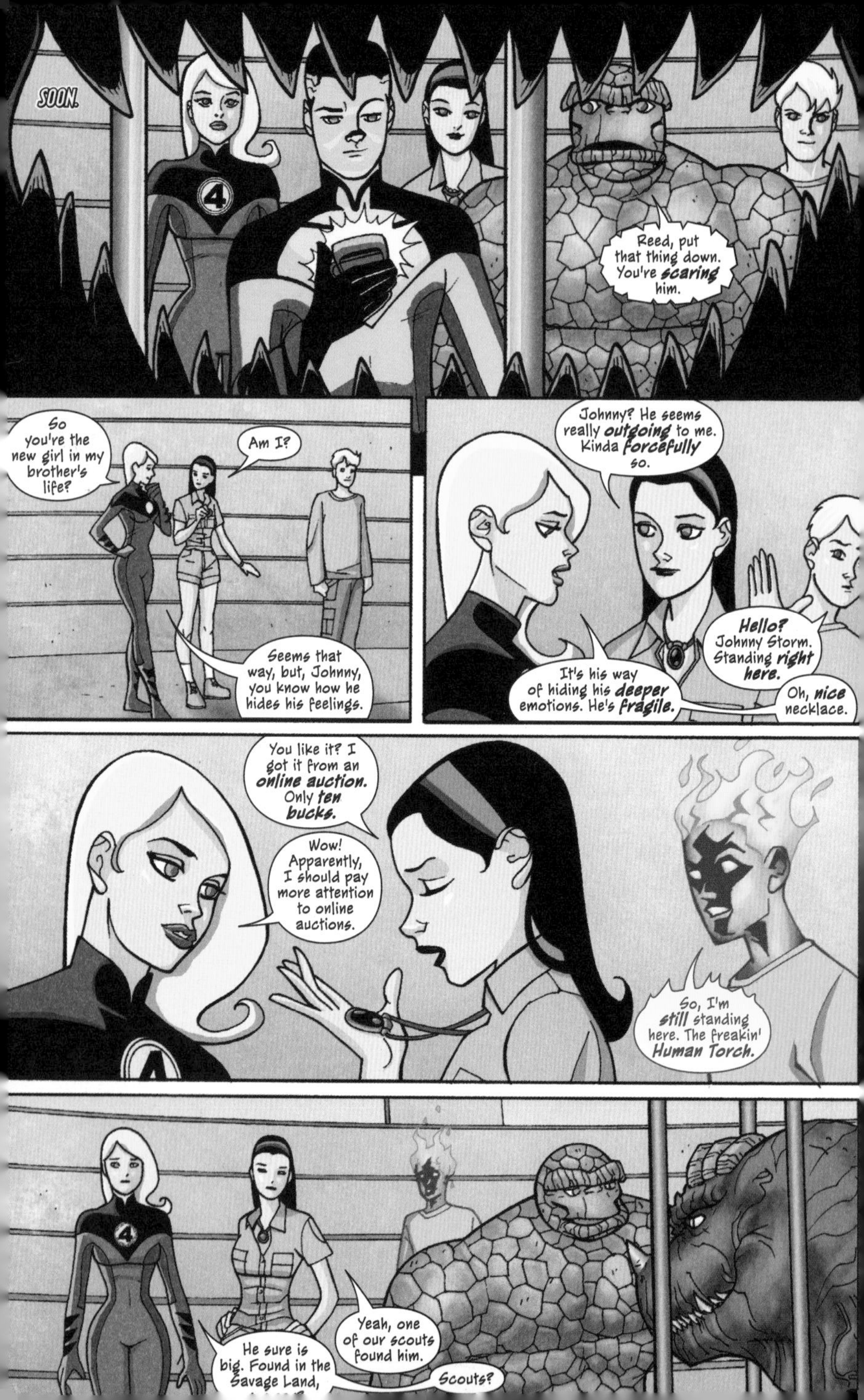

SOON.
Reed, put that thing down. You're *scaring* him.
So you're the new girl in my brother's life?
Am I?
Seems that way, but, Johnny, you know how he hides his feelings.
Johnny? He seems really *outgoing* to me. Kinda *forcefully* so.
It's his way of hiding his *deeper* emotions. He's *fragile*.
Hello? Johnny Storm. Standing *right here*.
Oh, *nice* necklace.
You like it? I got it from an *online auction*. Only *ten bucks*.
Wow! Apparently, I should pay more attention to online auctions.
So, I'm *still* standing here. The freakin' *Human Torch*.
He sure is big. Found in the Savage Land,
Yeah, one of our scouts found him.
Scouts?

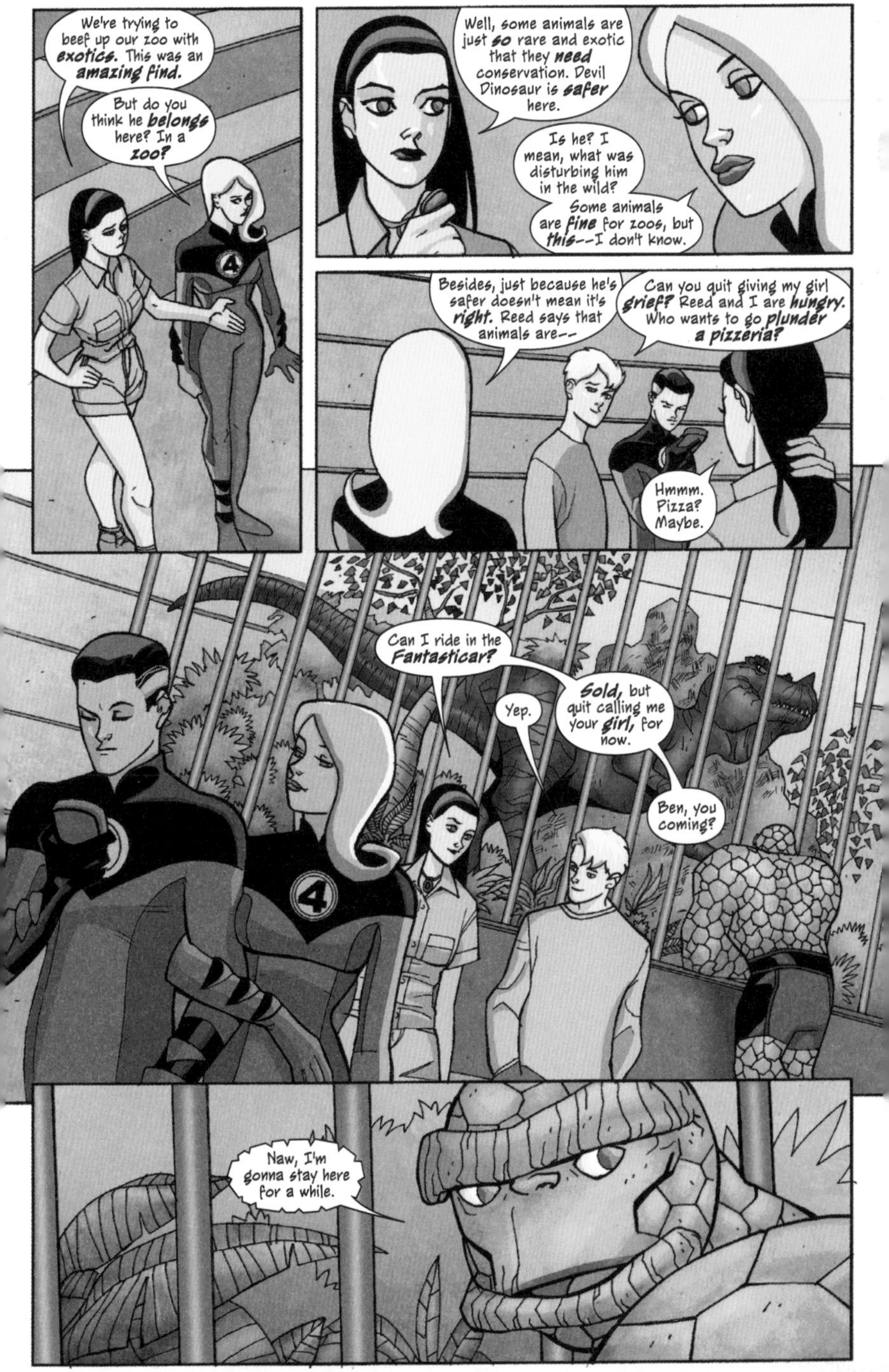

We're trying to beef up our zoo with exotics. This was an amazing find.
But do you think he belongs here? In a zoo?
Well, some animals are just so rare and exotic that they need conservation. Devil Dinosaur is safer here.
Is he? I mean, what was disturbing him in the wild?
Some animals are fine for zoos, but this--I don't know.
Besides, just because he's safer doesn't mean it's right. Reed says that animals are--
Can you quit giving my girl grief? Reed and I are hungry. Who wants to go plunder a pizzeria?
Hmmm. Pizza? Maybe.
Can I ride in the Fantasticar?
Yep.
Sold, but quit calling me your girl, for now.
Ben, you coming?
Naw, I'm gonna stay here for a while.

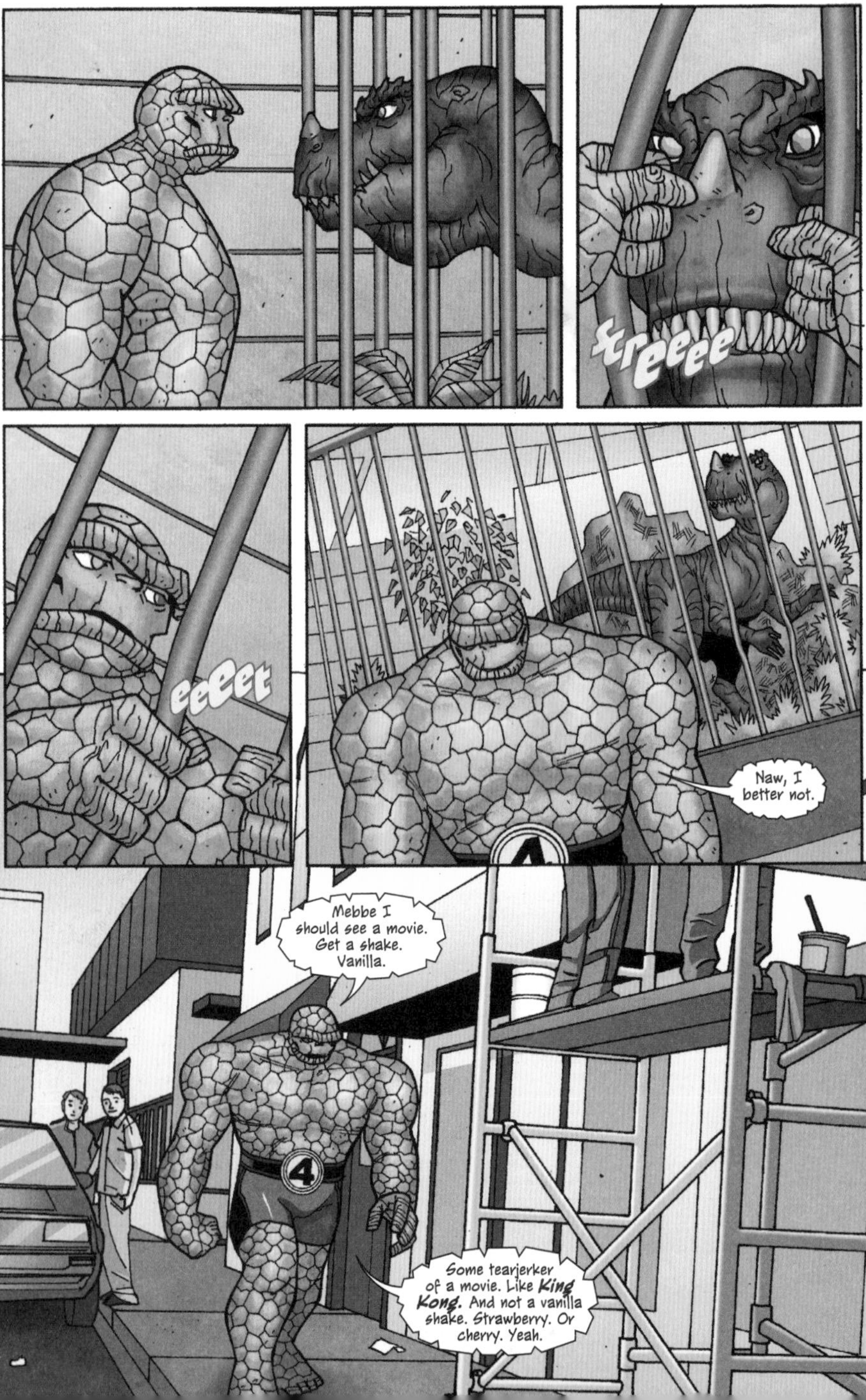
screeeee
eeeet
Naw, I better not.
Mebbe I should see a movie. Get a shake. Vanilla.
Some tearjerker of a movie. Like **King Kong.** And not a vanilla shake. Strawberry. Or cherry. Yeah.

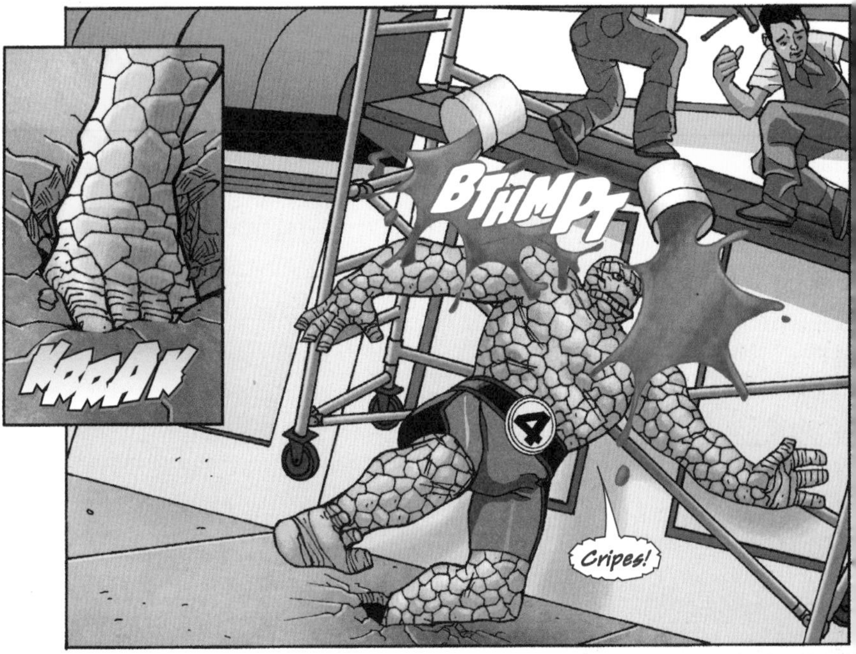
KRRAK
BTHMPT
Cripes!

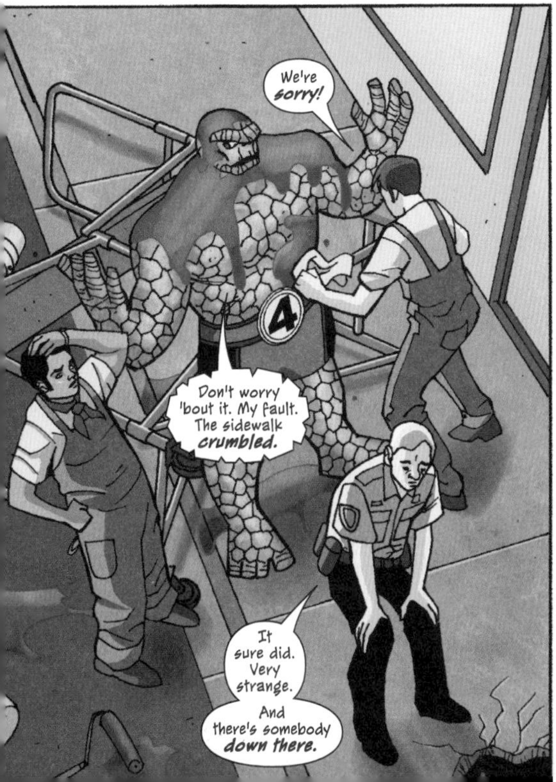
We're sorry!
Don't worry 'bout it. My fault. The sidewalk crumbled.
It sure did. Very strange.
And there's somebody down there.

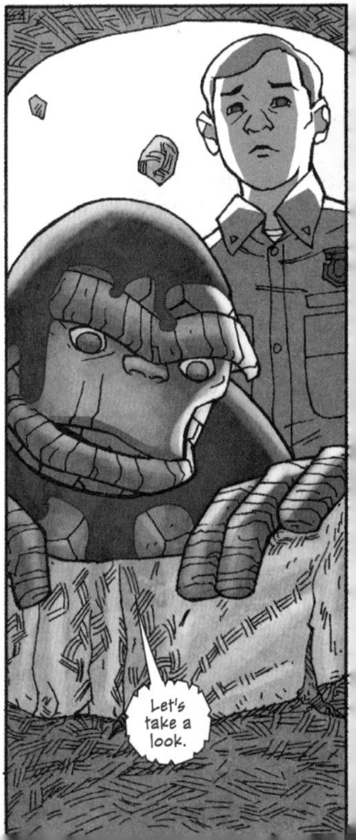
Let's take a look.

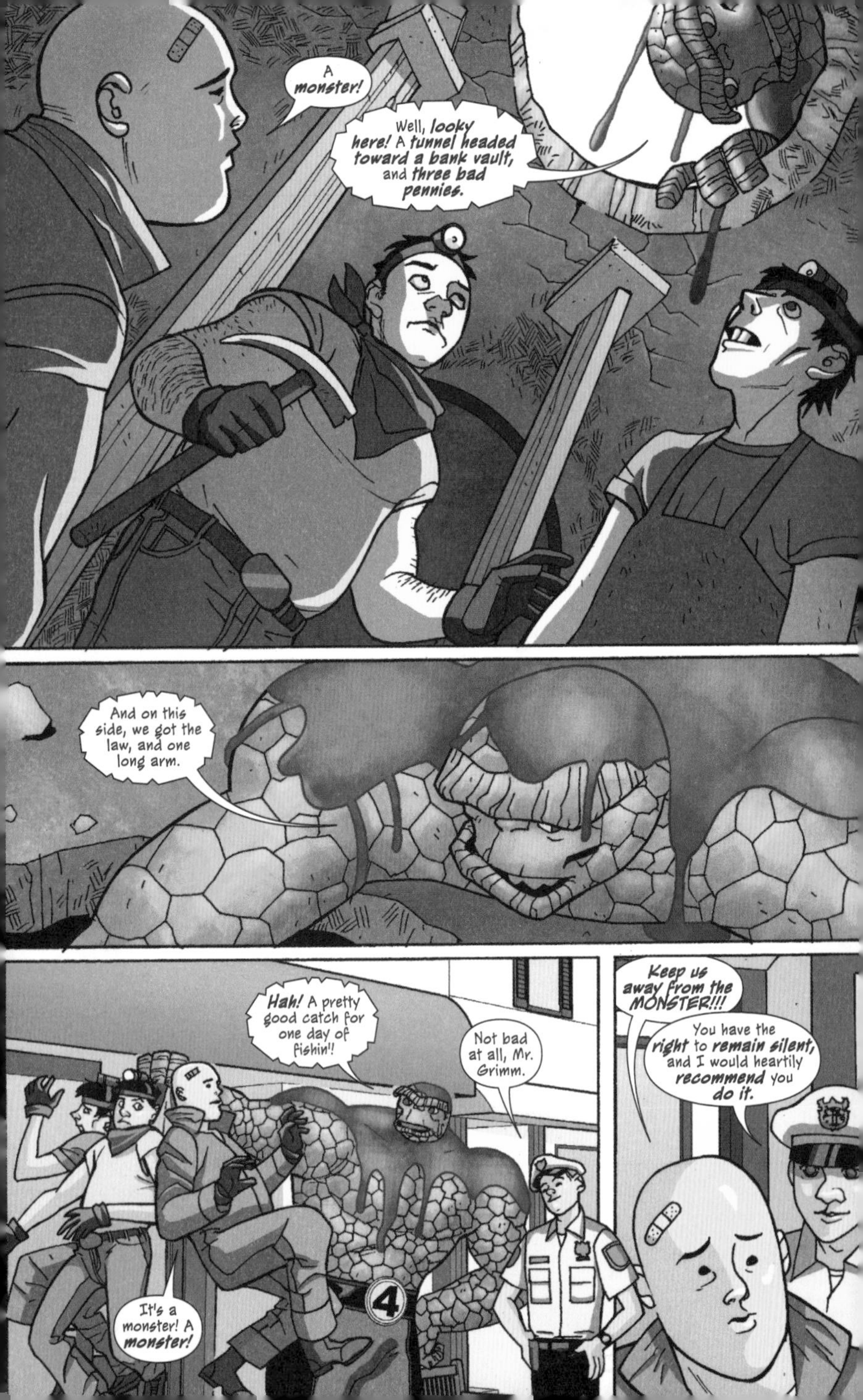
A *monster!*
Well, ***looky here!*** A ***tunnel headed toward a bank vault,*** and ***three bad pennies.***
And on this side, we got the law, and one long arm.
Hah! A pretty good catch for one day of fishin'!
Not bad at all, Mr. Grimm.
It's a monster! A ***monster!***
Keep us away from the MONSTER!!!
You have the ***right*** to ***remain silent,*** and I would heartily ***recommend*** you ***do it.***
4

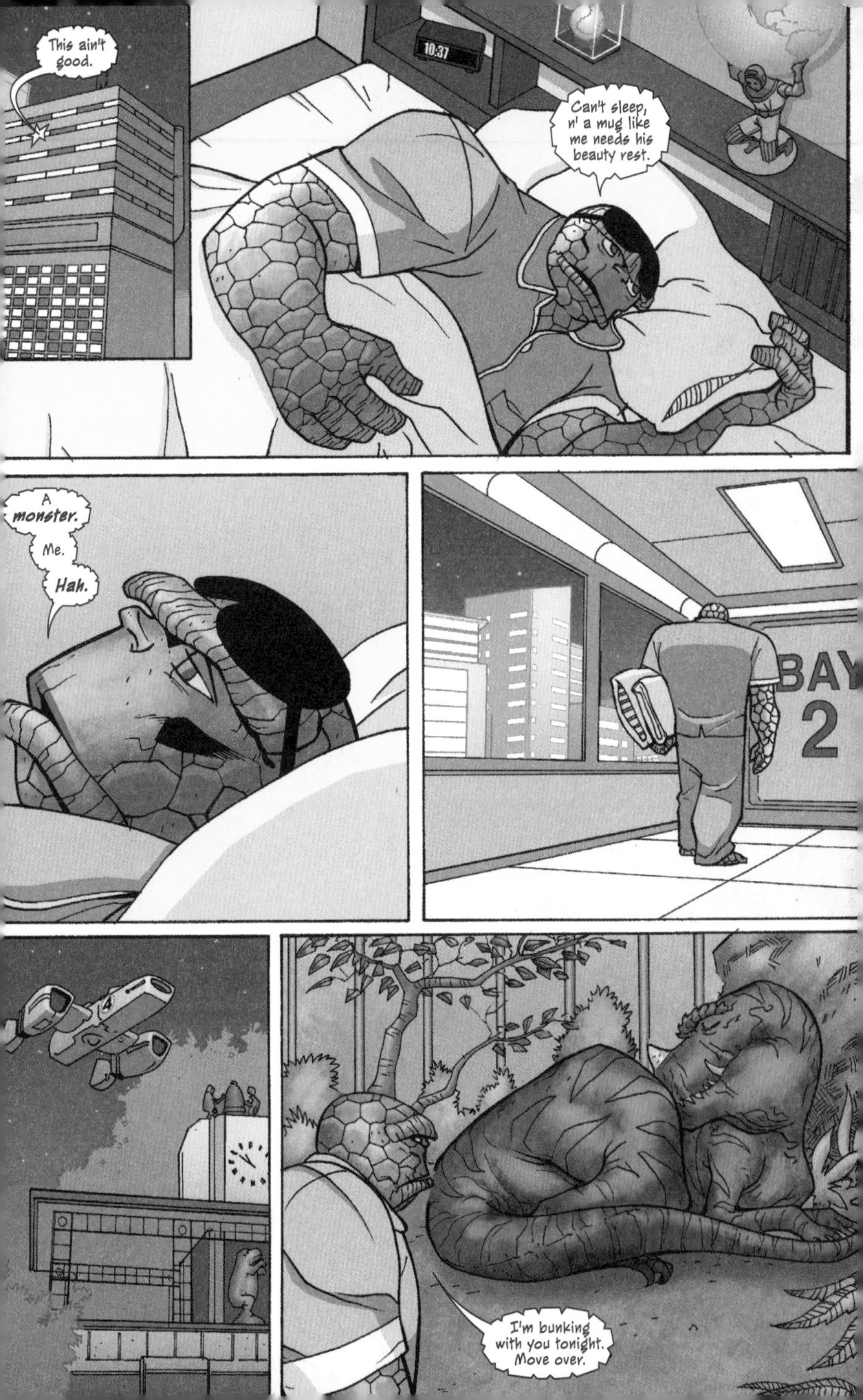
This ain't good.
10:37
Can't sleep, n' a mug like me needs his beauty rest.
A *monster.*
Me.
Hah.
BAY 2
4
I'm bunking with you tonight. Move over.

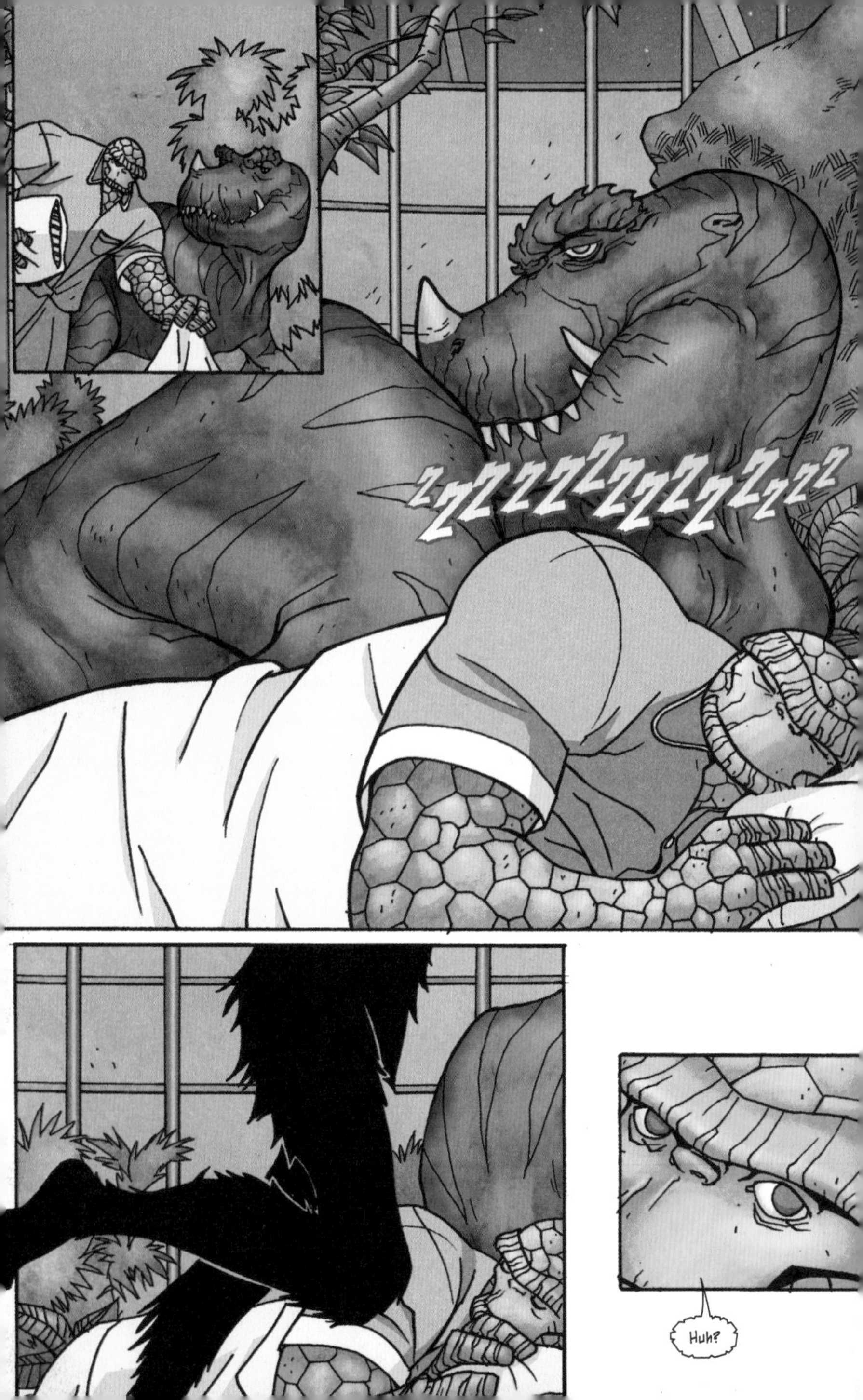
ZZZZZZZZZZZZZZ
Huh?

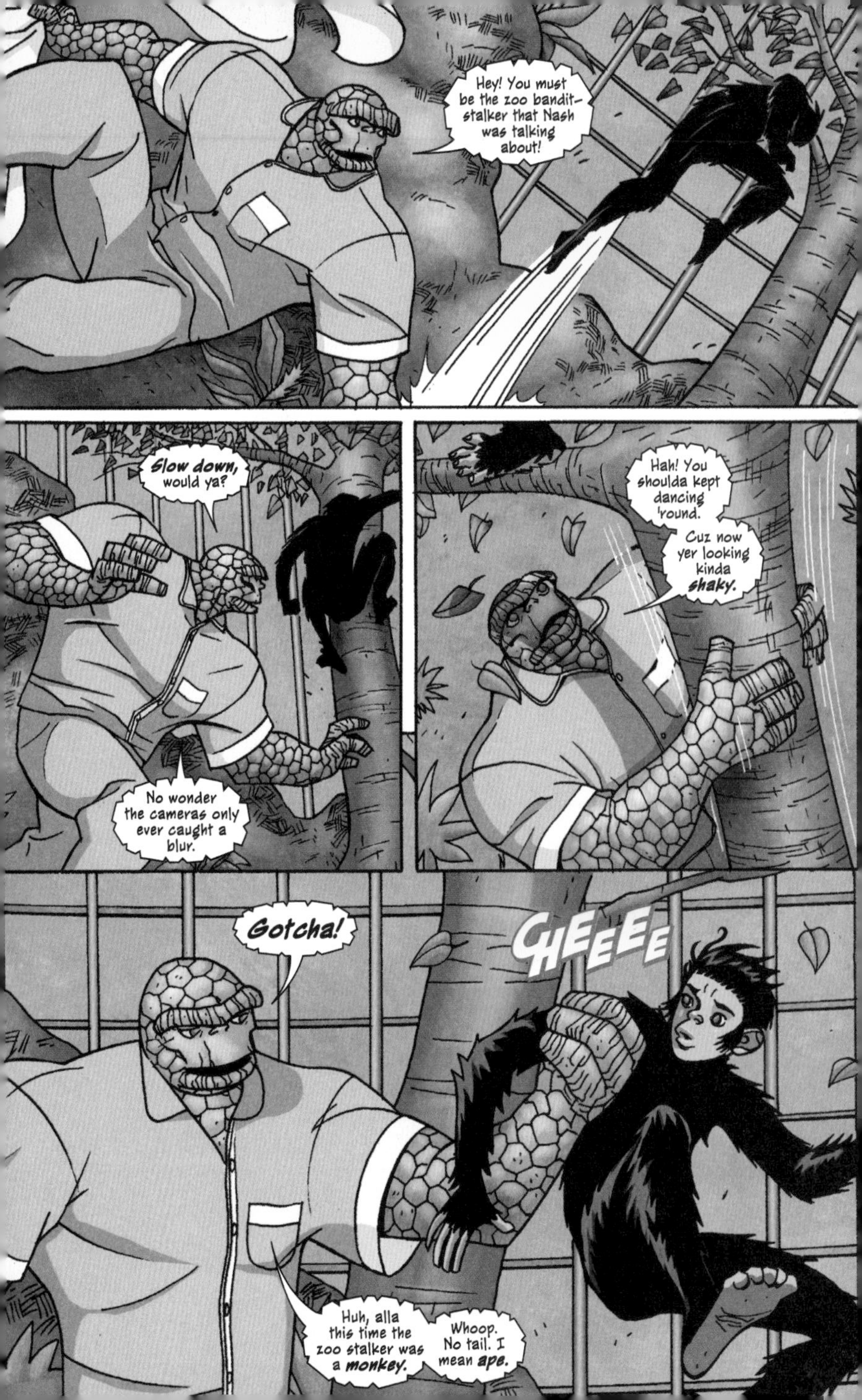
Hey! You must be the zoo bandit-stalker that Nash was talking about!
Slow down, would ya?
No wonder the cameras only ever caught a blur.
Hah! You shoulda kept dancing 'round.
Cuz now yer looking kinda shaky.
Gotcha!
CHEEEE
Huh, alla this time the zoo stalker was a monkey.
Whoop. No tail. I mean ape.

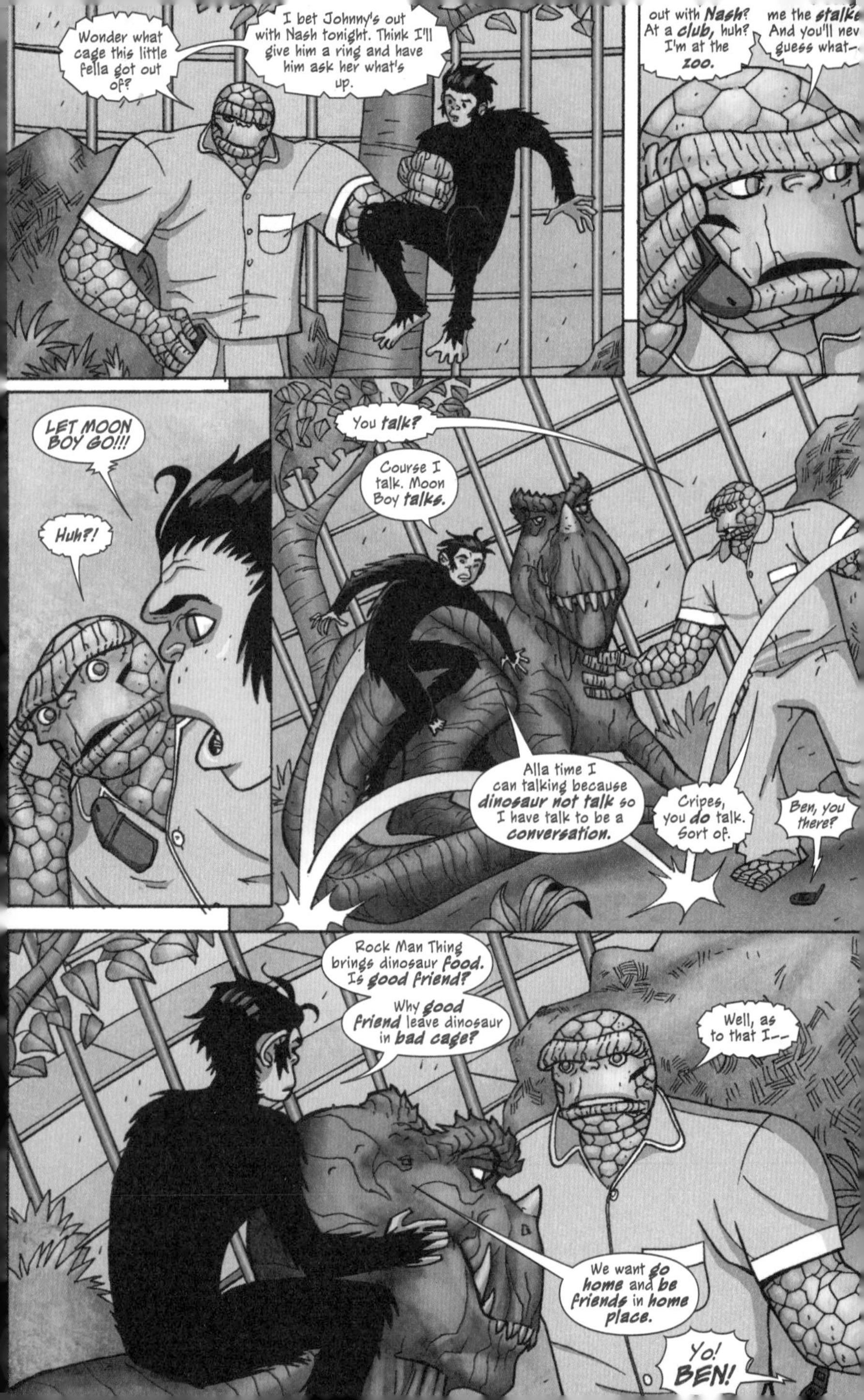

Wonder what cage this little fella got out of?
I bet Johnny's out with Nash tonight. Think I'll give him a ring and have him ask her what's up.
out with Nash? At a club, huh? I'm at the zoo.
me the stalke And you'll nev guess what--
LET MOON BOY GO!!!
Huh?!
You talk?
Course I talk. Moon Boy talks.
Alla time I can talking because dinosaur not talk so I have talk to be a conversation.
Cripes, you do talk. Sort of.
Ben, you there?
Rock Man Thing brings dinosaur food. Is good friend?
Why good friend leave dinosaur in bad cage?
Well, as to that I--
We want go home and be friends in home place.
Yo! BEN!

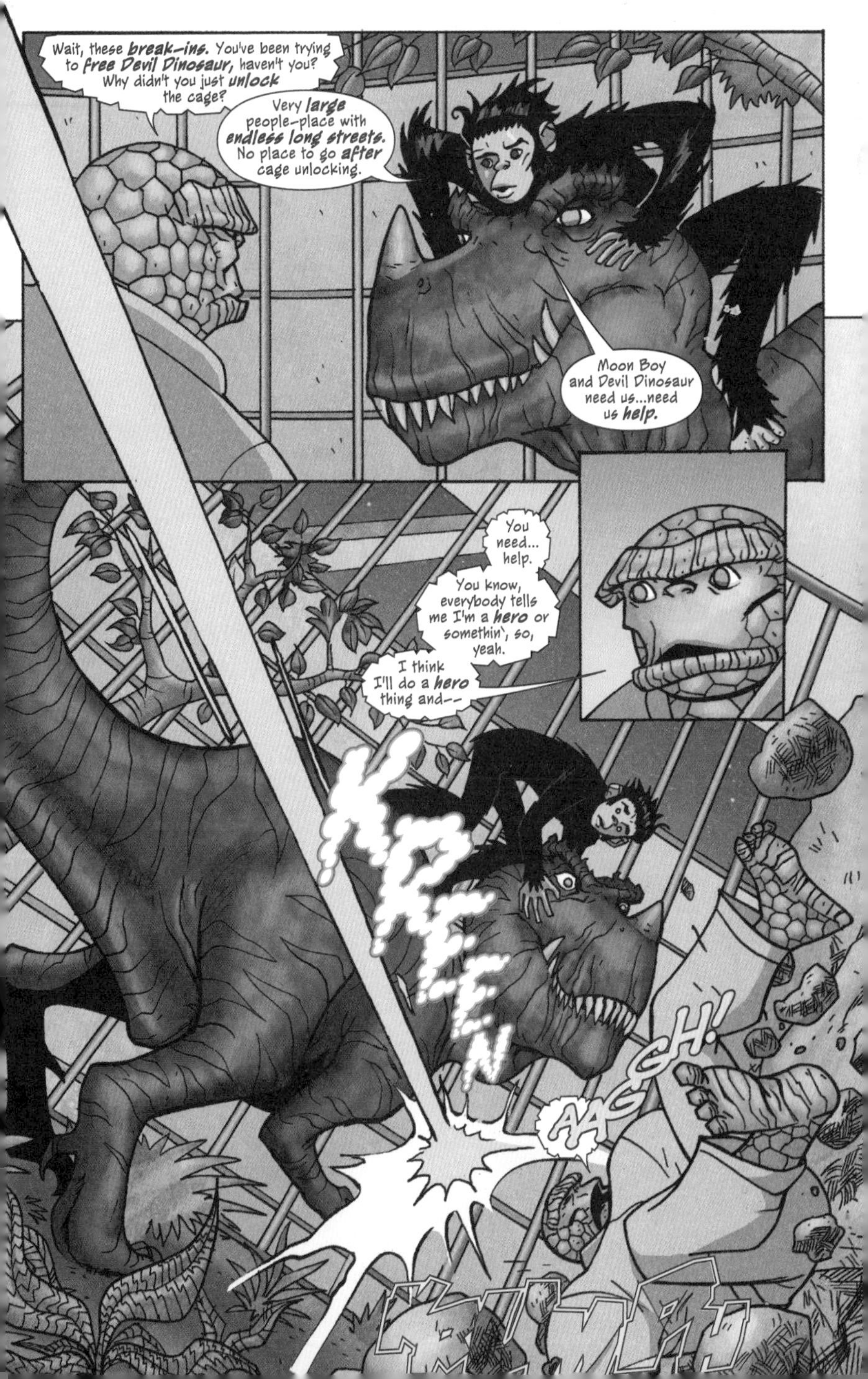
Wait, these break-ins. You've been trying to free Devil Dinosaur, haven't you? Why didn't you just unlock the cage?
Very large people-place with endless long streets. No place to go after cage unlocking.
Moon Boy and Devil Dinosaur need us...need us help.
You need... help.
You know, everybody tells me I'm a hero or somethin', so, yeah.
I think I'll do a hero thing and--
KREEEN
AAAGGH!

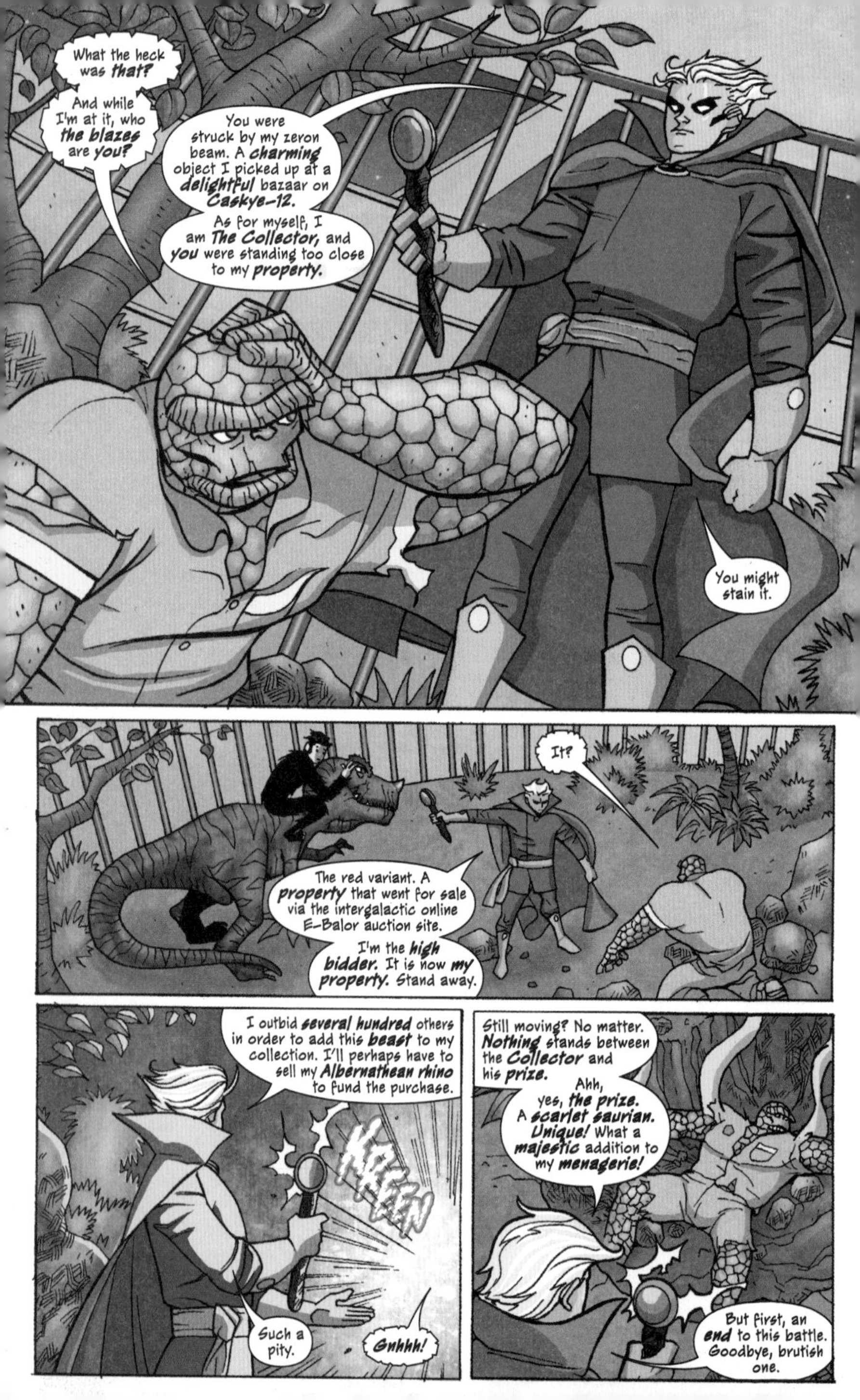
What the heck was that?
And while I'm at it, who the blazes are you?
You were struck by my zeron beam. A charming object I picked up at a delightful bazaar on Caskye-12.
As for myself, I am The Collector, and you were standing too close to my property.
You might stain it.
It?
The red variant. A property that went for sale via the intergalactic online E-Balor auction site.
I'm the high bidder. It is now my property. Stand away.
I outbid several hundred others in order to add this beast to my collection. I'll perhaps have to sell my Albernathean rhino to fund the purchase.
Such a pity.
Gnhhh!
Still moving? No matter. Nothing stands between the Collector and his prize.
Ahh, yes, the prize. A scarlet saurian. Unique! What a majestic addition to my menagerie!
But first, an end to this battle. Goodbye, brutish one.

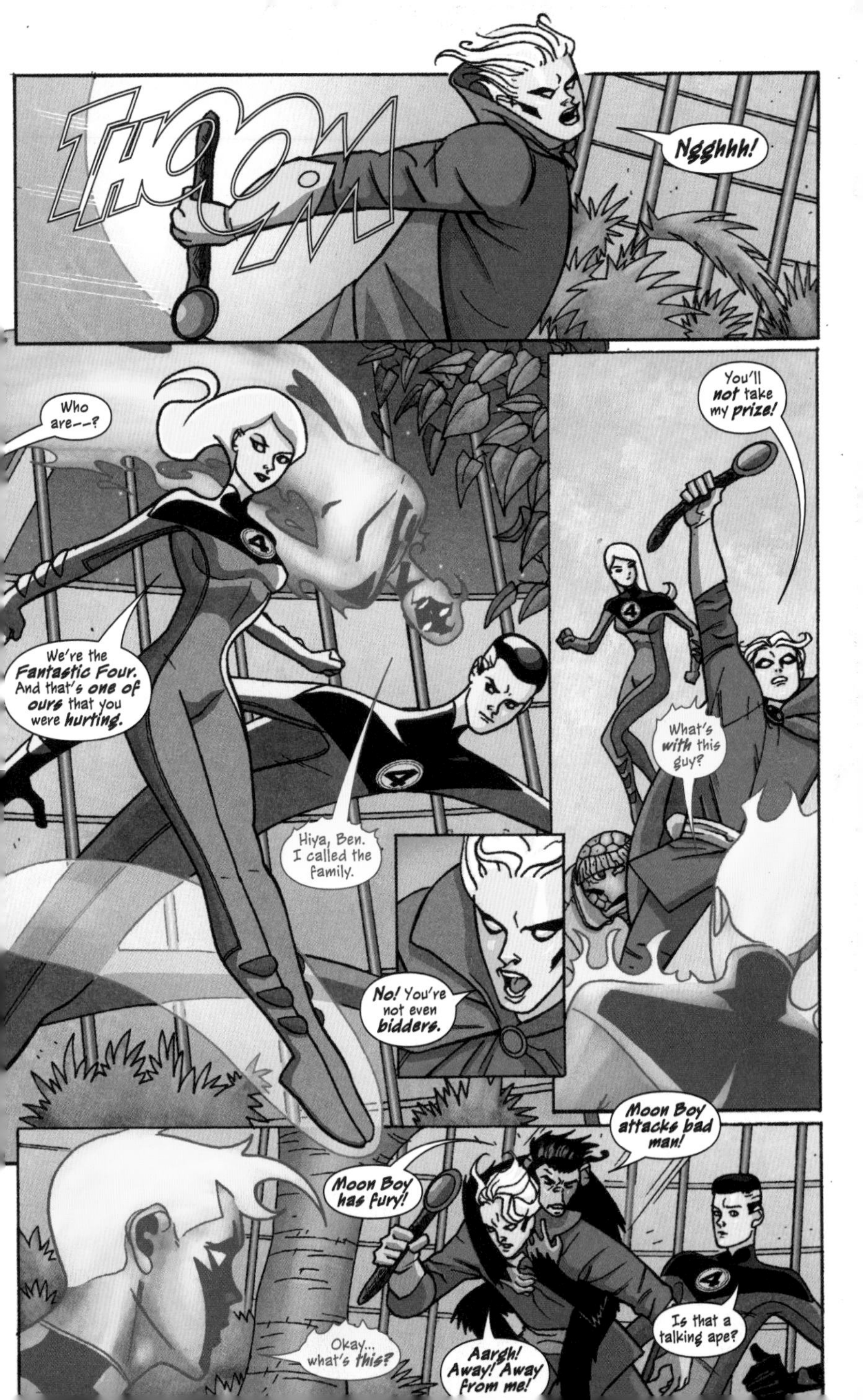
THOOM
Ngghhh!
Who are--?
We're the Fantastic Four. And that's one of ours that you were hurting.
Hiya, Ben. I called the family.
You'll not take my prize!
What's with this guy?
No! You're not even bidders.
Moon Boy attacks bad man!
Moon Boy has fury!
Is that a talking ape?
Okay... what's this?
Aargh! Away! Away from me!

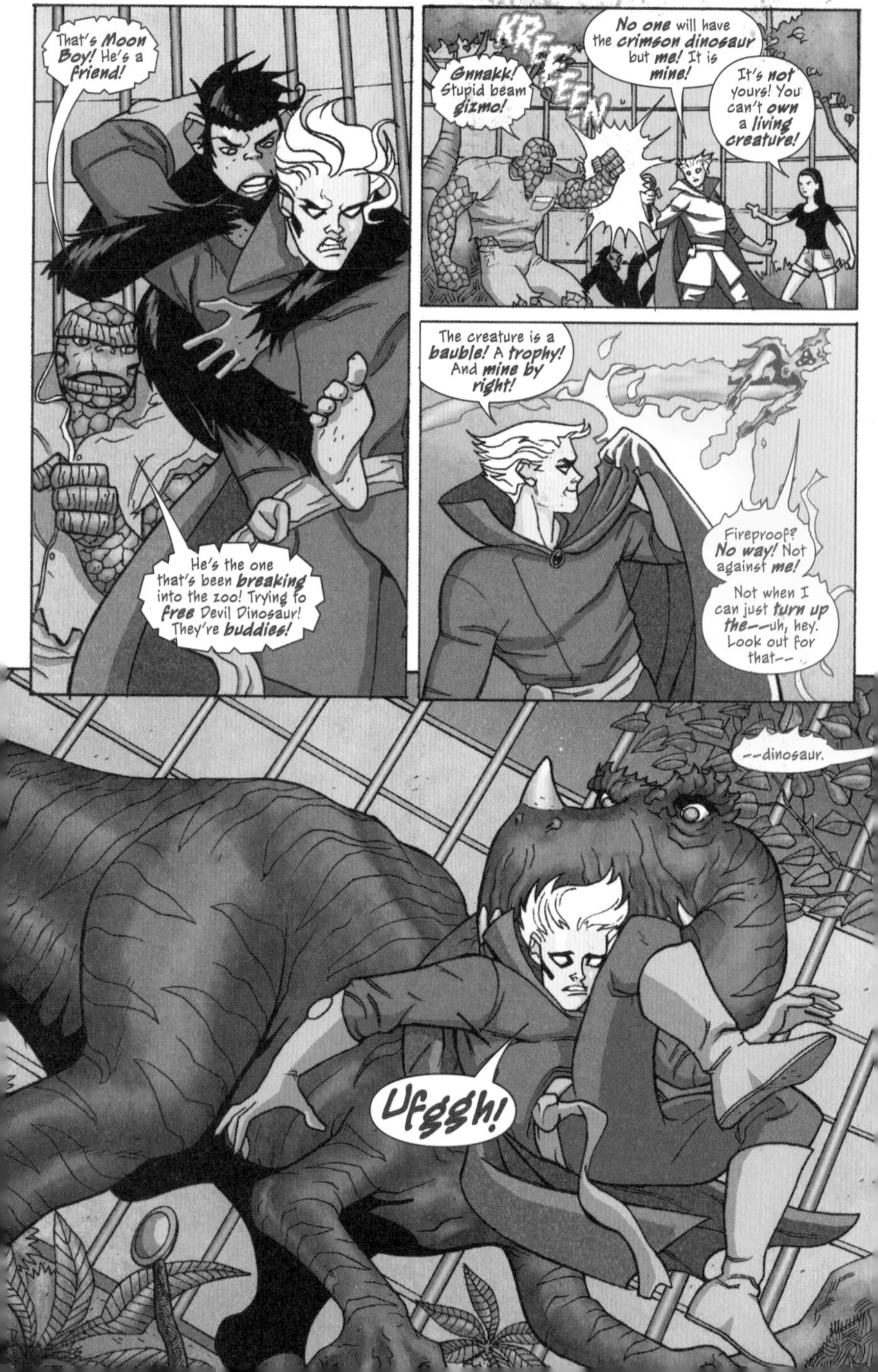

That's Moon Boy! He's a friend!
He's the one that's been breaking into the zoo! Trying to free Devil Dinosaur! They're buddies!
KREEEEN
Gnnakk! Stupid beam gizmo!
No one will have the crimson dinosaur but me! It is mine!
It's not yours! You can't own a living creature!
The creature is a bauble! A trophy! And mine by right!
Fireproof? No way! Not against me!
Not when I can just turn up the--uh, hey. Look out for that--
--dinosaur.
Ufggh!

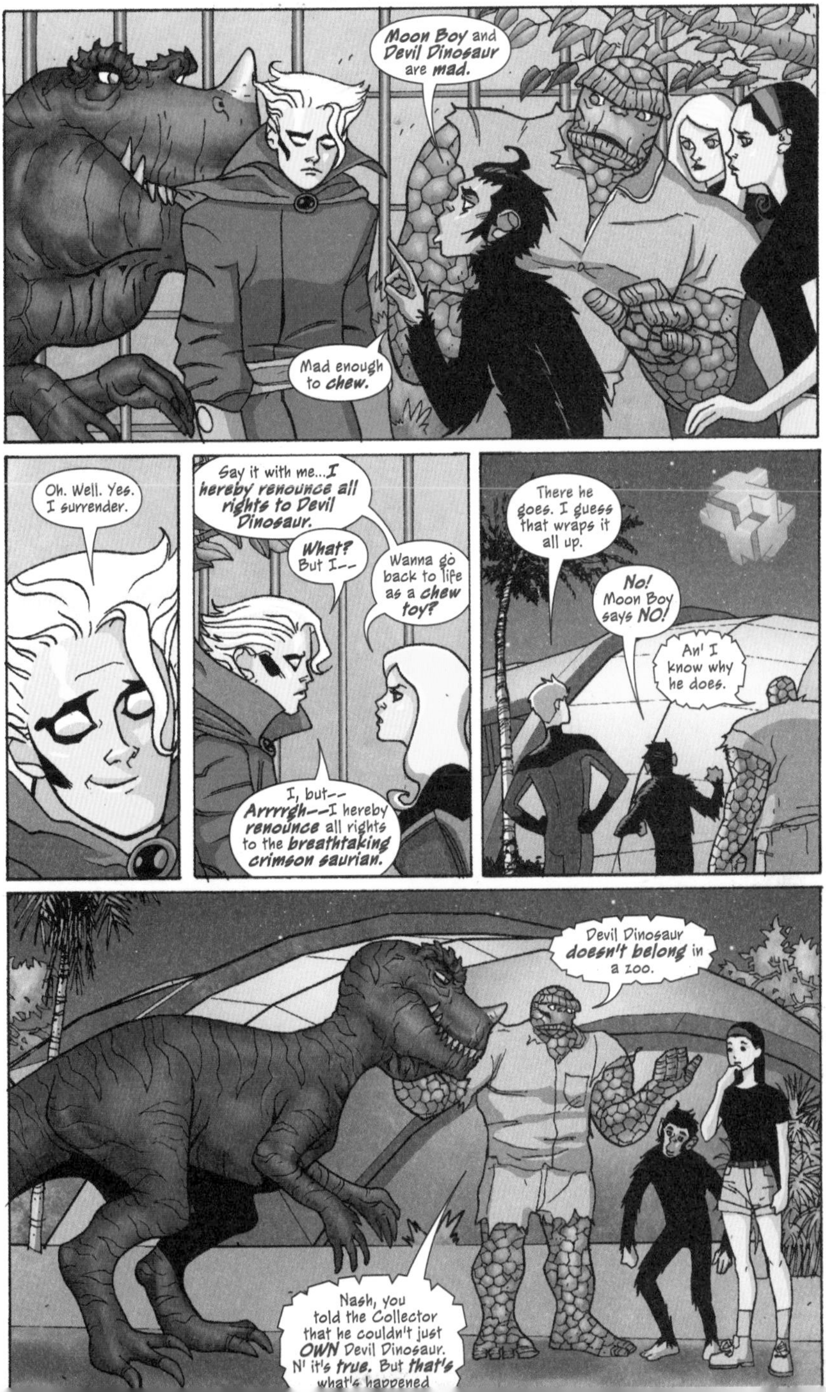

Moon Boy and Devil Dinosaur are mad.
Mad enough to chew.
Oh. Well. Yes. I surrender.
Say it with me...I hereby renounce all rights to Devil Dinosaur.
What? But I--
Wanna go back to life as a chew toy?
I, but-- Arrrrgh--I hereby renounce all rights to the breathtaking crimson saurian.
There he goes. I guess that wraps it all up.
No! Moon Boy says NO!
An' I know why he does.
Devil Dinosaur doesn't belong in a zoo.
Nash, you told the Collector that he couldn't just OWN Devil Dinosaur. N' it's true. But that's what's happened

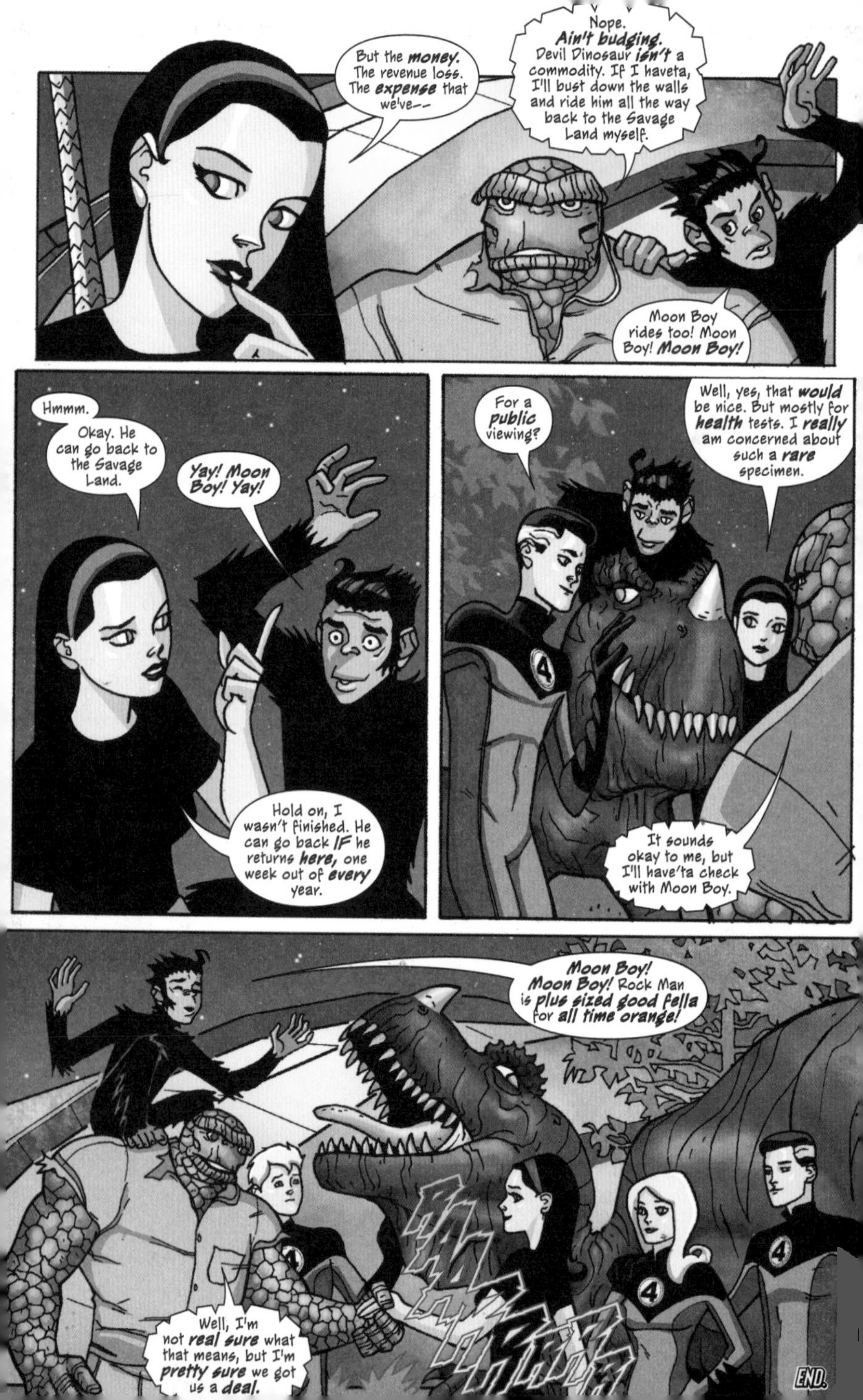

But the money. The revenue loss. The expense that we've--
Nope. Ain't budging. Devil Dinosaur isn't a commodity. If I haveta, I'll bust down the walls and ride him all the way back to the Savage Land myself.
Moon Boy rides too! Moon Boy! Moon Boy!
Hmmm.
Okay. He can go back to the Savage Land.
Yay! Moon Boy! Yay!
Hold on, I wasn't finished. He can go back IF he returns here, one week out of every year.
For a public viewing?
Well, yes, that would be nice. But mostly for health tests. I really am concerned about such a rare specimen.
It sounds okay to me, but I'll have'ta check with Moon Boy.
Moon Boy! Moon Boy! Rock Man is plus sized good fella for all time orange!
Well, I'm not real sure what that means, but I'm pretty sure we got us a deal.
END.

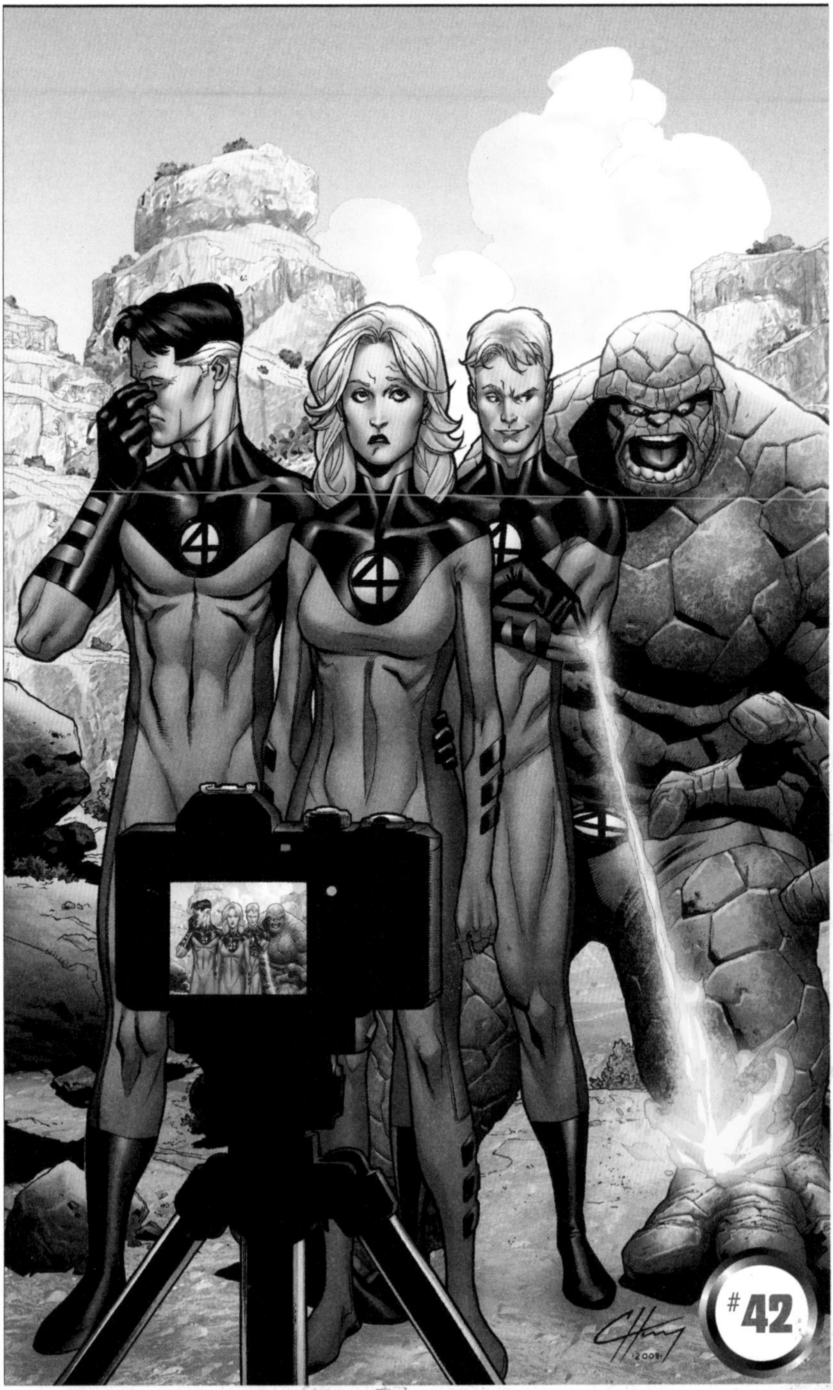
#42

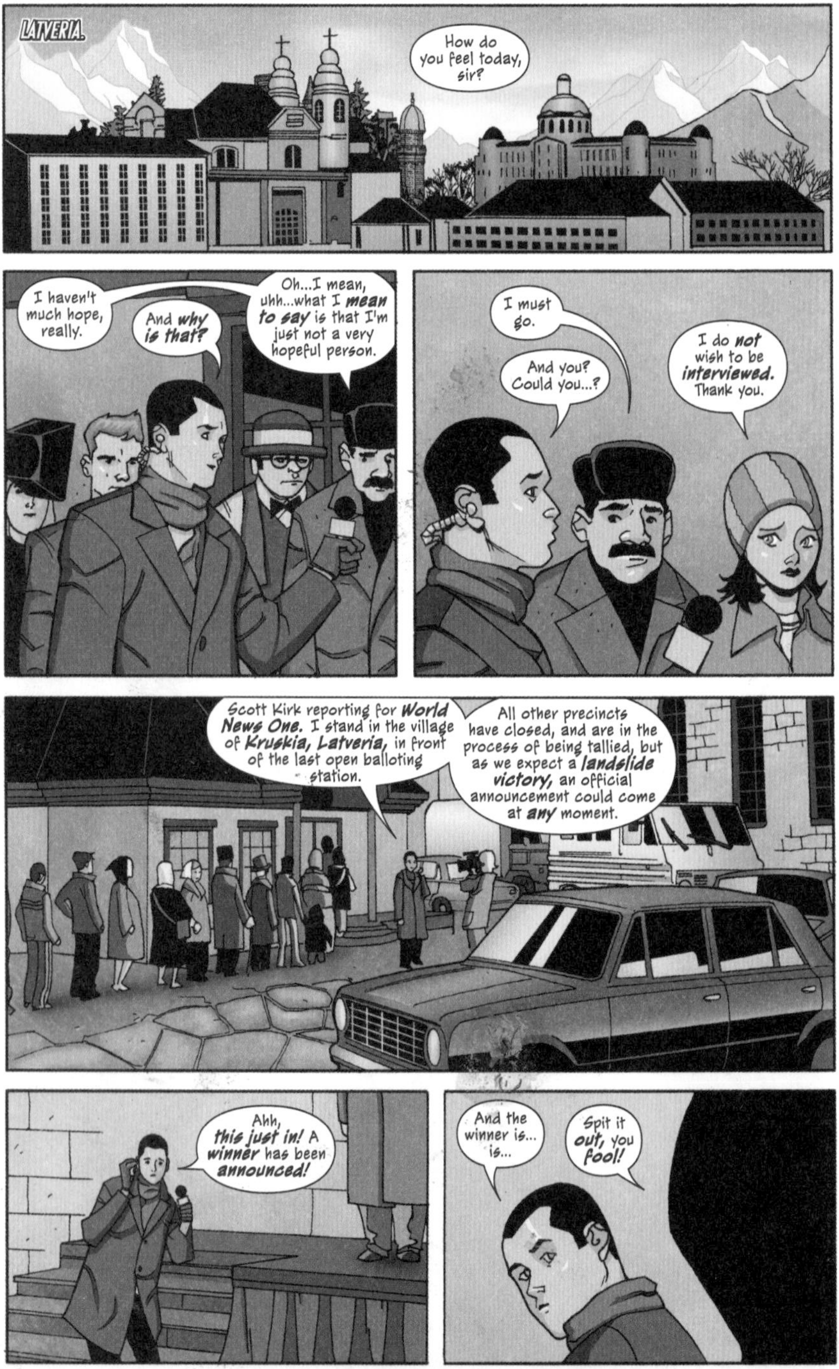
LATVERIA.
How do you feel today, sir?
I haven't much hope, really.
And why is that?
Oh...I mean, uhh...what I mean to say is that I'm just not a very hopeful person.
I must go.
And you? Could you...?
I do not wish to be interviewed. Thank you.
Scott Kirk reporting for World News One. I stand in the village of Kruskia, Latveria, in front of the last open balloting station.
All other precincts have closed, and are in the process of being tallied, but as we expect a landslide victory, an official announcement could come at any moment.
Ahh, this just in! A winner has been announced!
And the winner is... is...
Spit it out, you fool!

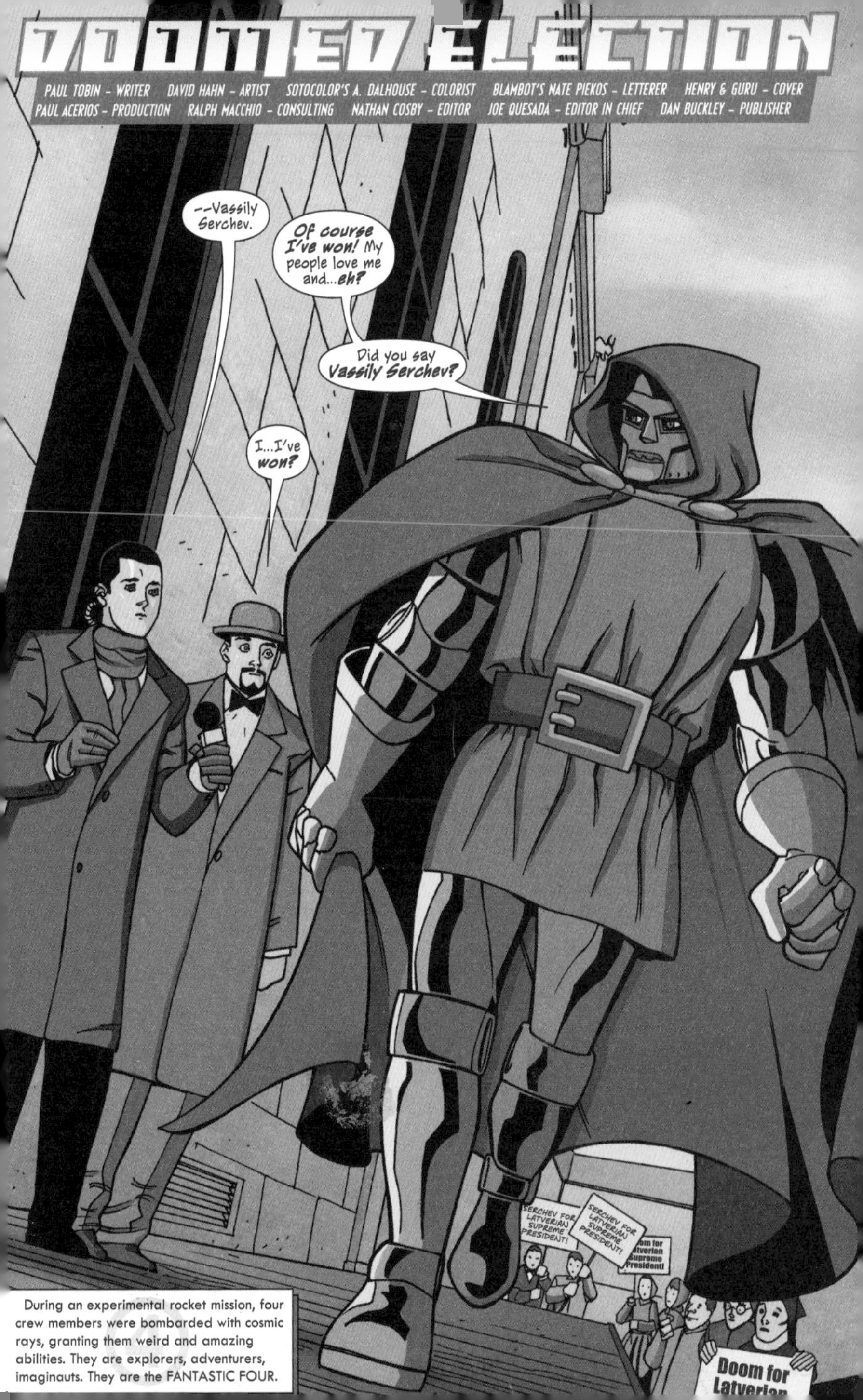
DOOMED ELECTION
PAUL TOBIN - WRITER DAVID HAHN - ARTIST SOTOCOLOR'S A. DALHOUSE - COLORIST BLAMBOT'S NATE PIEKOS - LETTERER HENRY & GURU - COVER
PAUL ACERIOS - PRODUCTION RALPH MACCHIO - CONSULTING NATHAN COSBY - EDITOR JOE QUESADA - EDITOR IN CHIEF DAN BUCKLEY - PUBLISHER
--Vassily Serchev.
Of course I've won! My people love me and...eh?
Did you say Vassily Serchev?
I...I've won?
SERCHEV FOR LATVERIAN SUPREME PRESIDENT!
SERCHEV FOR LATVERIAN SUPREME PRESIDENT!
Doom for Latverian Supreme President!
Doom for Latverian
During an experimental rocket mission, four crew members were bombarded with cosmic rays, granting them weird and amazing abilities. They are explorers, adventurers, imaginauts. They are the FANTASTIC FOUR.

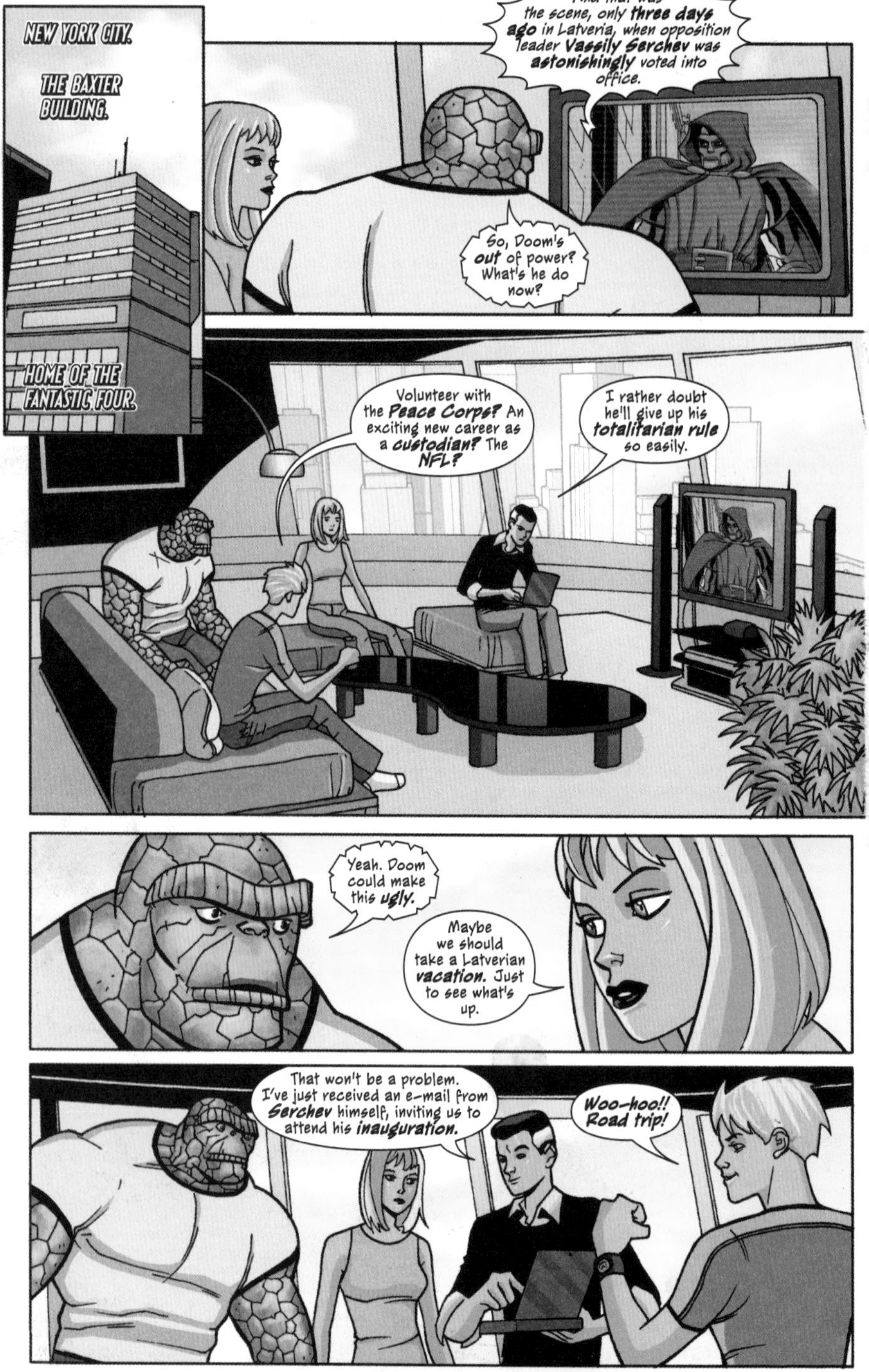
NEW YORK CITY.
THE BAXTER BUILDING.
HOME OF THE FANTASTIC FOUR.
And that was the scene, only three days ago in Latveria, when opposition leader Vassily Serchev was astonishingly voted into office.
So, Doom's out of power? What's he do now?
Volunteer with the Peace Corps? An exciting new career as a custodian? The NFL?
I rather doubt he'll give up his totalitarian rule so easily.
Yeah. Doom could make this ugly.
Maybe we should take a Latverian vacation. Just to see what's up.
That won't be a problem. I've just received an e-mail from Serchev himself, inviting us to attend his inauguration.
Woo-hoo!! Road trip!

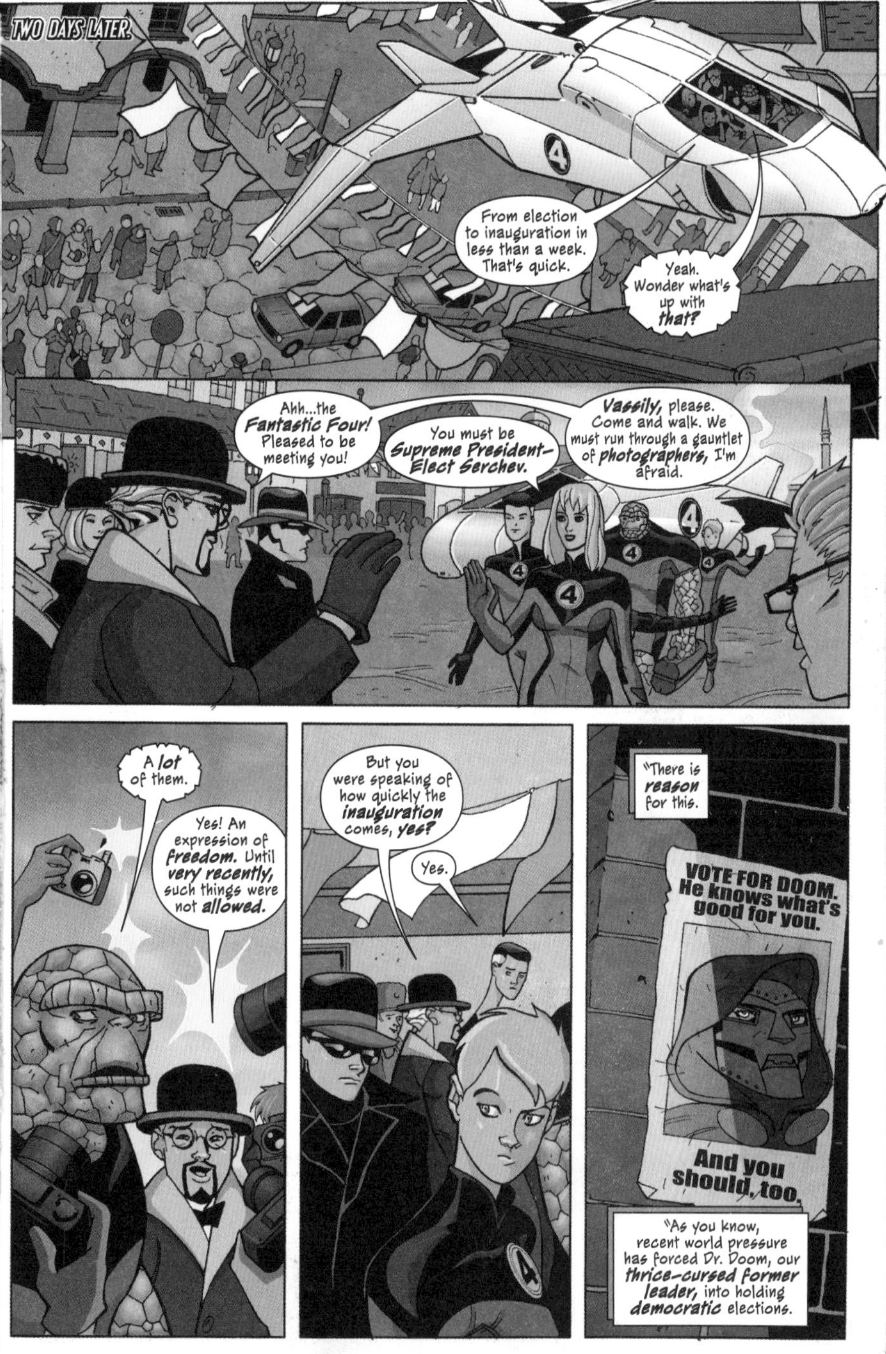
TWO DAYS LATER.
From election to inauguration in less than a week. That's quick.
Yeah. Wonder what's up with *that?*
Ahh...the *Fantastic Four!* Pleased to be meeting you!
You must be *Supreme President-Elect Serchev.*
Vassily, please. Come and walk. We must run through a gauntlet of *photographers,* I'm afraid.
A *lot* of them.
Yes! An expression of **freedom.** Until *very recently,* such things were not **allowed.**
But you were speaking of how quickly the *inauguration* comes, *yes?*
Yes.
"There is *reason* for this.
VOTE FOR DOOM. He knows what's good for you.
And you should, too.
"As you know, recent world pressure has forced Dr. Doom, our *thrice-cursed former leader,* into holding *democratic* elections.

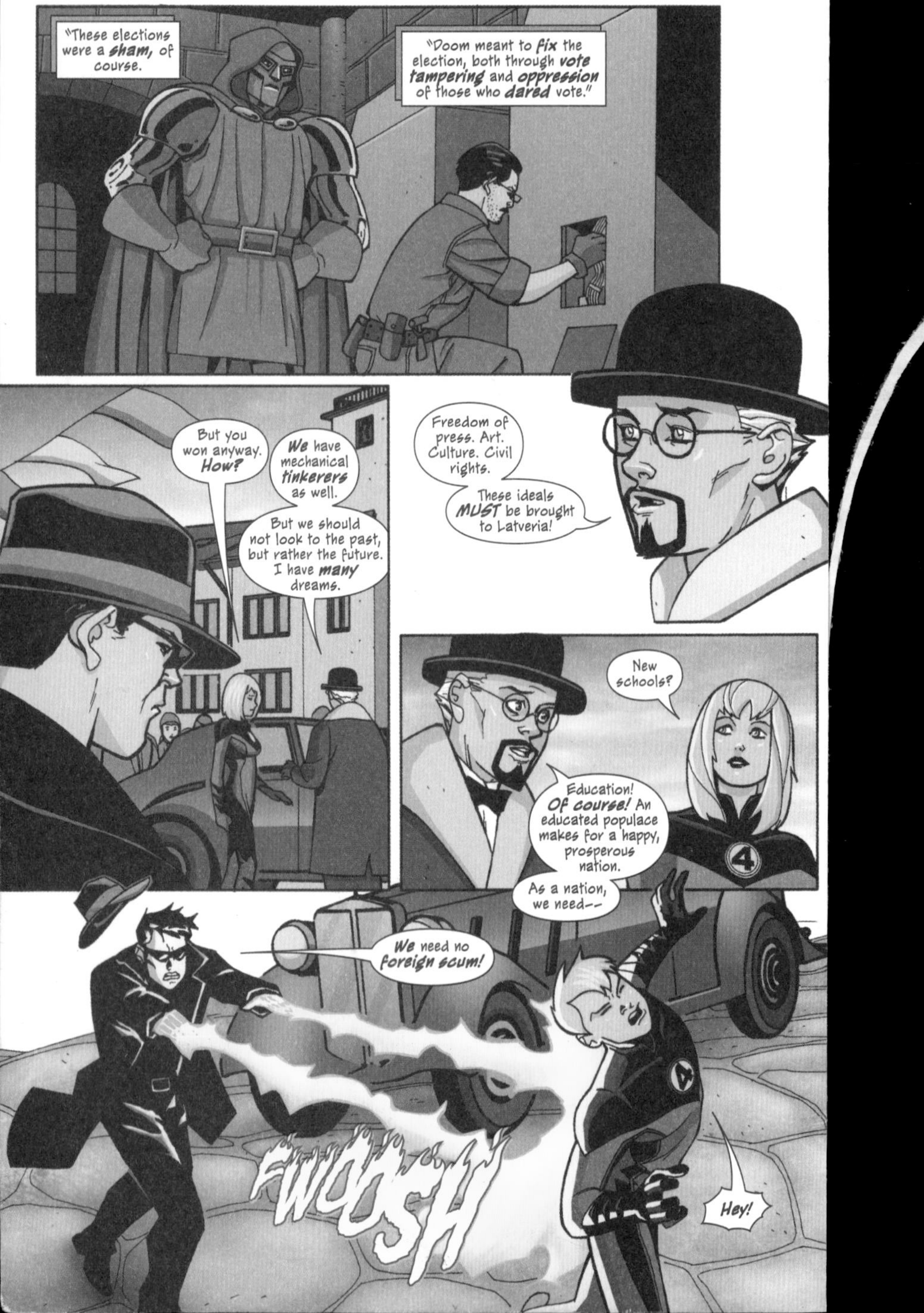
"These elections were a *sham,* of course.
"Doom meant to *fix* the election, both through *vote tampering* and *oppression* of those who *dared* vote."
But you won anyway. *How?*
We have mechanical *tinkerers* as well.
But we should not look to the past, but rather the future. I have *many* dreams.
Freedom of press. Art. Culture. Civil rights.
These ideals *MUST* be brought to Latveria!
New schools?
Education! *Of course!* An educated populace makes for a happy, prosperous nation.
As a nation, we need--
We need no *foreign scum!*
FWOOSH
Hey!

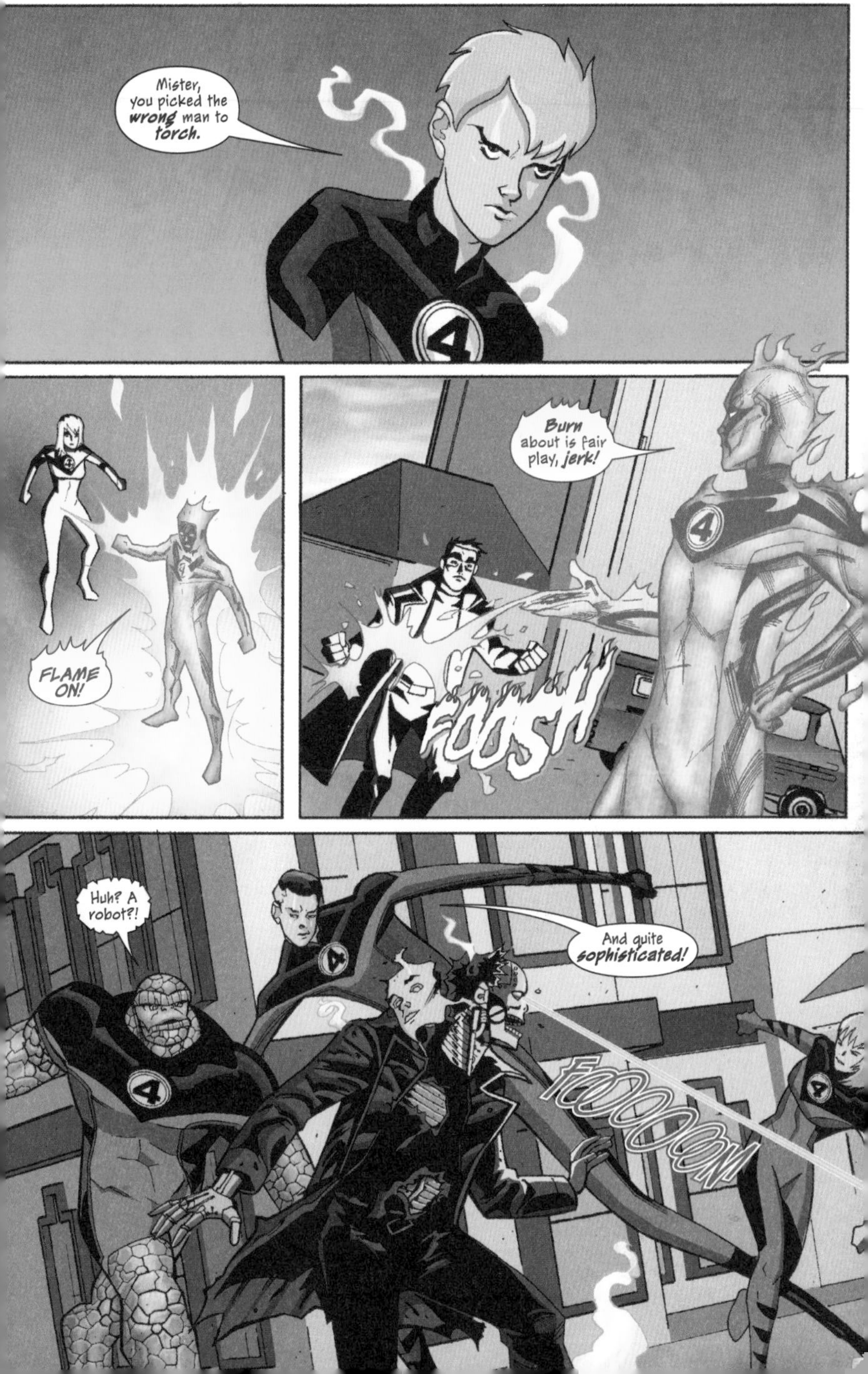

Mister, you picked the wrong man to torch.
FLAME ON!
Burn about is fair play, jerk!
FOOSH
Huh? A robot?!
And quite sophisticated!
FOOOOOOM

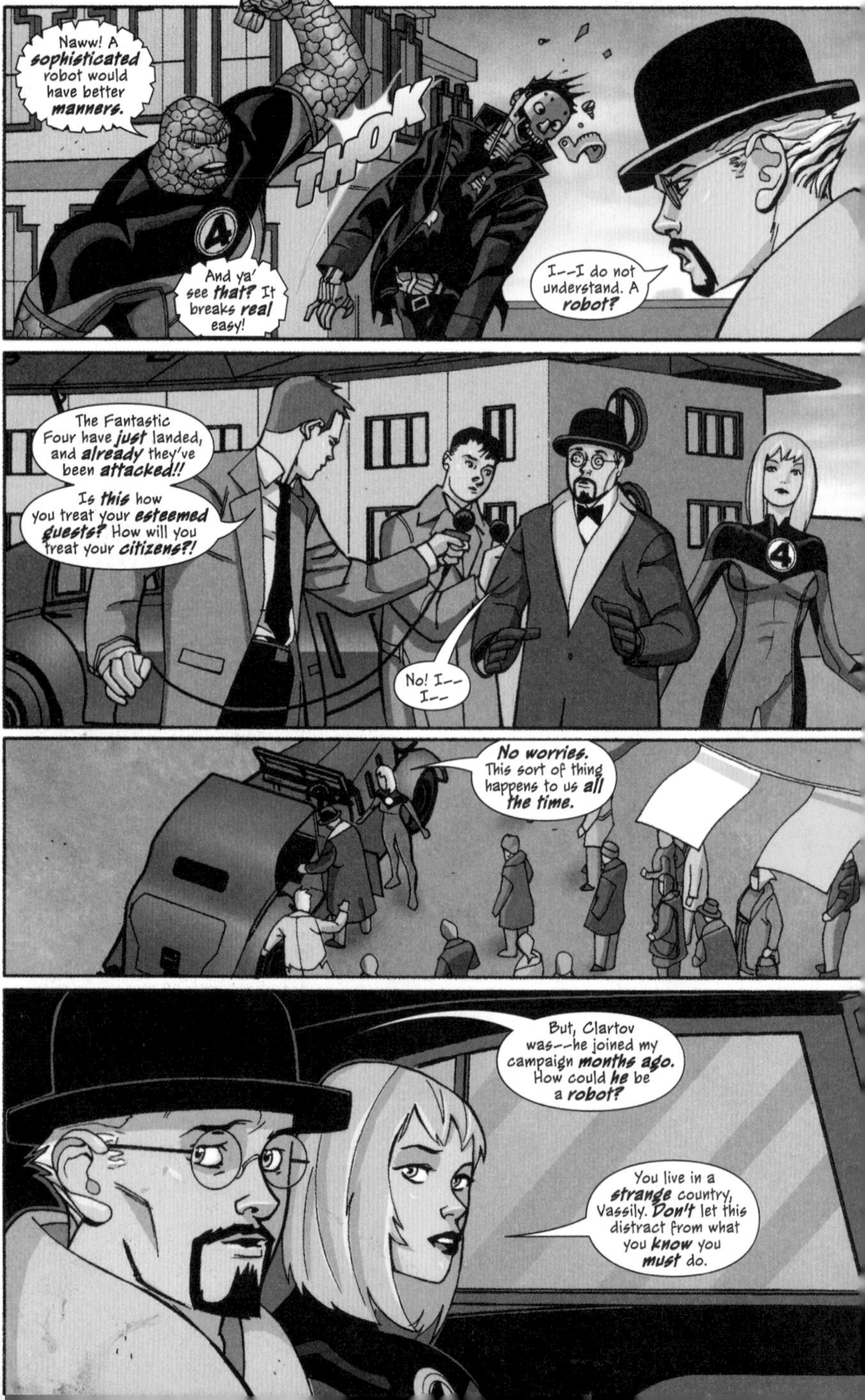
Naww! A sophisticated robot would have better manners.
THOK
And ya' see that? It breaks real easy!
I--I do not understand. A robot?
The Fantastic Four have just landed, and already they've been attacked!!
Is this how you treat your esteemed guests? How will you treat your citizens?!
No! I-- I--
No worries. This sort of thing happens to us all the time.
But, Clartov was--he joined my campaign months ago. How could he be a robot?
You live in a strange country, Vassily. Don't let this distract from what you know you must do.

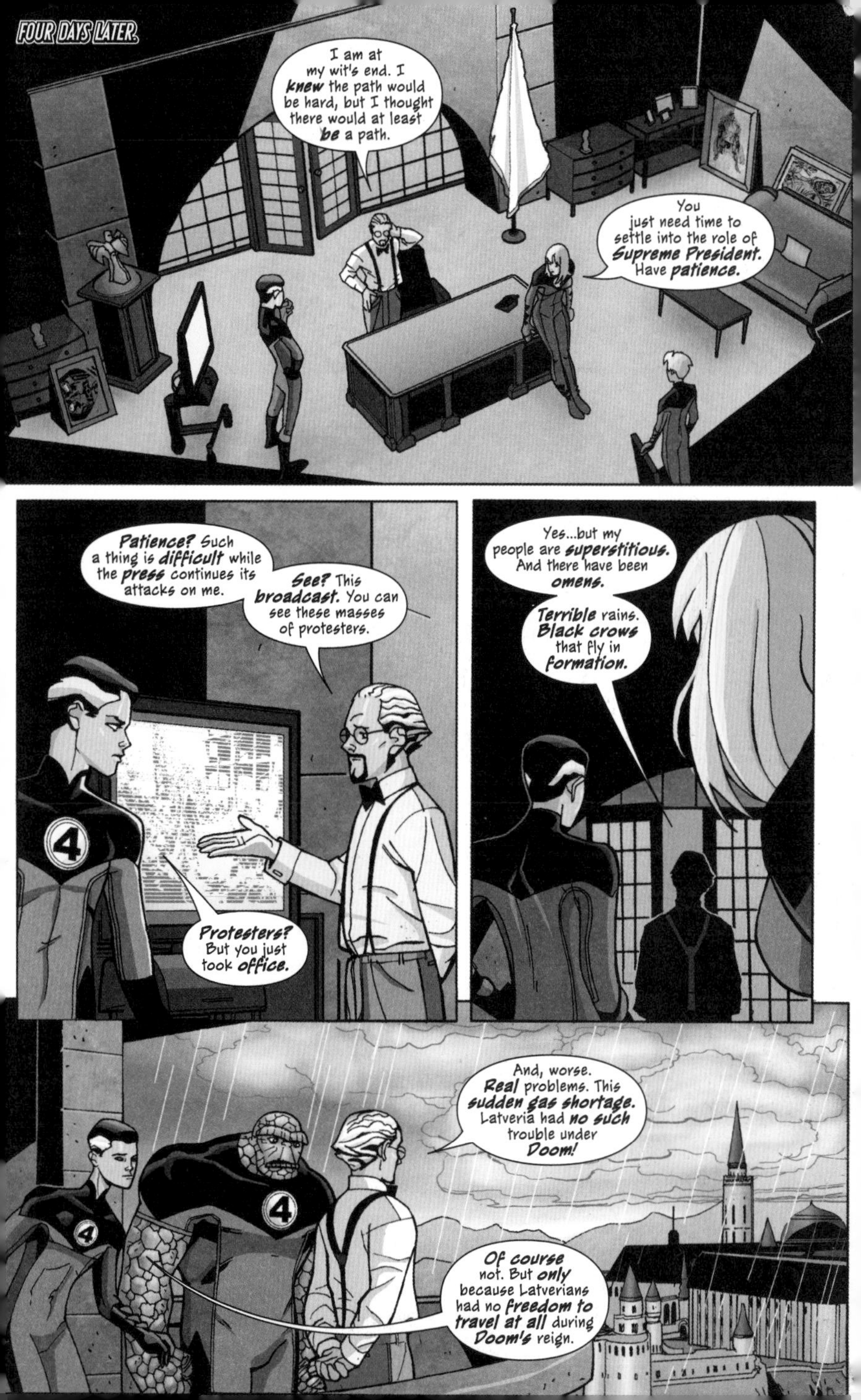

FOUR DAYS LATER.
I am at my wit's end. I knew the path would be hard, but I thought there would at least be a path.
You just need time to settle into the role of Supreme President. Have patience.
Patience? Such a thing is difficult while the press continues its attacks on me.
See? This broadcast. You can see these masses of protesters.
Protesters? But you just took office.
Yes...but my people are superstitious. And there have been omens.
Terrible rains. Black crows that fly in formation.
And, worse. Real problems. This sudden gas shortage. Latveria had no such trouble under Doom!
Of course not. But only because Latverians had no freedom to travel at all during Doom's reign.

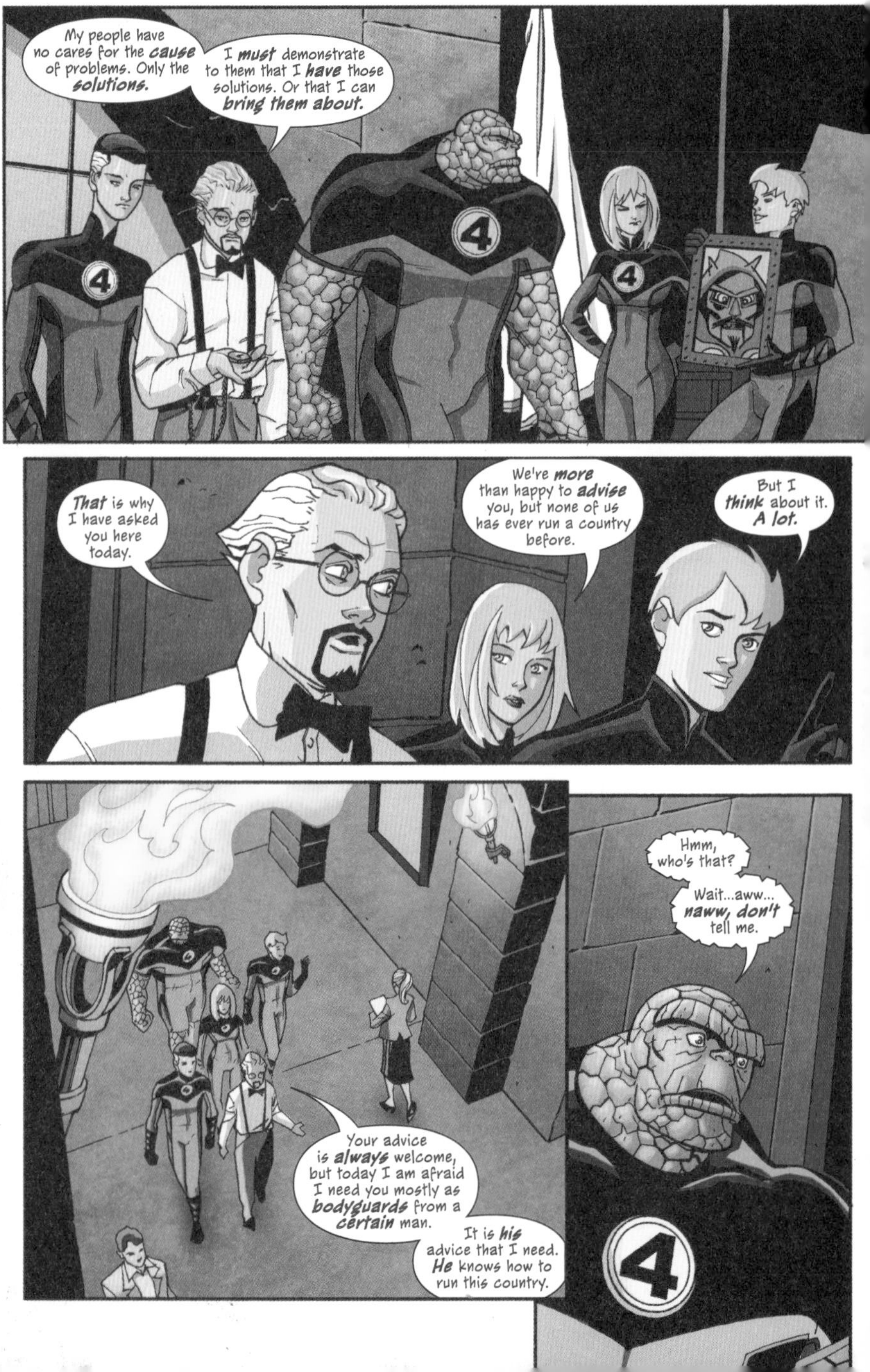

My people have no cares for the *cause* of problems. Only the *solutions.*
I *must* demonstrate to them that I *have* those solutions. Or that I can *bring them about.*
That is why I have asked you here today.
We're *more* than happy to *advise* you, but none of us has ever run a country before.
But I *think* about it. *A lot.*
Your advice is *always* welcome, but today I am afraid I need you mostly as *bodyguards* from a *certain* man.
It is *his* advice that I need. *He* knows how to run this country.
Hmm, who's that?
Wait...aww... *naww, don't* tell me.

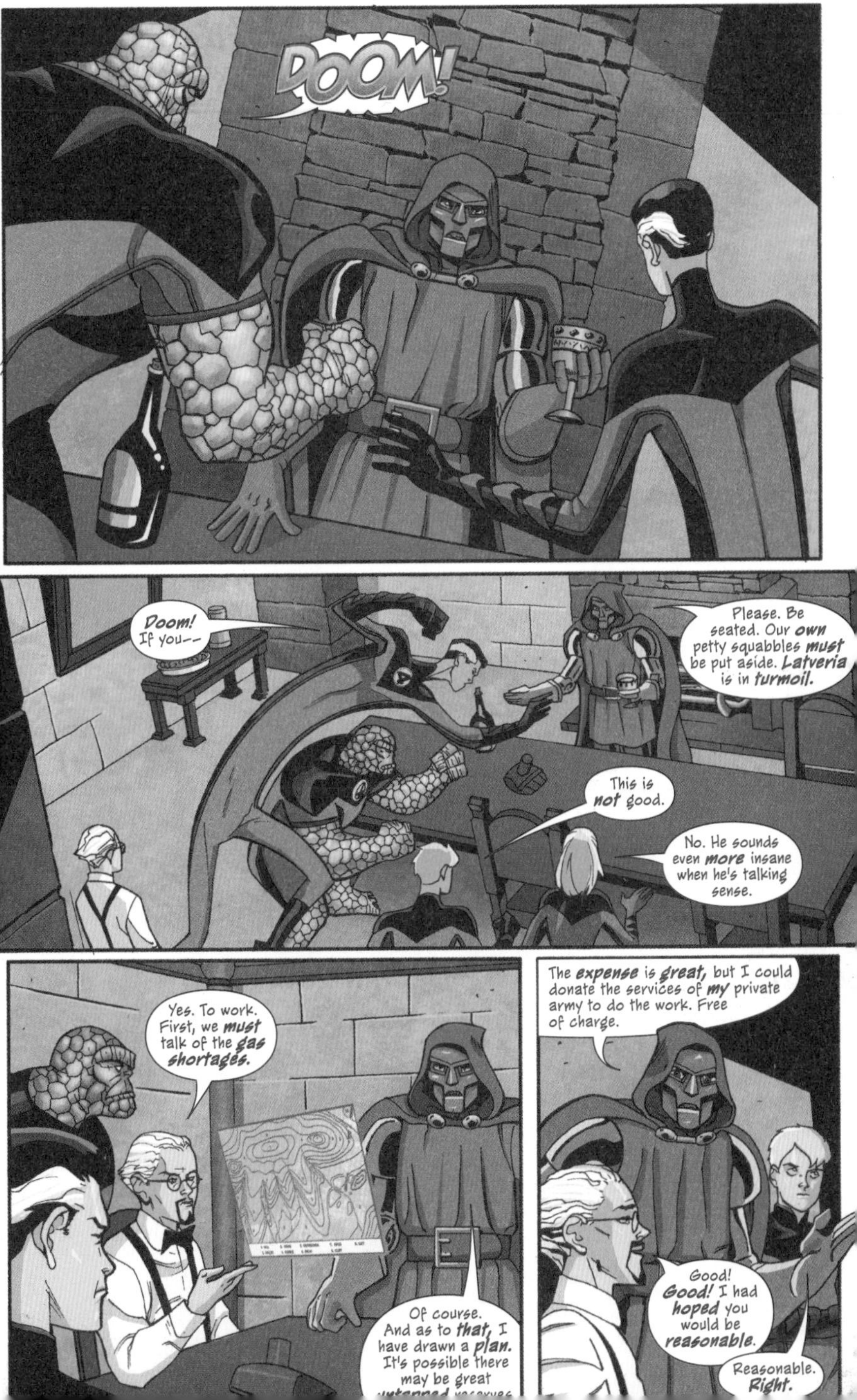
DOOM!
Doom! If you--
Please. Be seated. Our own petty squabbles must be put aside. Latveria is in turmoil.
This is not good.
No. He sounds even more insane when he's talking sense.
Yes. To work. First, we must talk of the gas shortages.
Of course. And as to that, I have drawn a plan. It's possible there may be great
The expense is great, but I could donate the services of my private army to do the work. Free of charge.
Good! Good! I had hoped you would be reasonable.
Reasonable. Right.

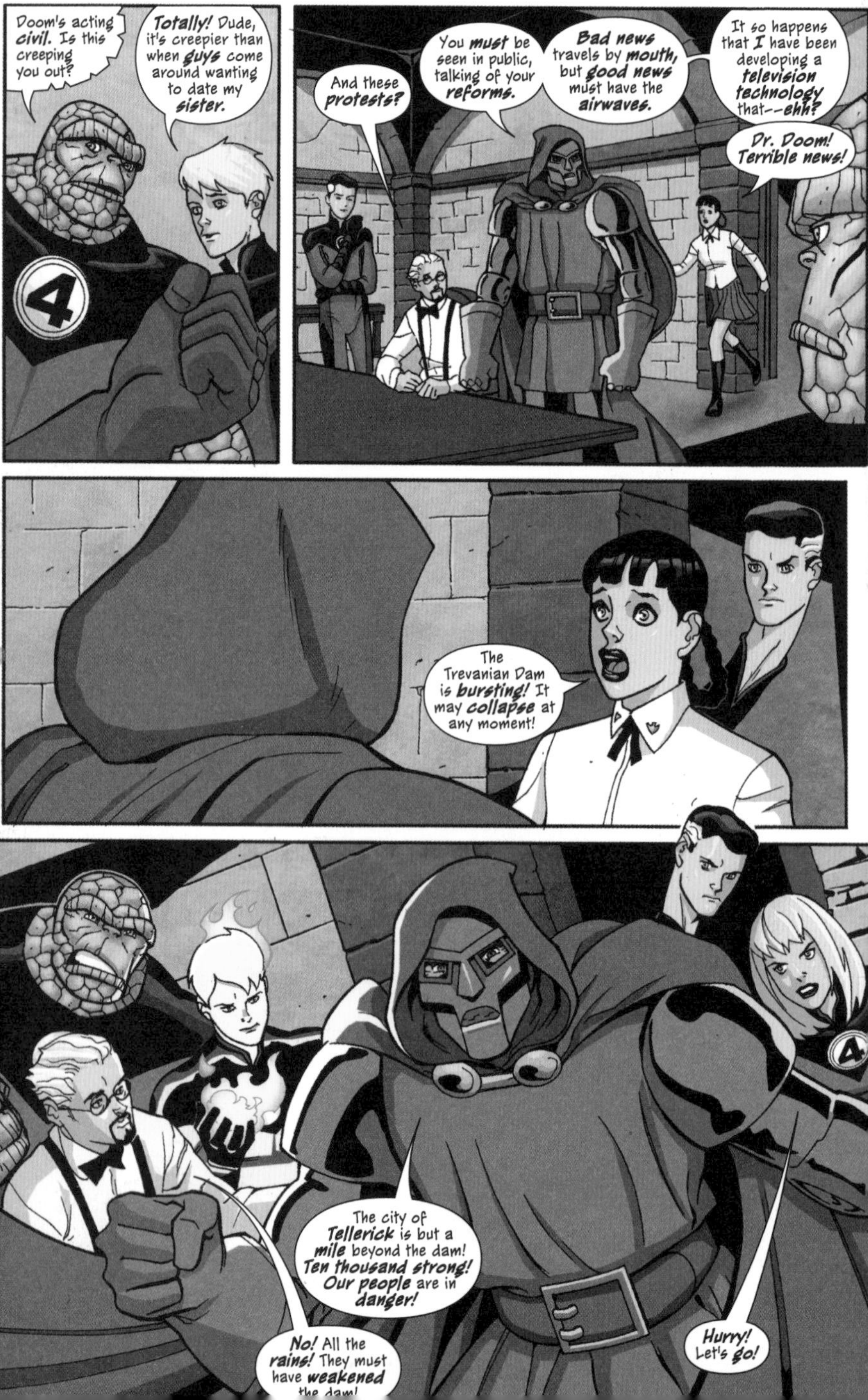
Doom's acting civil. Is this creeping you out?
Totally! Dude, it's creepier than when guys come around wanting to date my sister.
And these protests?
You must be seen in public, talking of your reforms.
Bad news travels by mouth, but good news must have the airwaves.
It so happens that I have been developing a television technology that--ehh?
Dr. Doom! Terrible news!
The Trevanian Dam is bursting! It may collapse at any moment!
The city of Tellerick is but a mile beyond the dam! Ten thousand strong! Our people are in danger!
No! All the rains! They must have weakened the dam!
Hurry! Let's go!

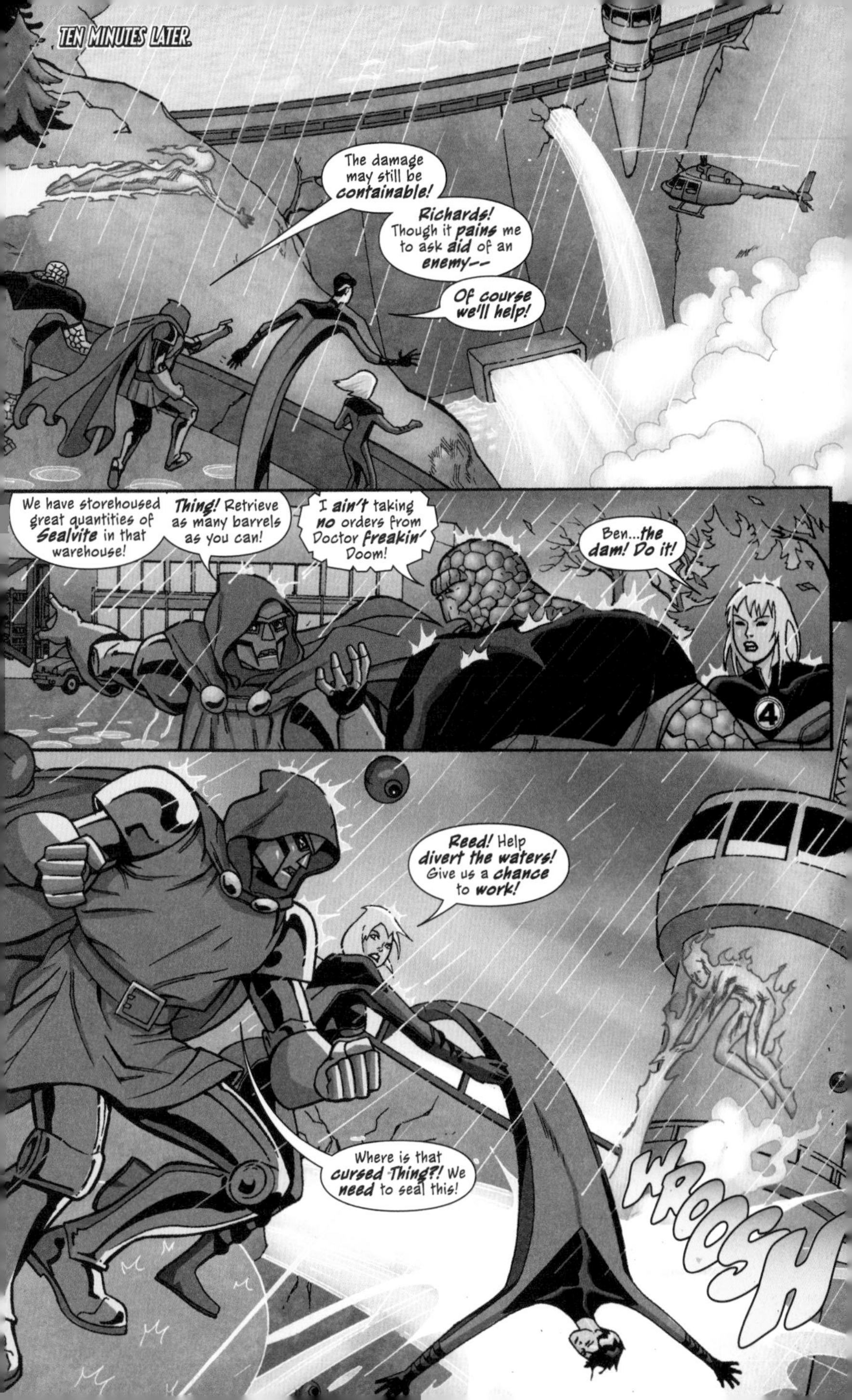

TEN MINUTES LATER.
The damage may still be containable!
Richards! Though it pains me to ask aid of an enemy--
Of course we'll help!
We have storehoused great quantities of Sealvite in that warehouse!
Thing! Retrieve as many barrels as you can!
I ain't taking no orders from Doctor freakin' Doom!
Ben...the dam! Do it!
Reed! Help divert the waters! Give us a chance to work!
Where is that cursed Thing?! We need to seal this!
WOOOCH

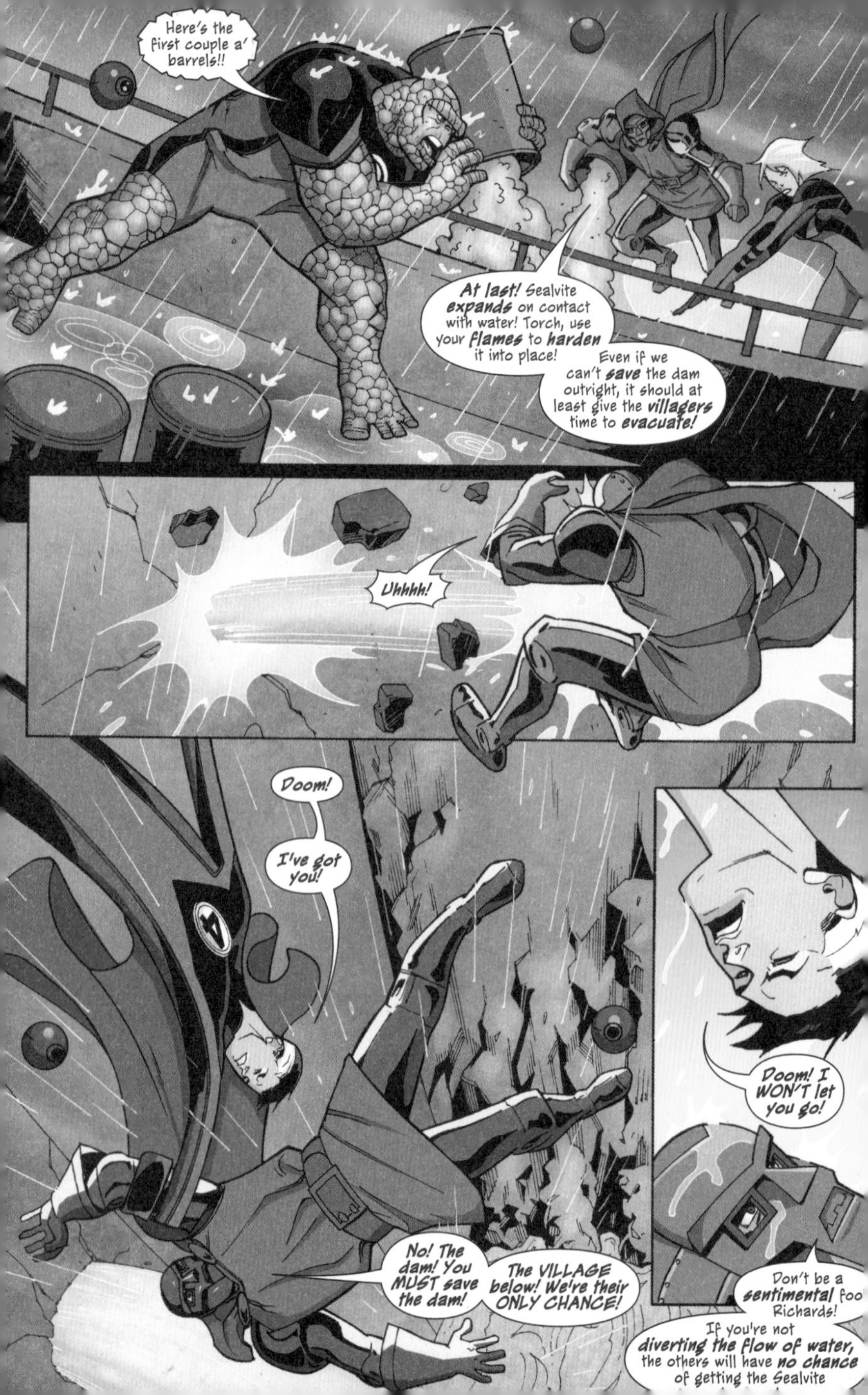
Here's the first couple a' barrels!!
At last! Sealvite expands on contact with water! Torch, use your flames to harden it into place!
Even if we can't save the dam outright, it should at least give the villagers time to evacuate!
Uhhhh!
Doom!
I've got you!
Doom! I WON'T let you go!
No! The dam! You MUST save the dam!
The VILLAGE below! We're their ONLY CHANCE!
Don't be a sentimental foo Richards!
If you're not diverting the flow of water, the others will have no chance of getting the Sealvite

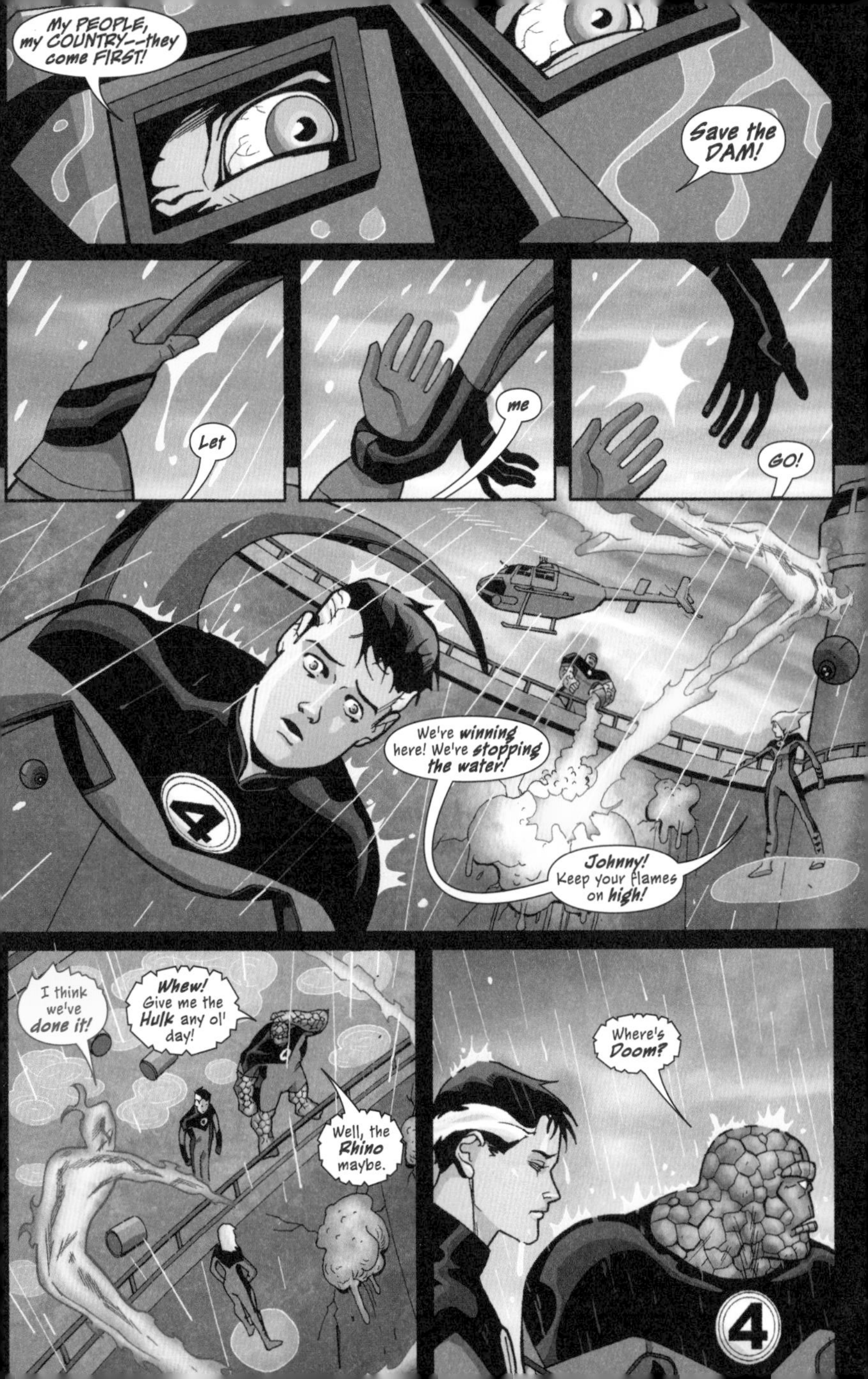
My PEOPLE, my COUNTRY--they come FIRST!
Save the DAM!
Let
me
GO!
We're winning here! We're stopping the water!
Johnny! Keep your flames on high!
I think we've done it!
Whew! Give me the Hulk any ol' day!
Well, the Rhino maybe.
Where's Doom?

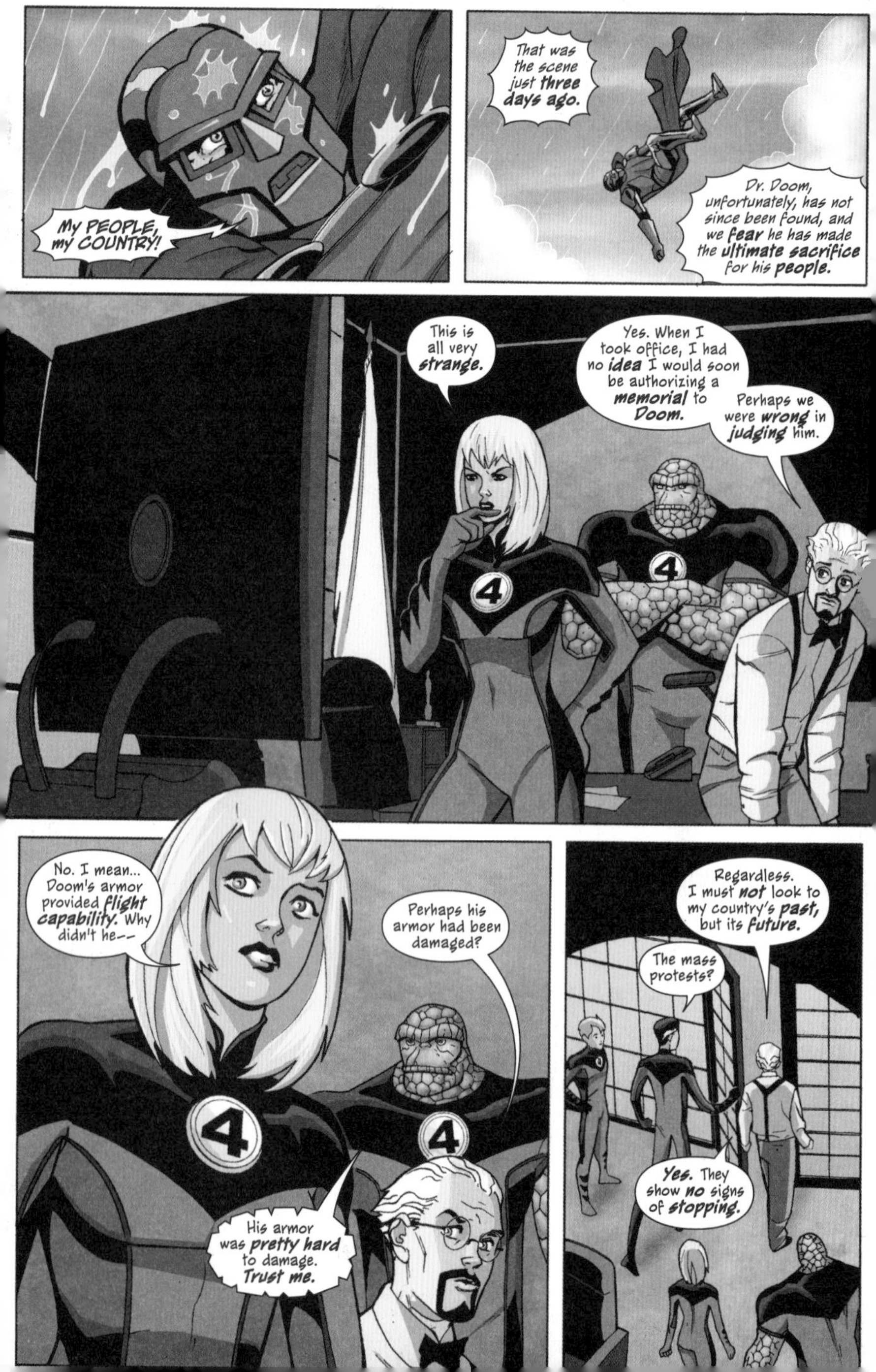

My PEOPLE, my COUNTRY!
That was the scene just three days ago.
Dr. Doom, unfortunately, has not since been found, and we fear he has made the ultimate sacrifice for his people.
This is all very strange.
Yes. When I took office, I had no idea I would soon be authorizing a memorial to Doom.
Perhaps we were wrong in judging him.
No. I mean... Doom's armor provided flight capability. Why didn't he--
Perhaps his armor had been damaged?
His armor was pretty hard to damage. Trust me.
Regardless. I must not look to my country's past, but its future.
The mass protests?
Yes. They show no signs of stopping.

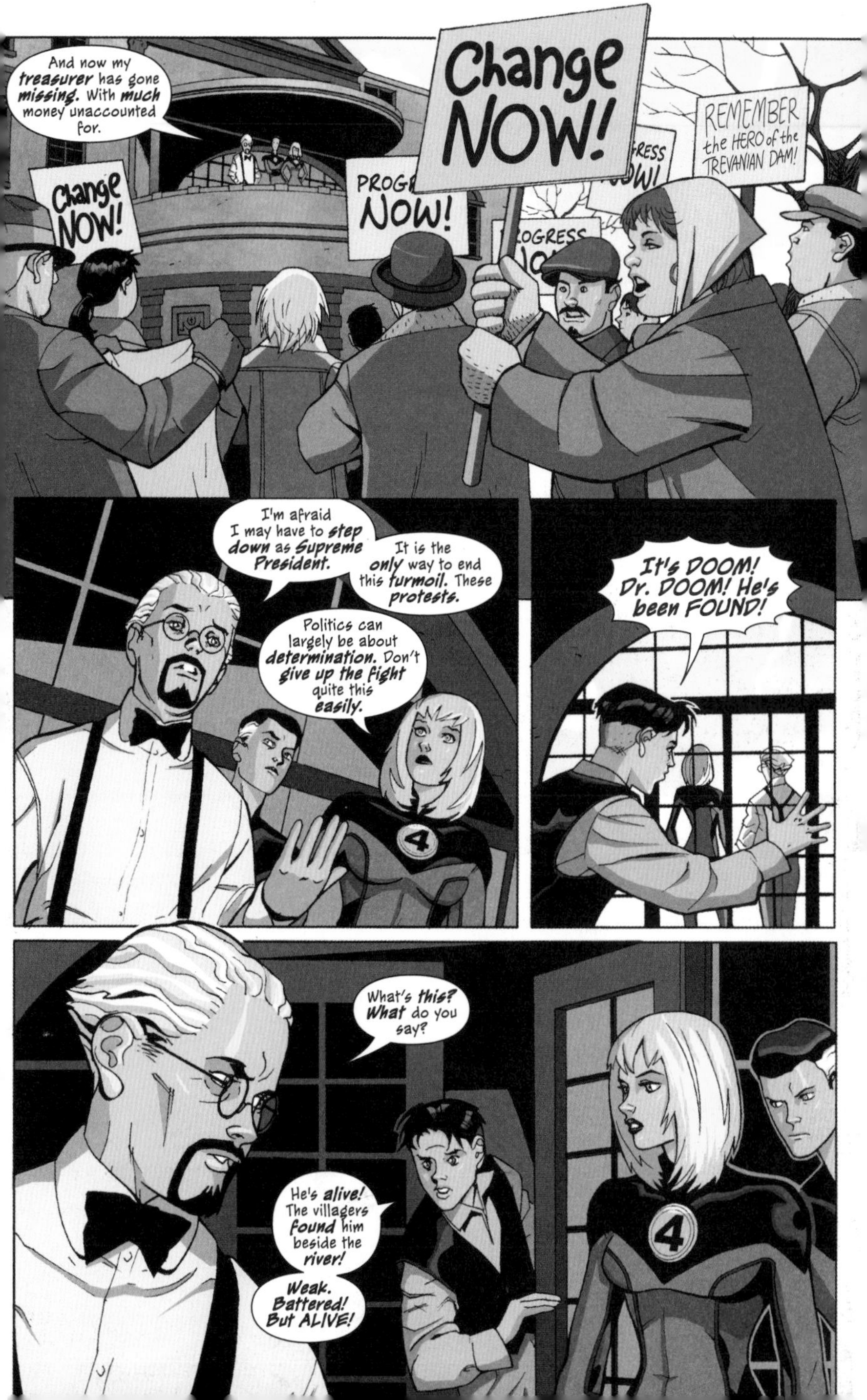
And now my treasurer has gone missing. With much money unaccounted for.
Change NOW!
Change NOW!
PROGRESS NOW!
PROGRESS NOW!
REMEMBER the HERO of the TREVANIAN DAM!
I'm afraid I may have to step down as Supreme President.
It is the only way to end this turmoil. These protests.
Politics can largely be about determination. Don't give up the fight quite this easily.
It's DOOM! Dr. DOOM! He's been FOUND!
What's this? What do you say?
He's alive! The villagers found him beside the river!
Weak. Battered! But ALIVE!

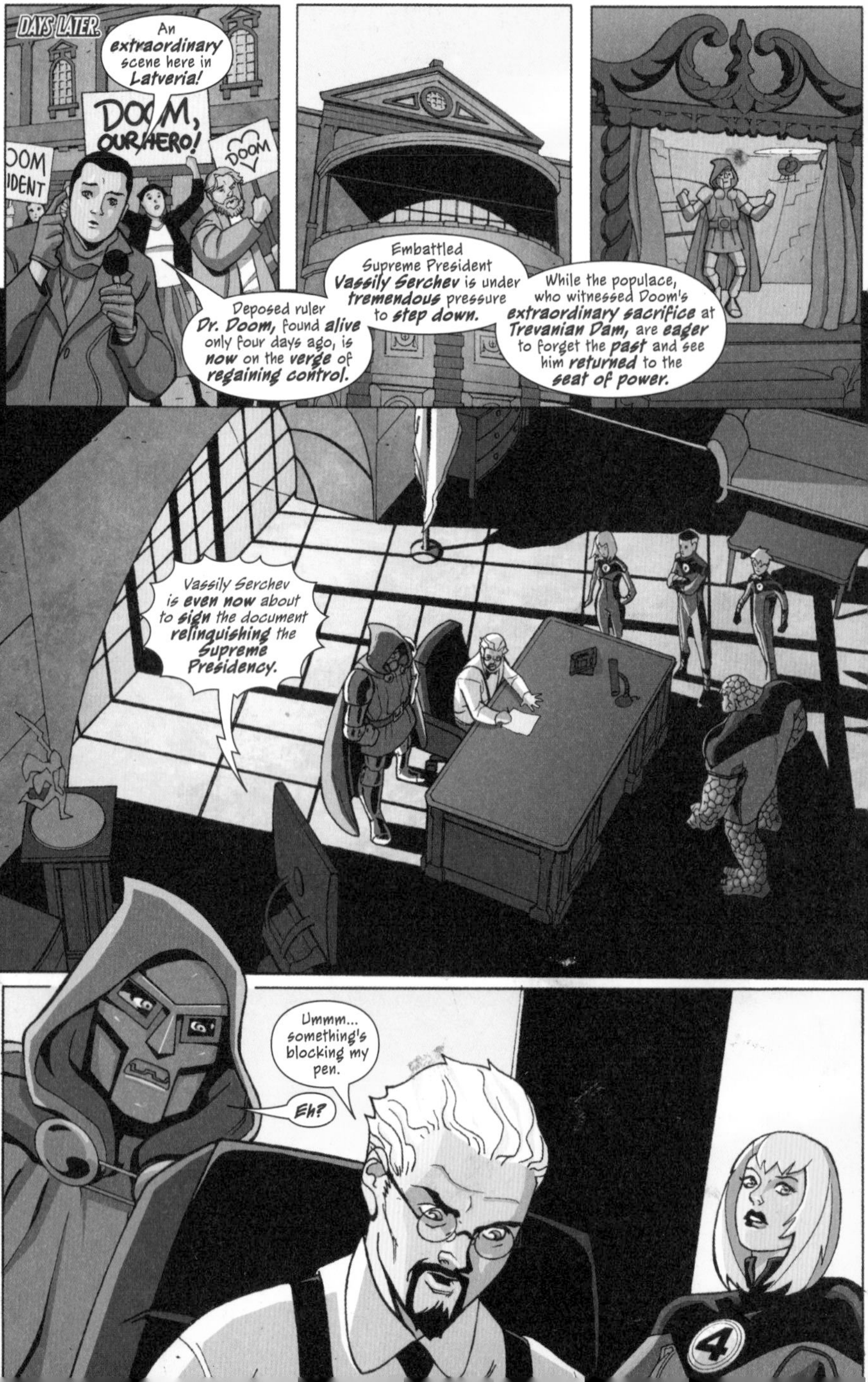
DAYS LATER.
An extraordinary scene here in Latveria!
DOOM, OUR HERO!
DOOM
Deposed ruler Dr. Doom, found alive only four days ago, is now on the verge of regaining control.
Embattled Supreme President Vassily Serchev is under tremendous pressure to step down.
While the populace, who witnessed Doom's extraordinary sacrifice at Trevanian Dam, are eager to forget the past and see him returned to the seat of power.
Vassily Serchev is even now about to sign the document relinquishing the Supreme Presidency.
Ummm... something's blocking my pen.
Eh?

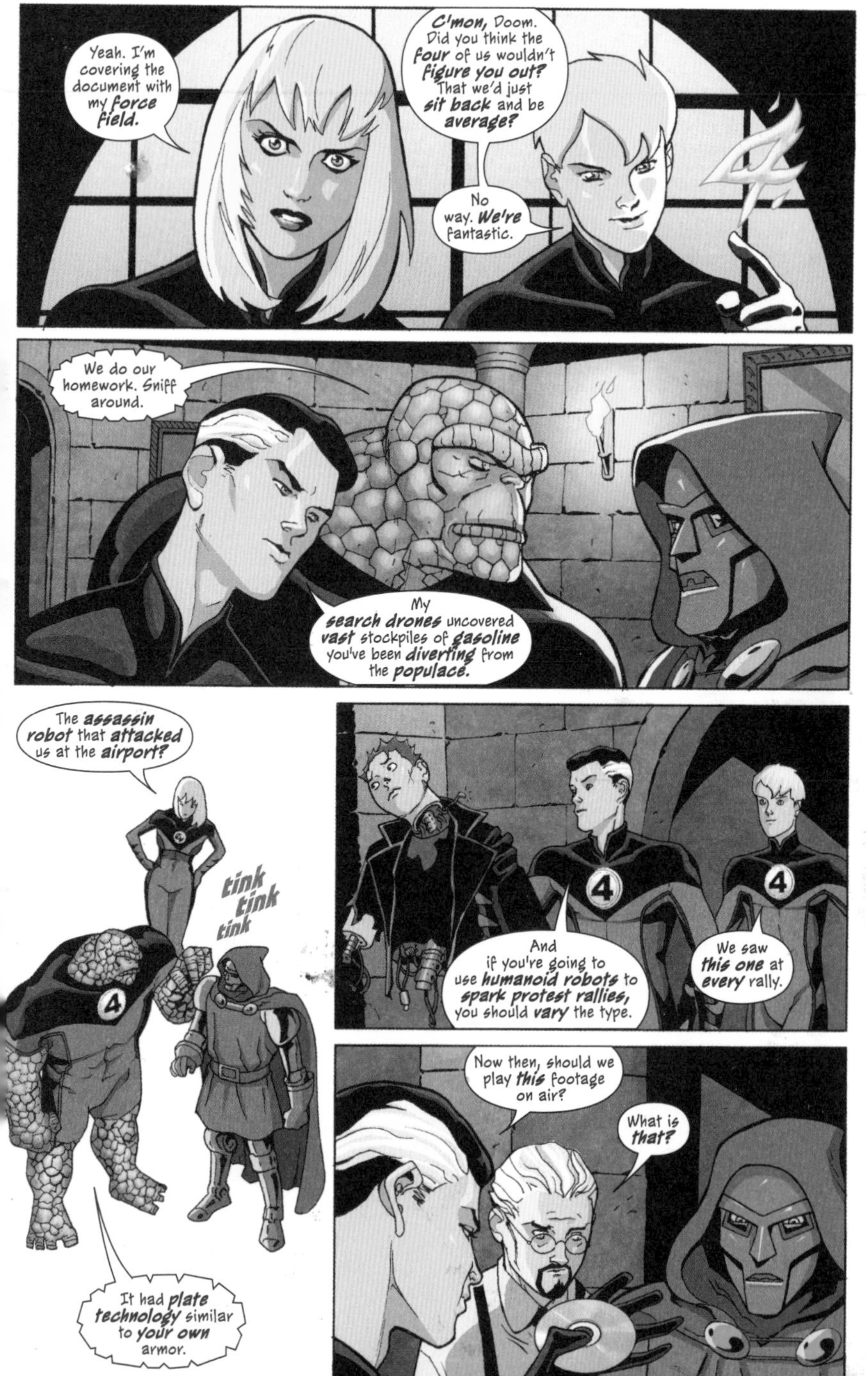

Yeah. I'm covering the document with my force field.
C'mon, Doom. Did you think the four of us wouldn't figure you out? That we'd just sit back and be average?
No way. We're fantastic.
We do our homework. Sniff around.
My search drones uncovered vast stockpiles of gasoline you've been diverting from the populace.
The assassin robot that attacked us at the airport?
tink tink tink
It had plate technology similar to your own armor.
And if you're going to use humanoid robots to spark protest rallies, you should vary the type.
We saw this one at every rally.
Now then, should we play this footage on air?
What is that?

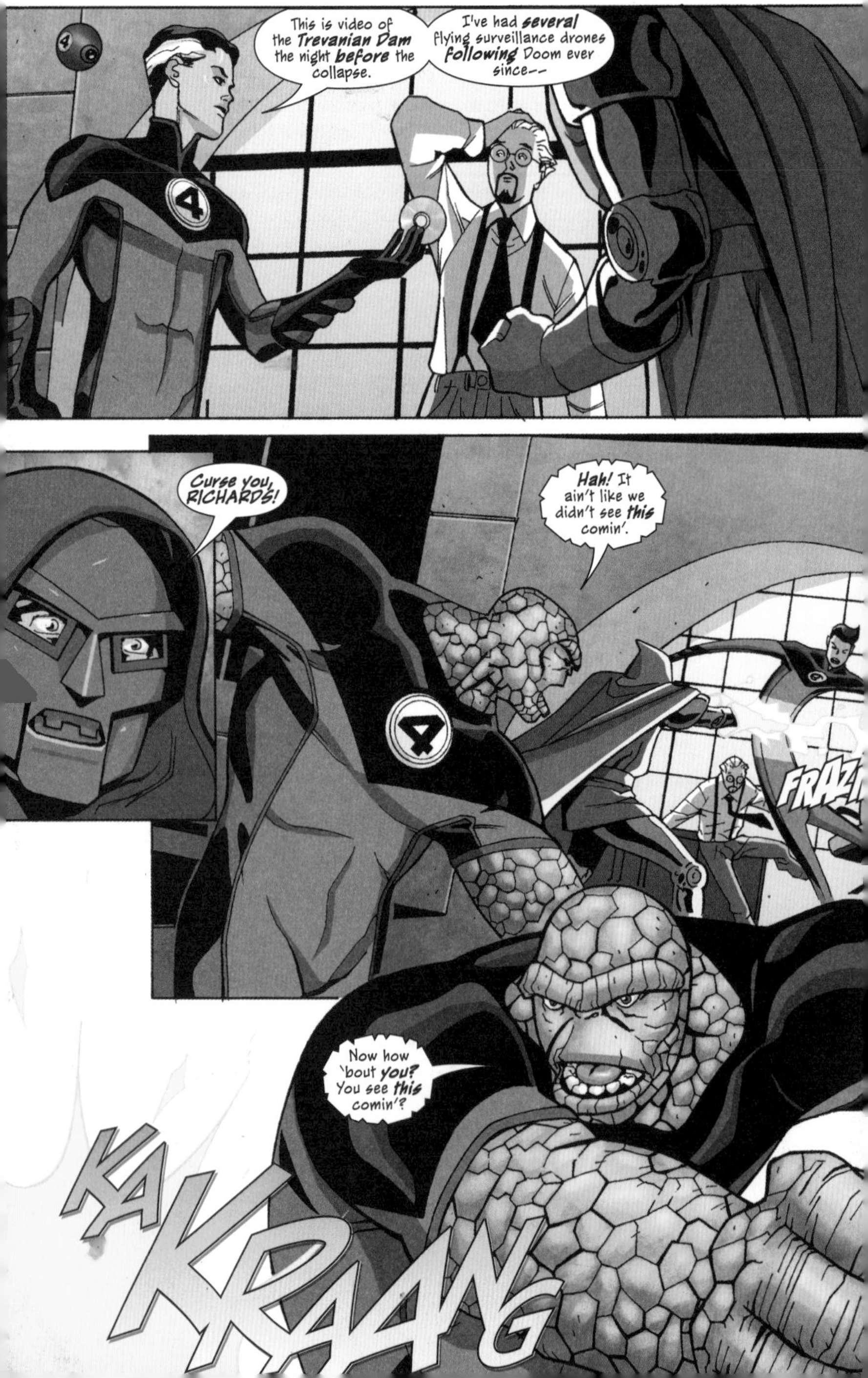
This is video of the Trevanian Dam the night before the collapse.
I've had several flying surveillance drones following Doom ever since--
Curse you, RICHARDS!
Hah! It ain't like we didn't see this comin'.
Now how 'bout you? You see this comin'?
KA KRAANG

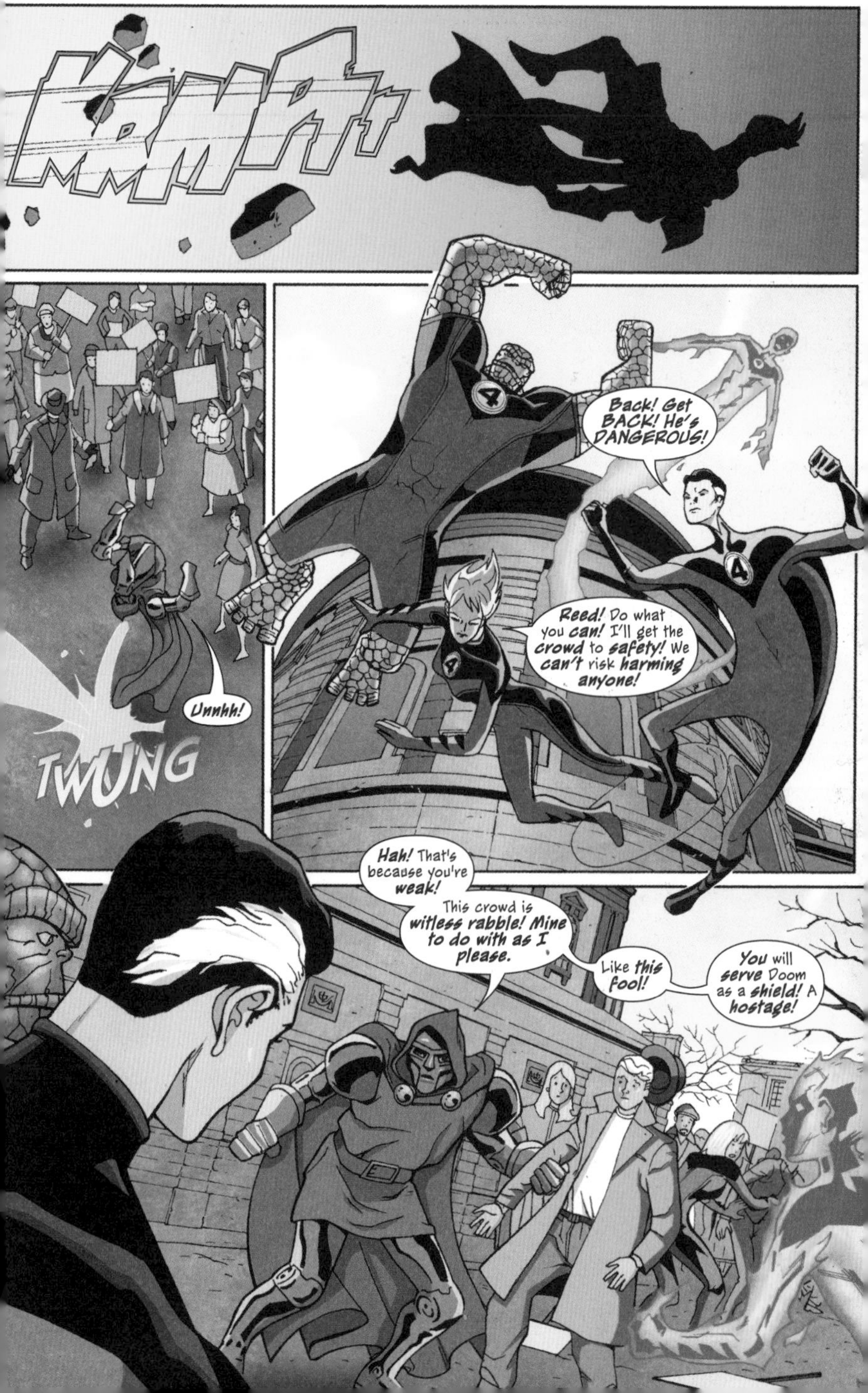

KAWHAM
Back! Get BACK! He's DANGEROUS!
Reed! Do what you can! I'll get the crowd to safety! We can't risk harming anyone!
Unnhh!
TWUNG
Hah! That's because you're weak!
This crowd is witless rabble! Mine to do with as I please.
Like this fool!
You will serve Doom as a shield! A hostage!

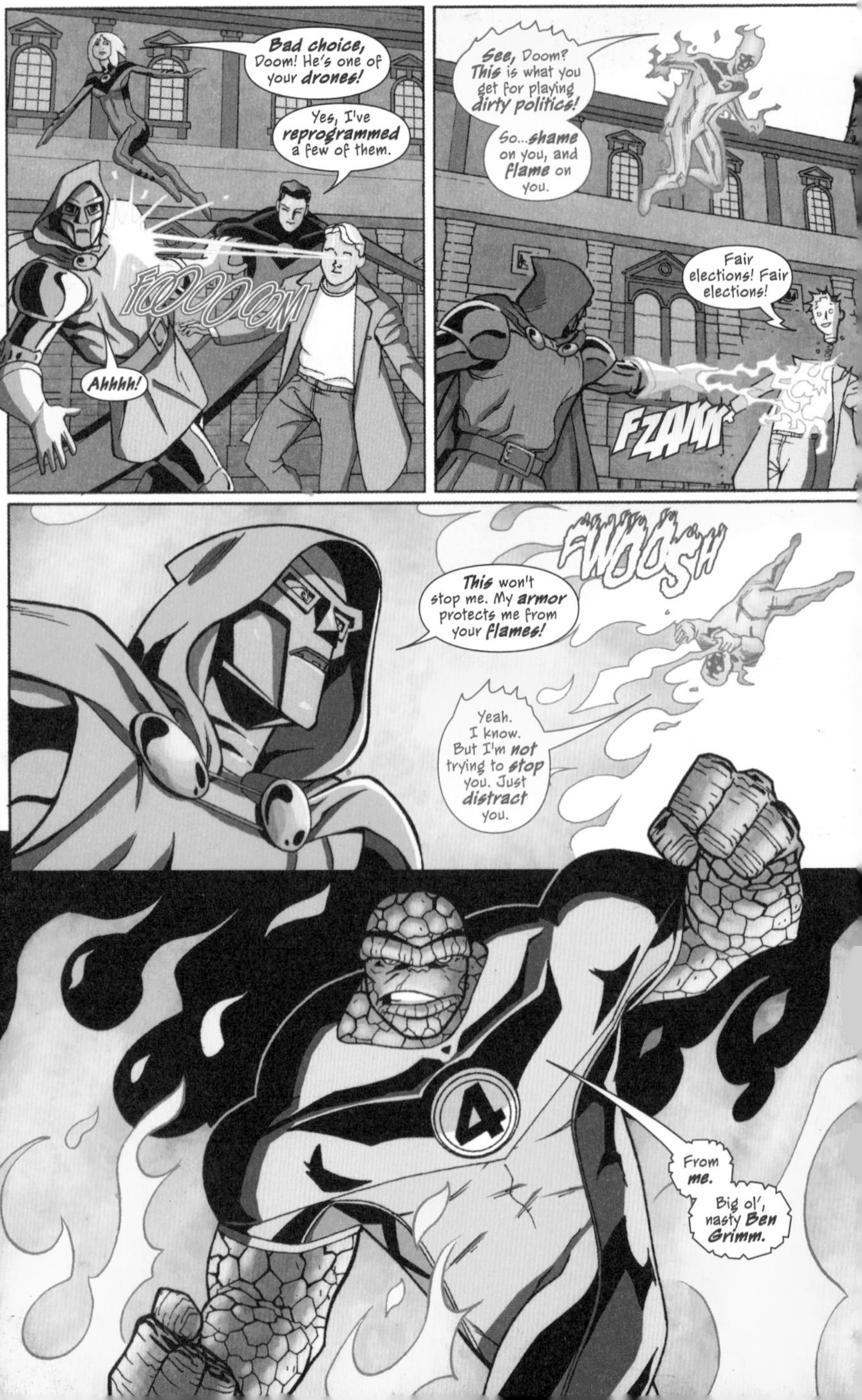
Bad choice, Doom! He's one of your drones!
Yes, I've reprogrammed a few of them.
FOOOOOOM
Ahhhh!
See, Doom? This is what you get for playing dirty politics!
So...shame on you, and flame on you.
Fair elections! Fair elections!
FZAKK
FWOOSH
This won't stop me. My armor protects me from your flames!
Yeah. I know. But I'm not trying to stop you. Just distract you.
From me.
Big ol', nasty Ben Grimm.

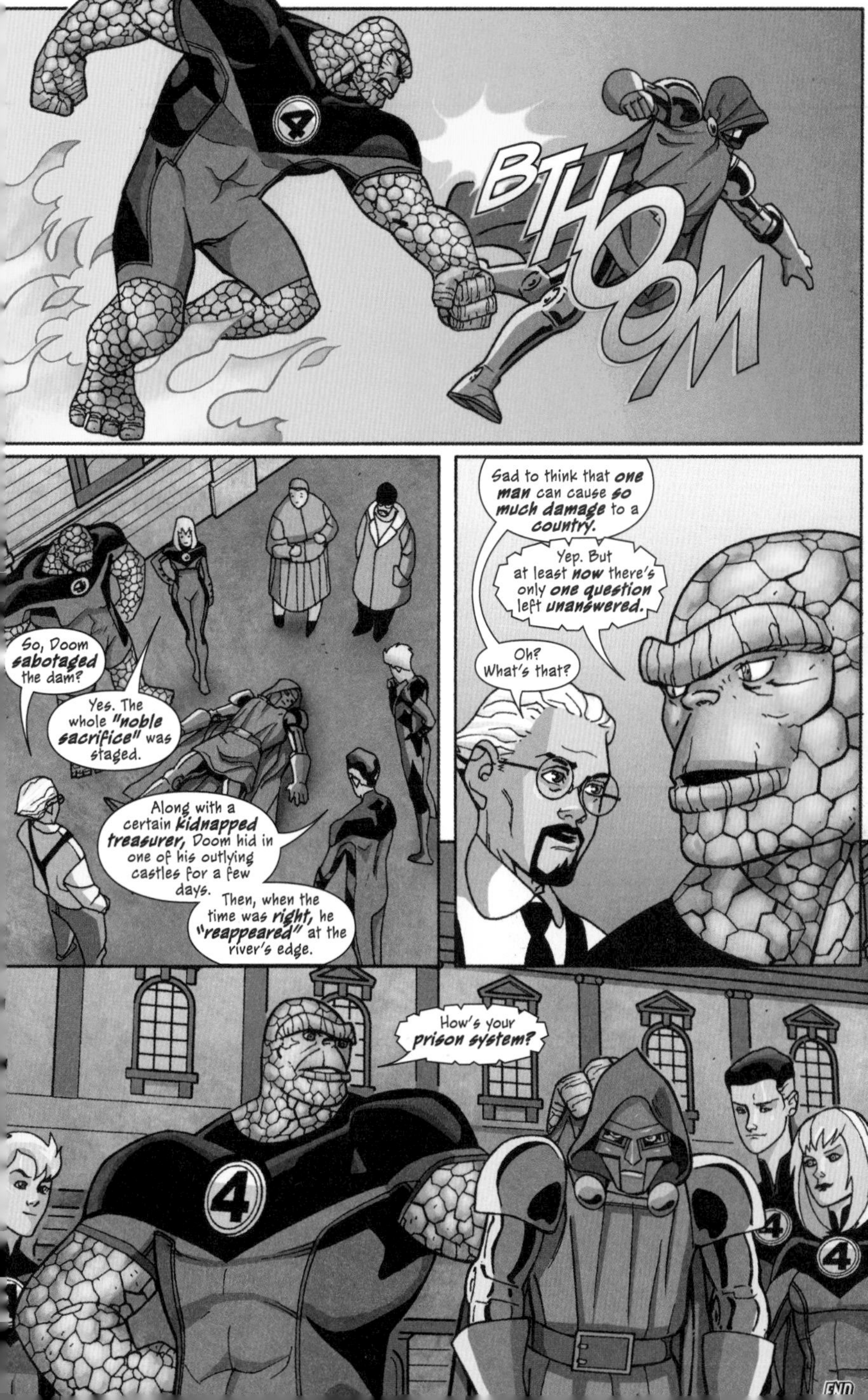
BTHOOM
So, Doom sabotaged the dam?
Yes. The whole "noble sacrifice" was staged.
Along with a certain kidnapped treasurer, Doom hid in one of his outlying castles for a few days.
Then, when the time was right, he "reappeared" at the river's edge.
Sad to think that one man can cause so much damage to a country.
Yep. But at least now there's only one question left unanswered.
Oh? What's that?
How's your prison system?
END

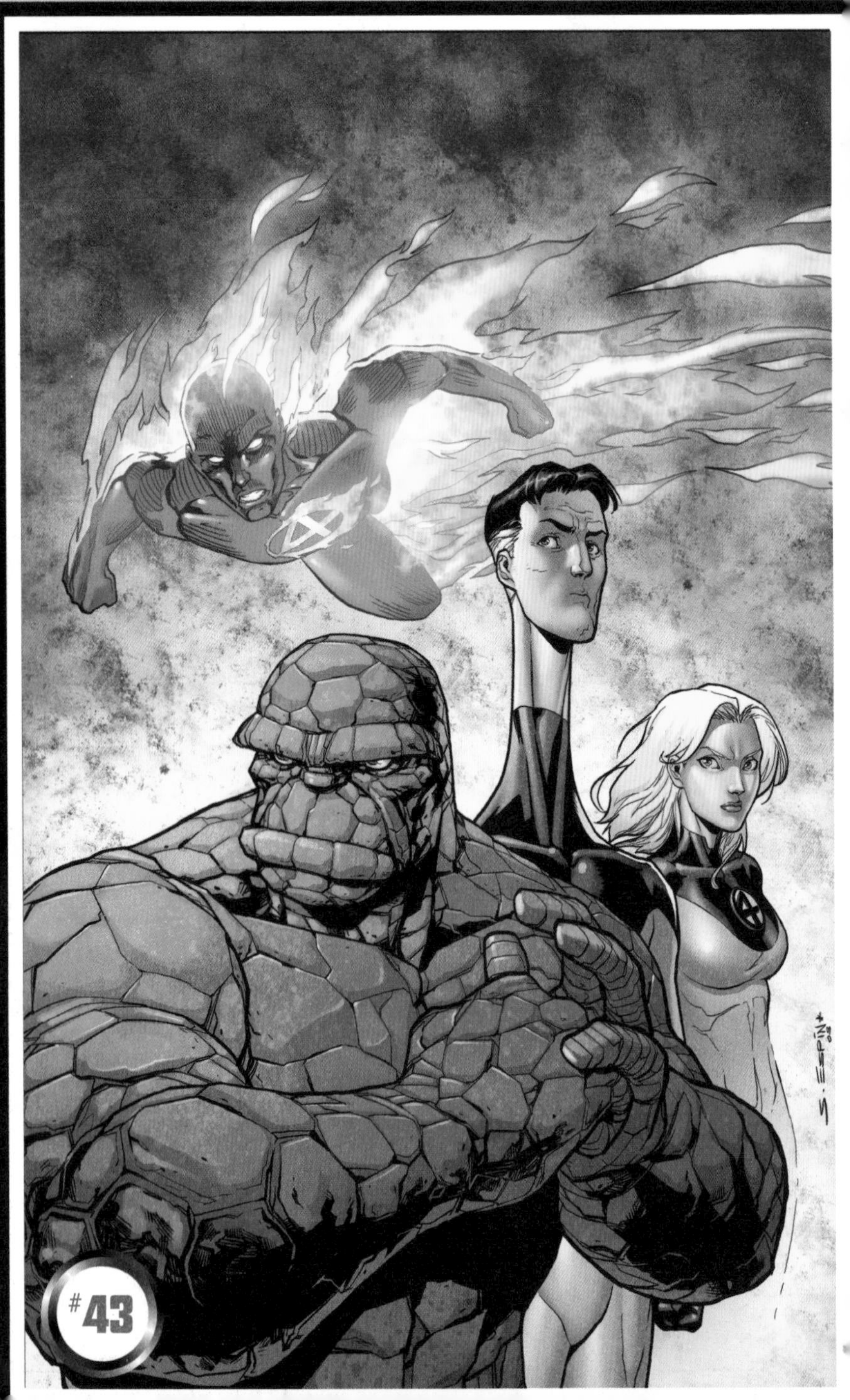
#43

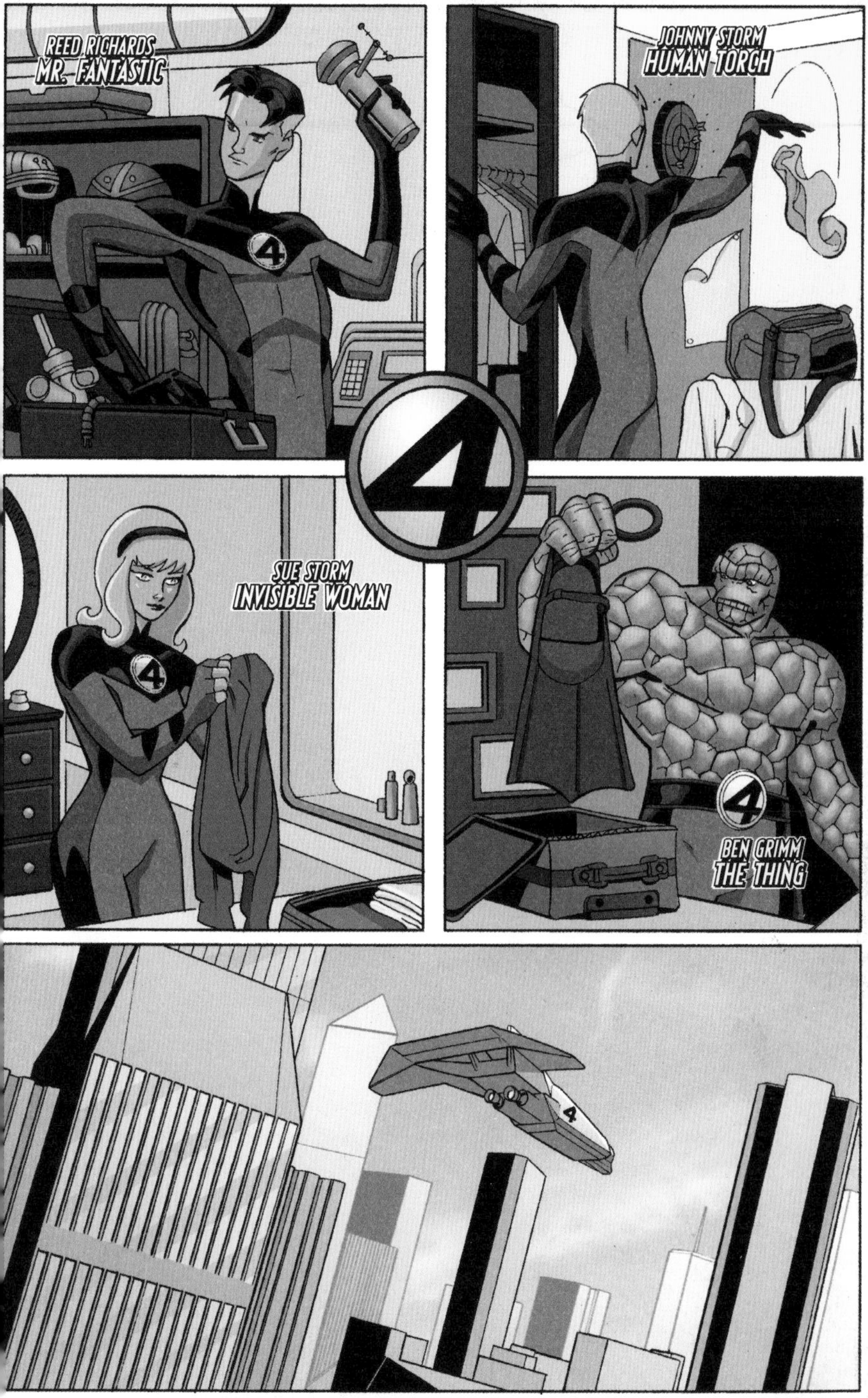
REED RICHARDS
MR. FANTASTIC
JOHNNY STORM
HUMAN TORCH
SUE STORM
INVISIBLE WOMAN
BEN GRIMM
THE THING

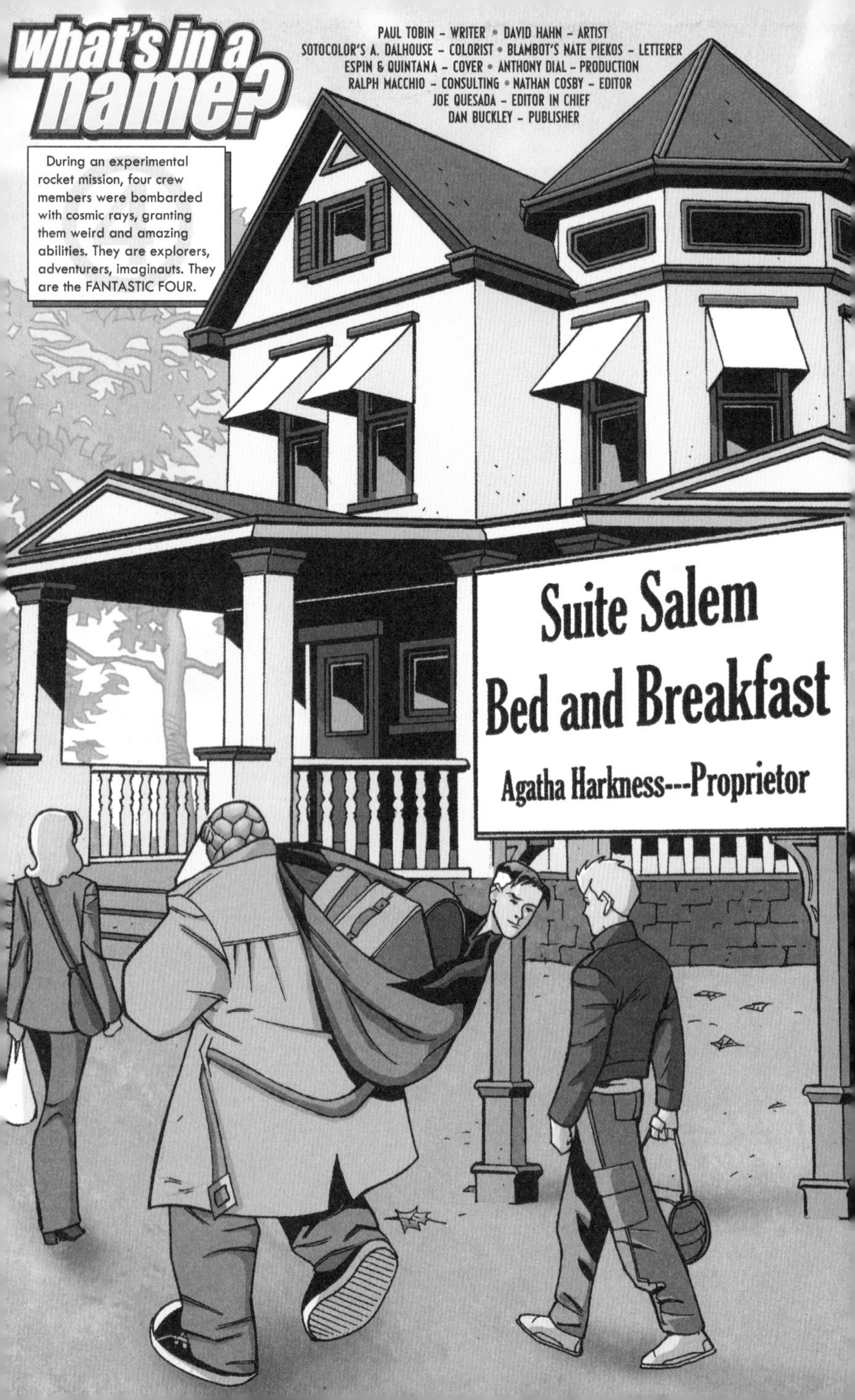
what's in a name?
PAUL TOBIN - WRITER • DAVID HAHN - ARTIST
SOTOCOLOR'S A. DALHOUSE - COLORIST • BLAMBOT'S NATE PIEKOS - LETTERER
ESPIN & QUINTANA - COVER • ANTHONY DIAL - PRODUCTION
RALPH MACCHIO - CONSULTING • NATHAN COSBY - EDITOR
JOE QUESADA - EDITOR IN CHIEF
DAN BUCKLEY - PUBLISHER
During an experimental rocket mission, four crew members were bombarded with cosmic rays, granting them weird and amazing abilities. They are explorers, adventurers, imaginauts. They are the FANTASTIC FOUR.
Suite Salem
Bed and Breakfast
Agatha Harkness---Proprietor

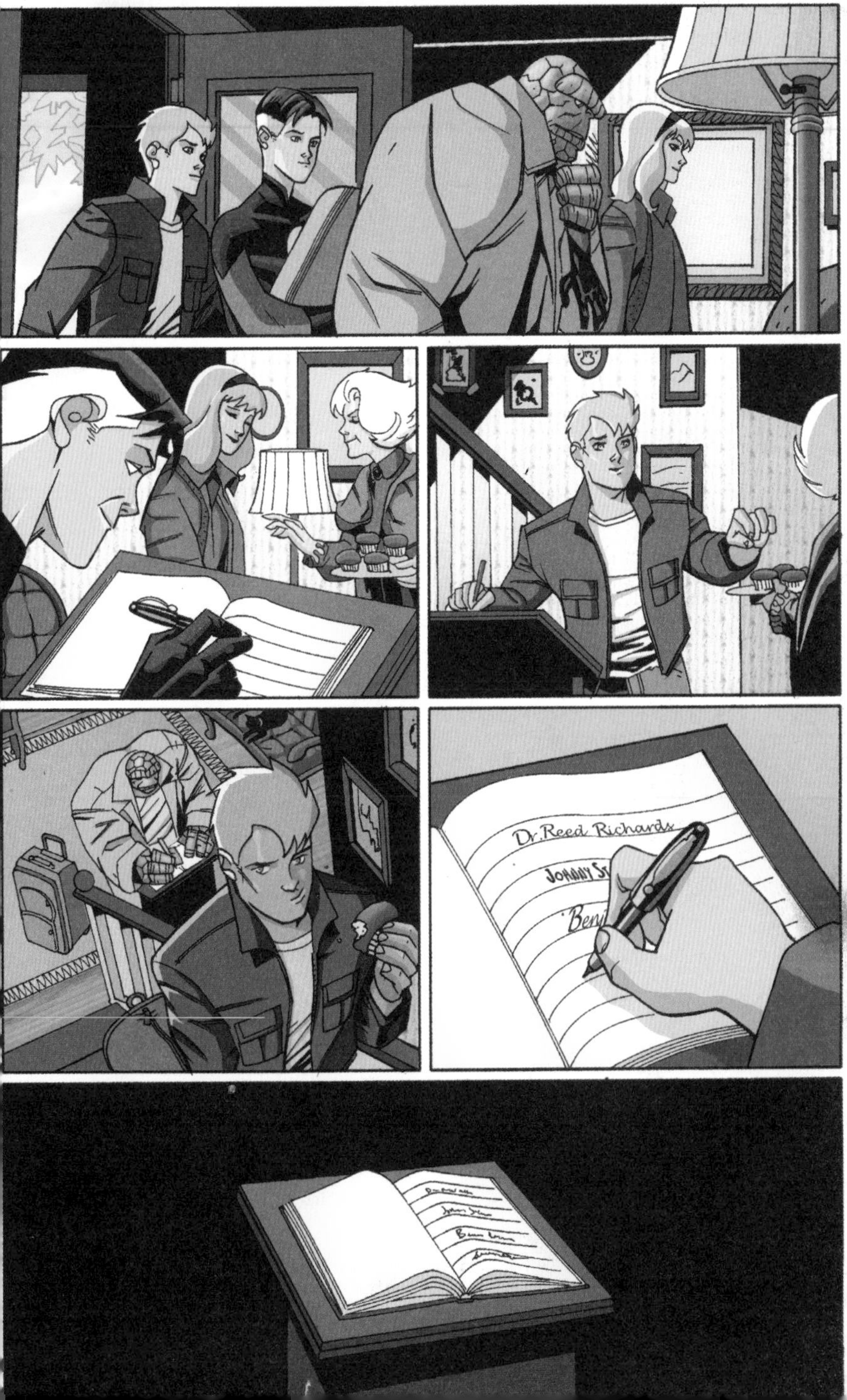
Dr. Reed Richards

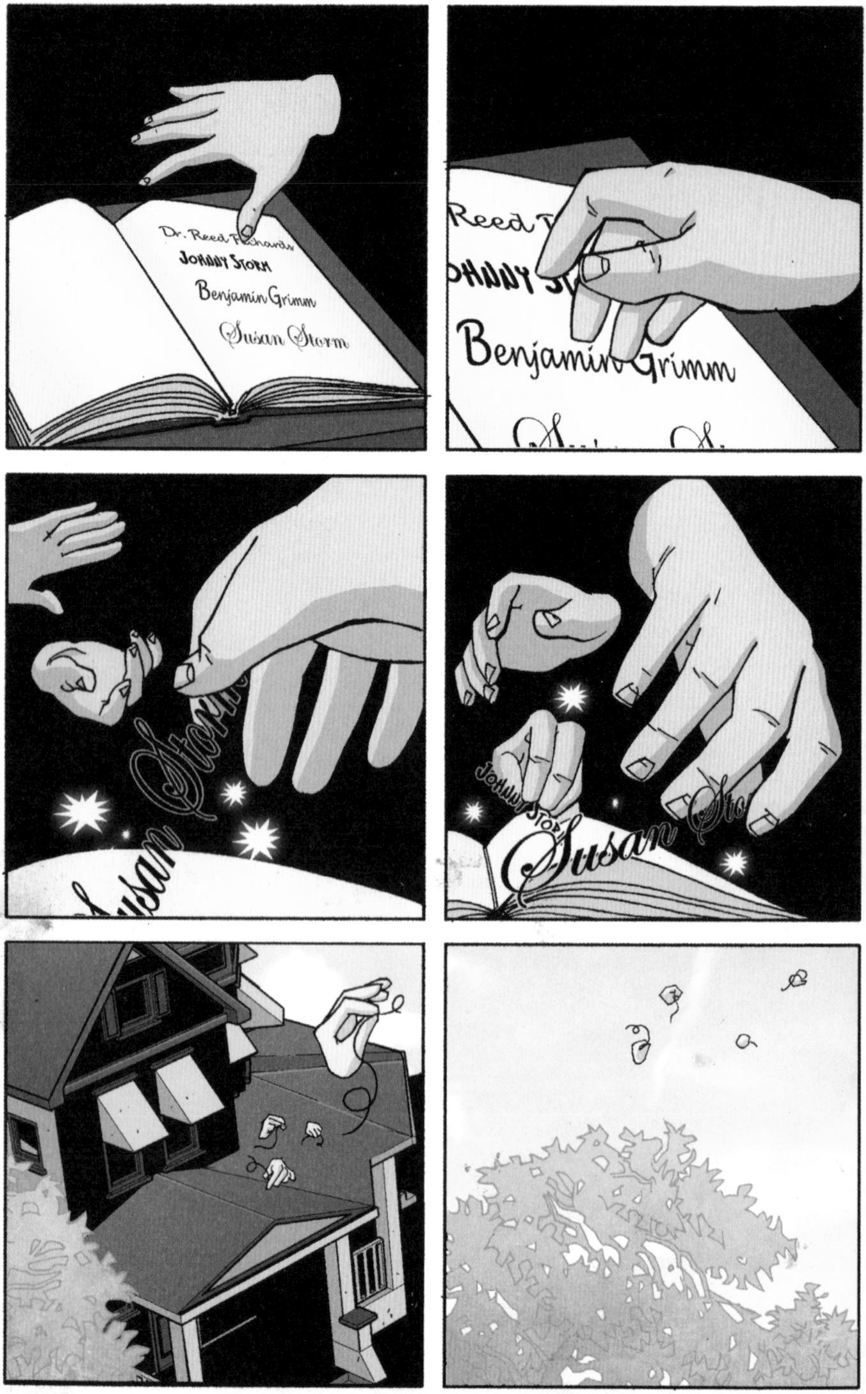
Dr. Reed Richards
JOHNNY STORM
Benjamin Grimm
Susan Storm
Benjamin Grimm
Susan

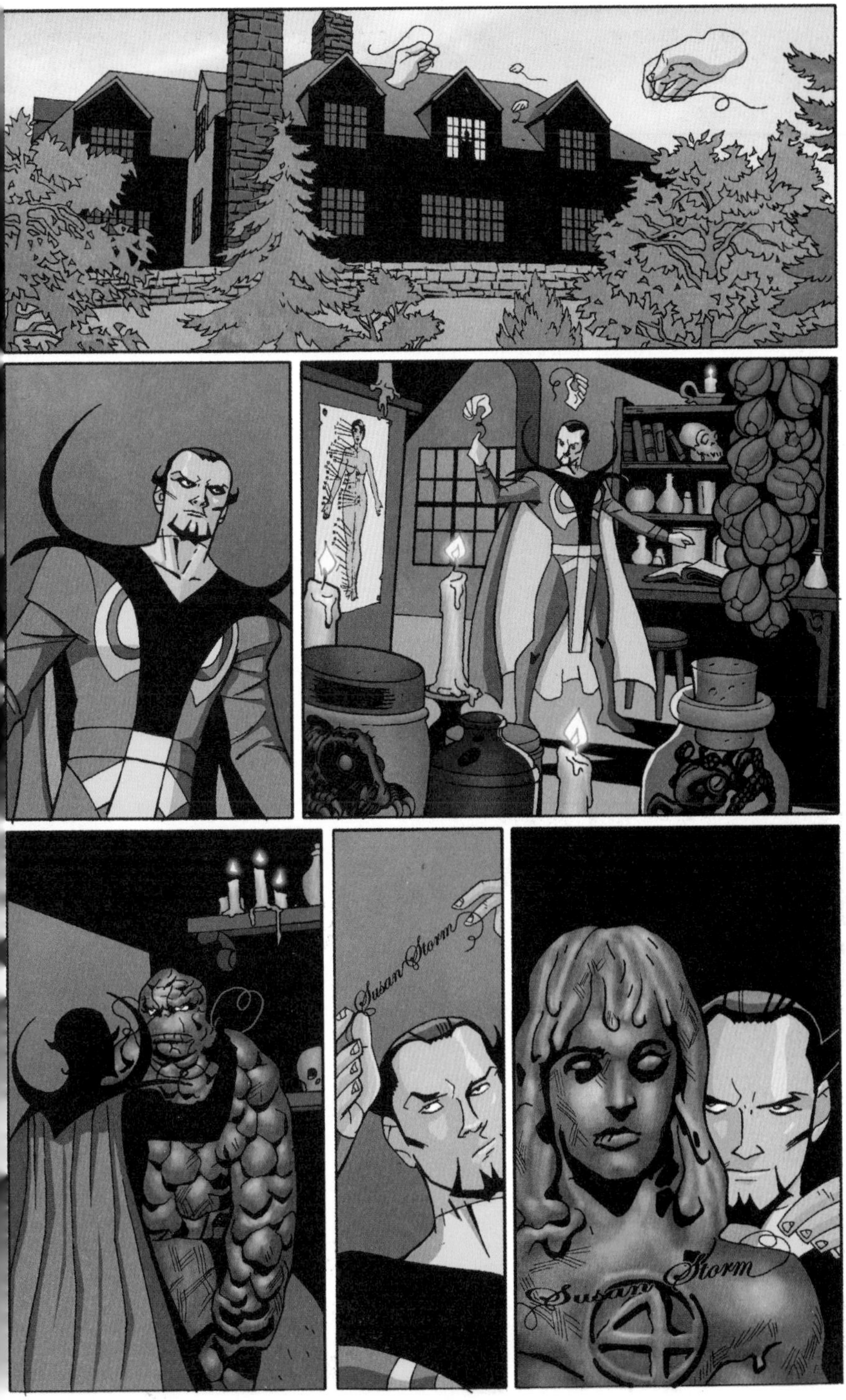
Susan Storm
Susan Storm

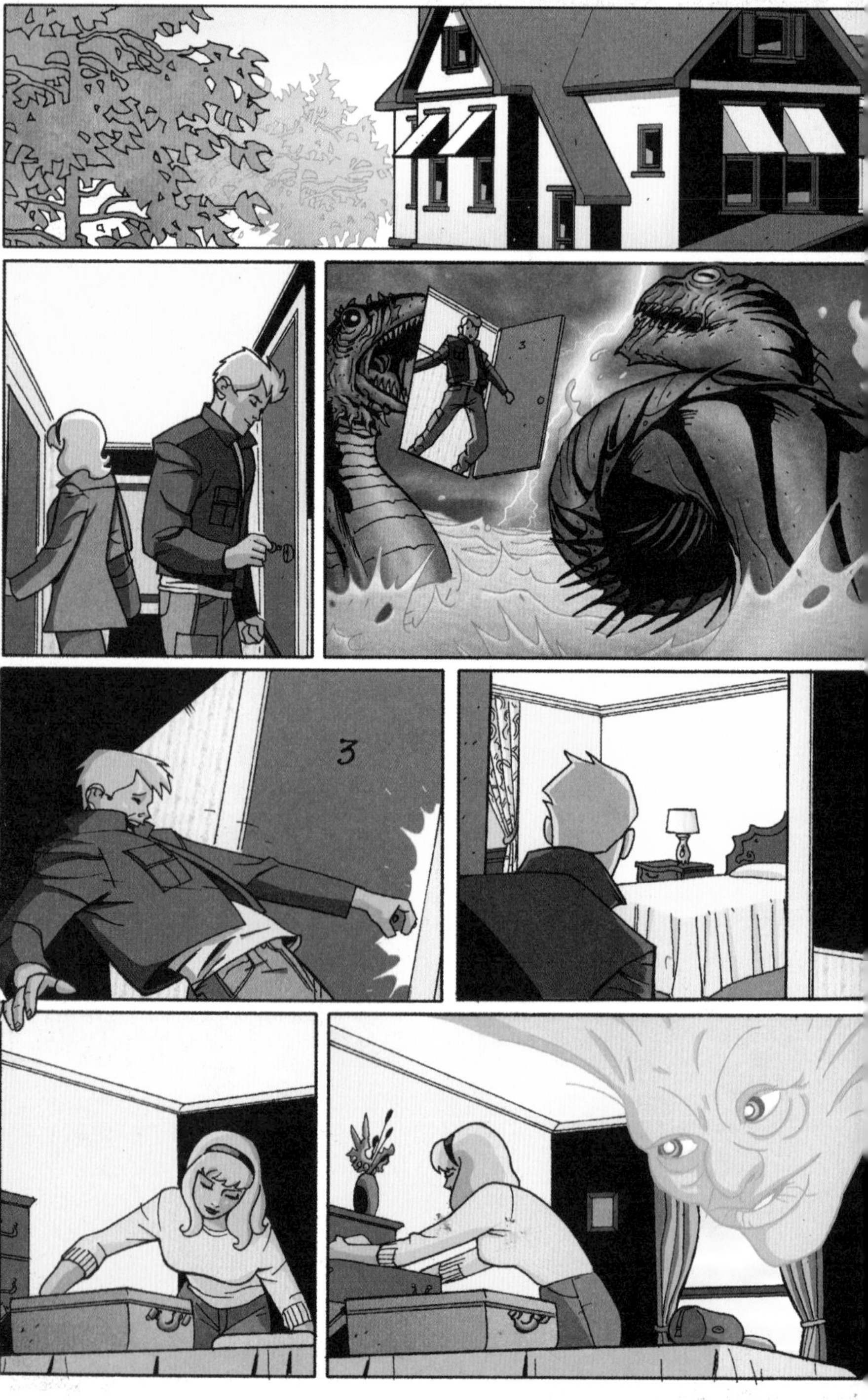
3

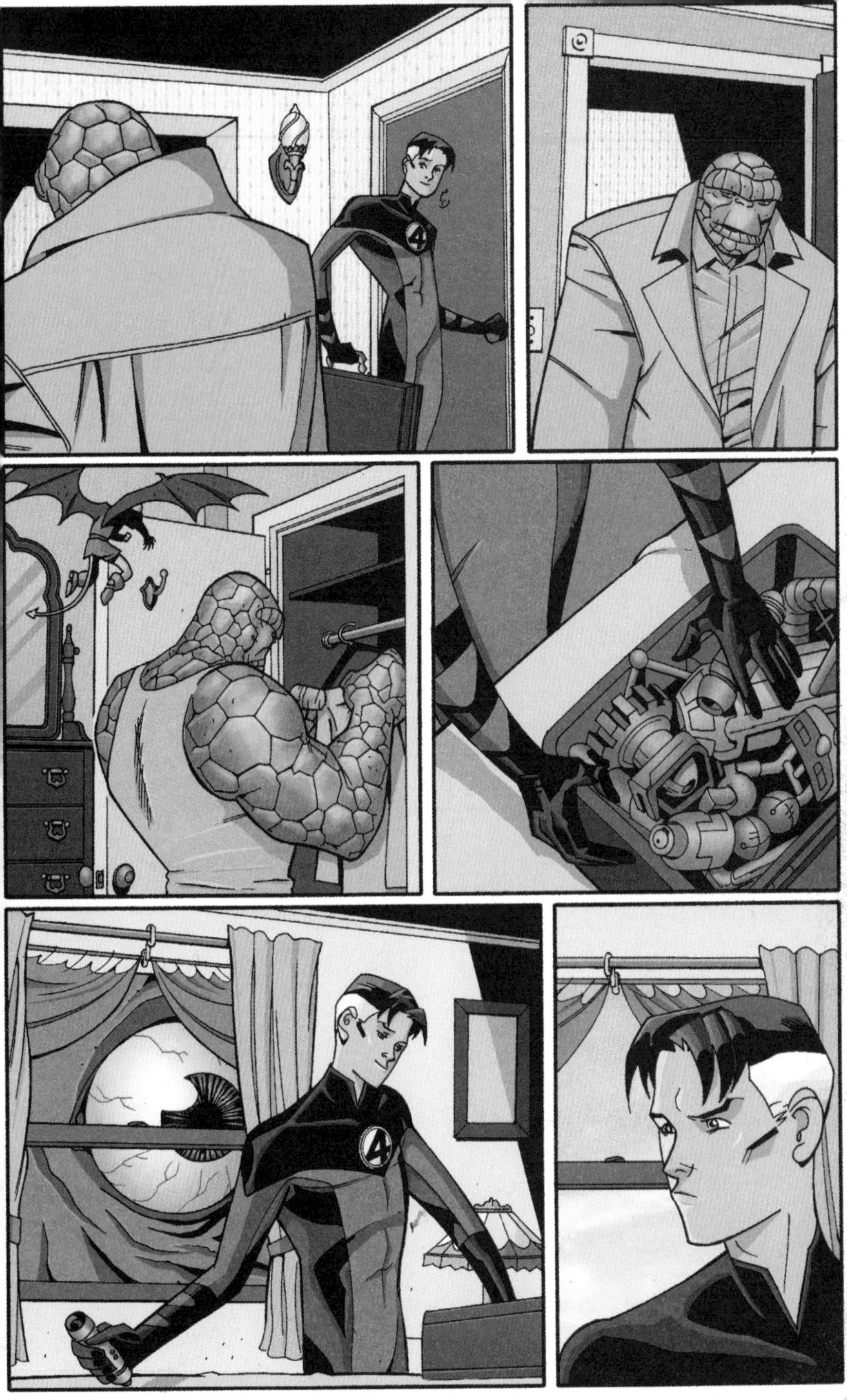

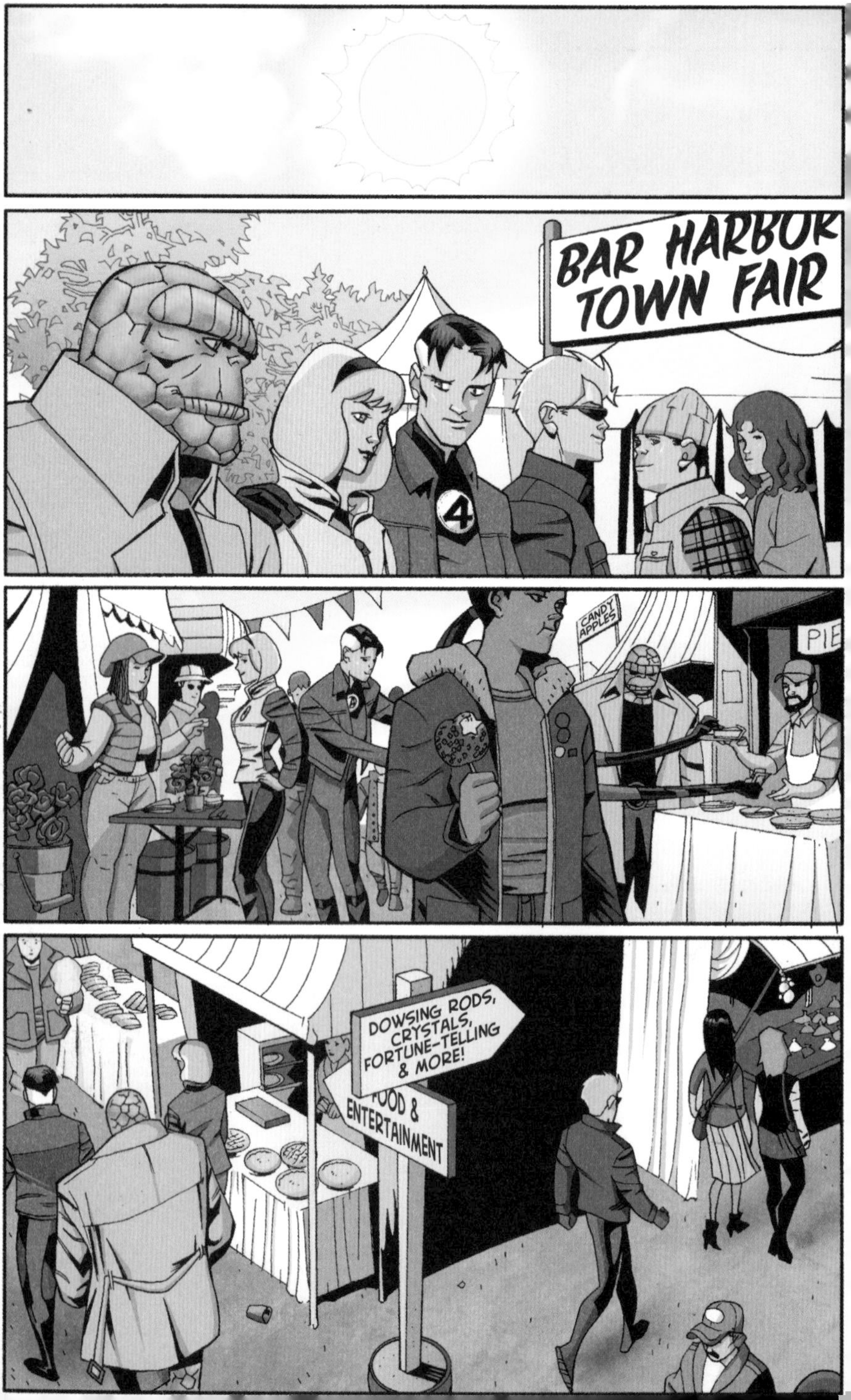
BAR HARBOR
TOWN FAIR
CANDY APPLES
PIE
DOWSING RODS, CRYSTALS, FORTUNE-TELLING & MORE!
FOOD & ENTERTAINMENT

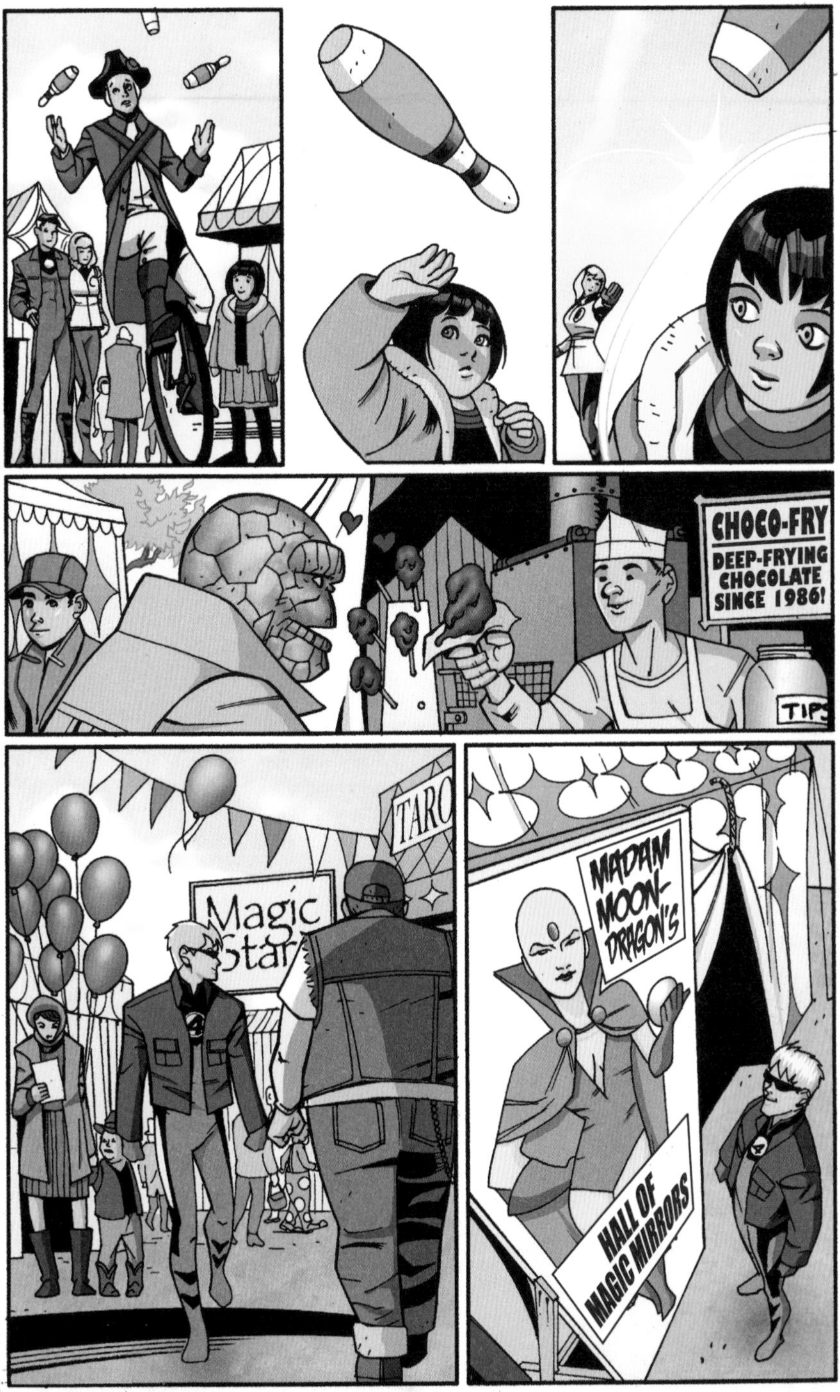
CHOCO-FRY
DEEP-FRYING CHOCOLATE SINCE 1986!
TIPS
TARO
Magic Star
MADAM MOON-DRAGON'S
HALL OF MAGIC MIRRORS

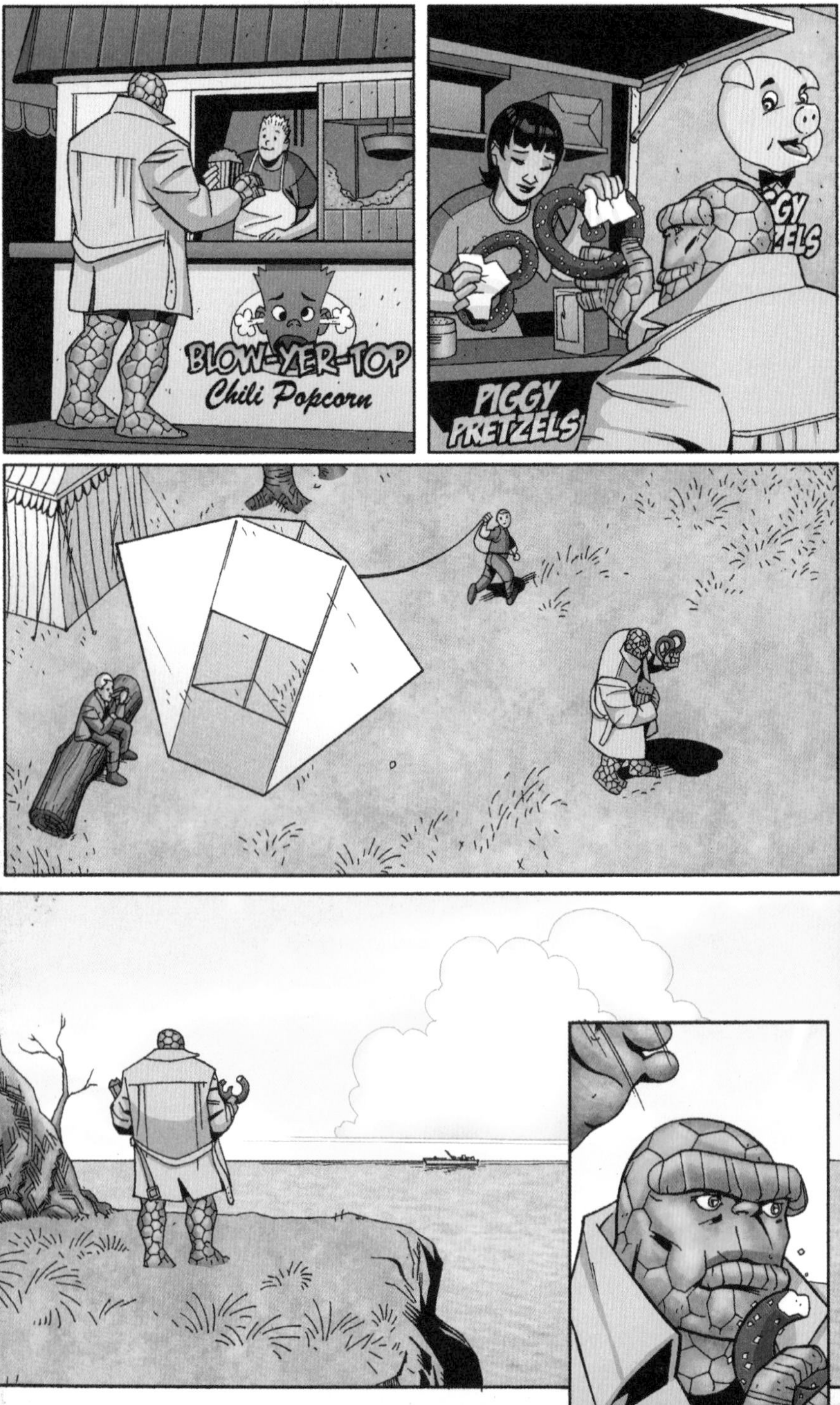
BLOW-YER-TOP
Chili Popcorn
PIGGY PRETZELS

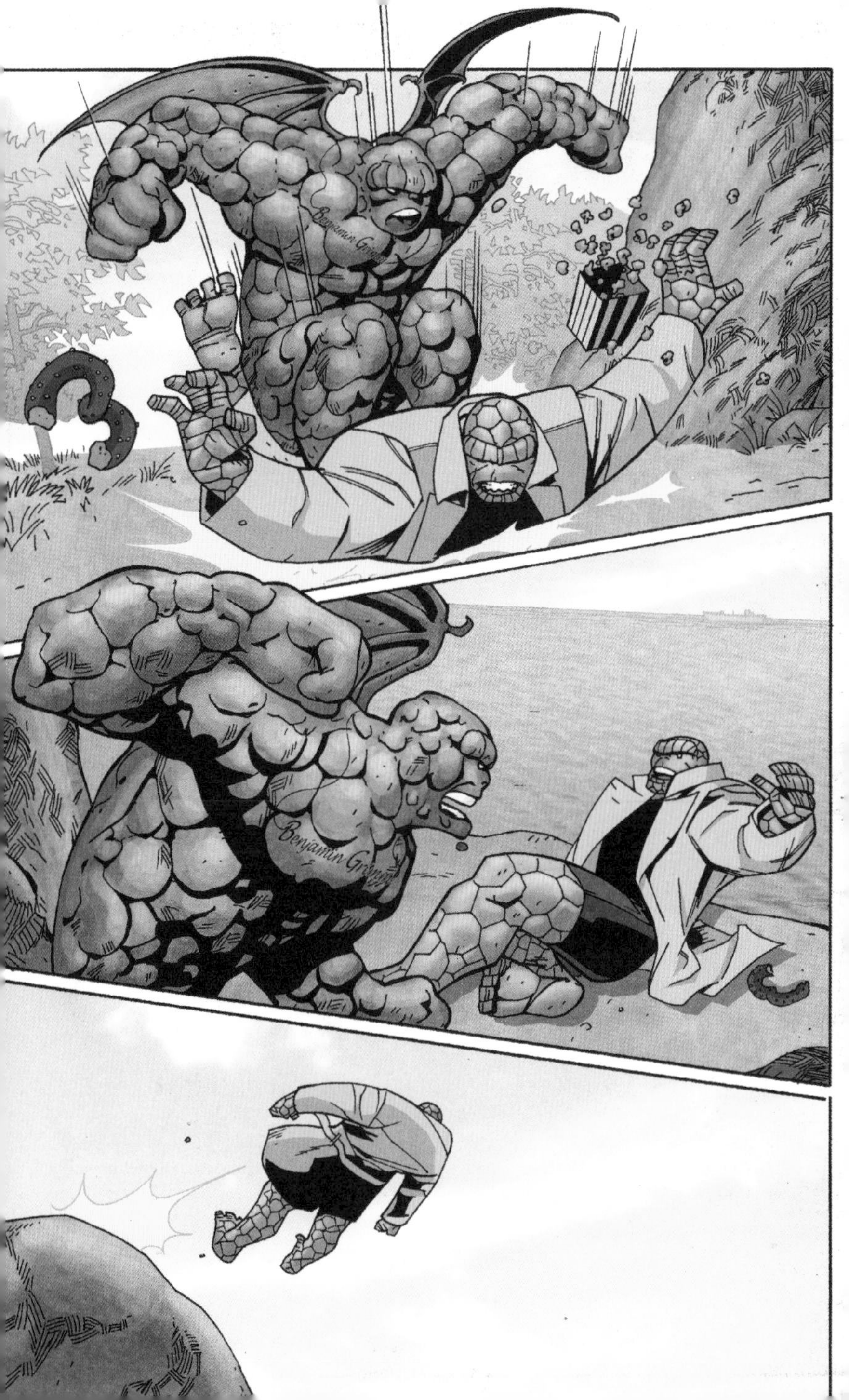

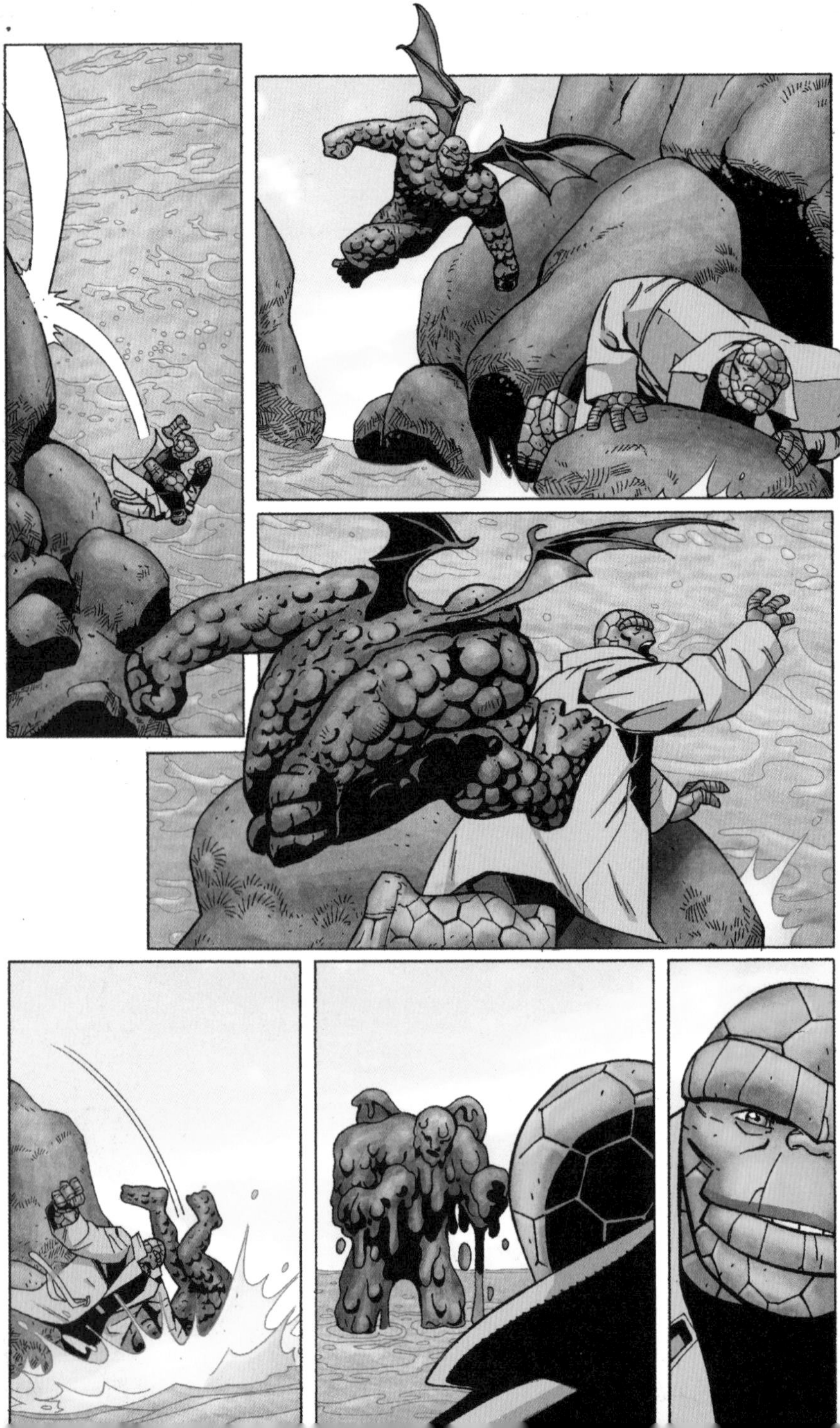

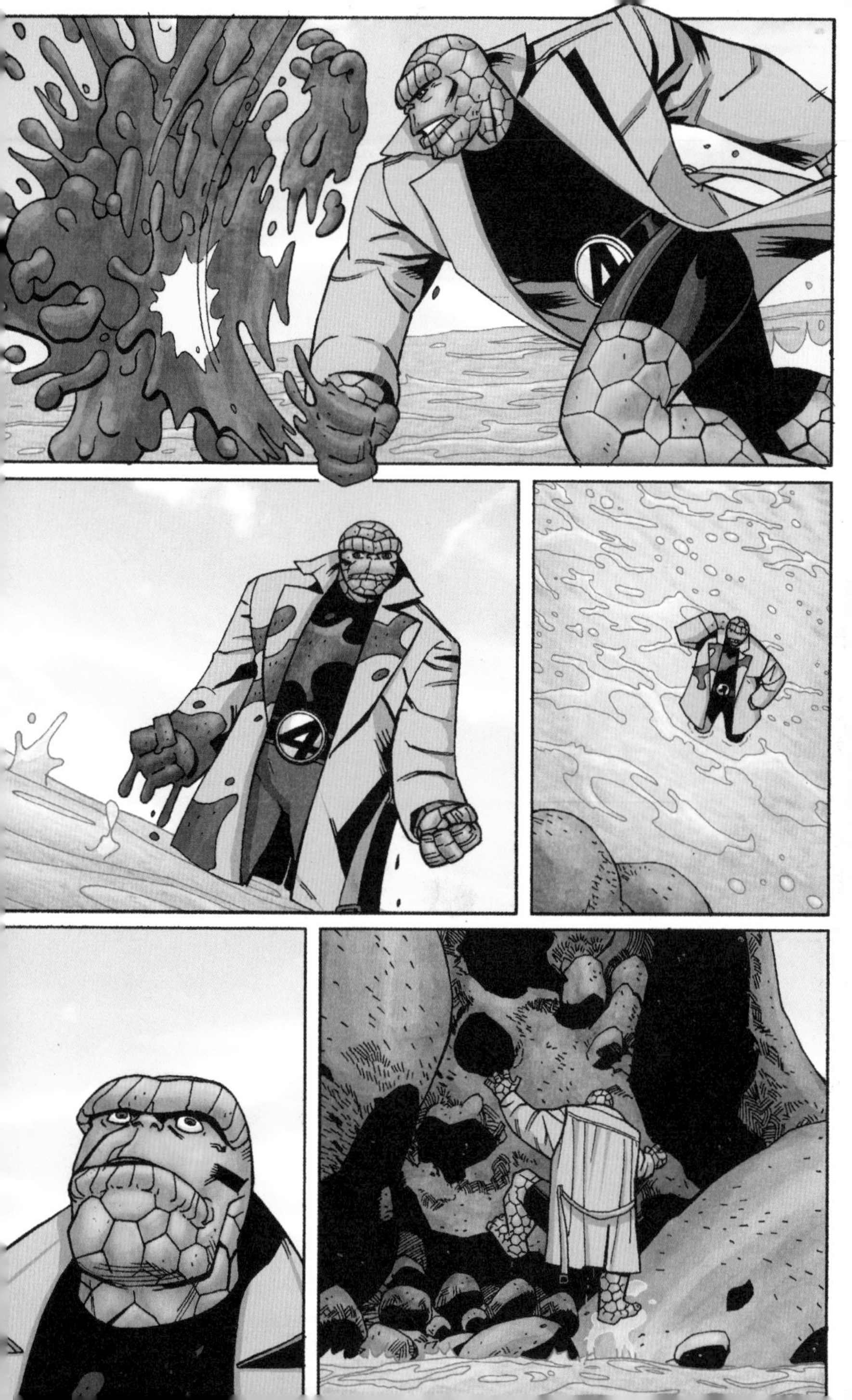

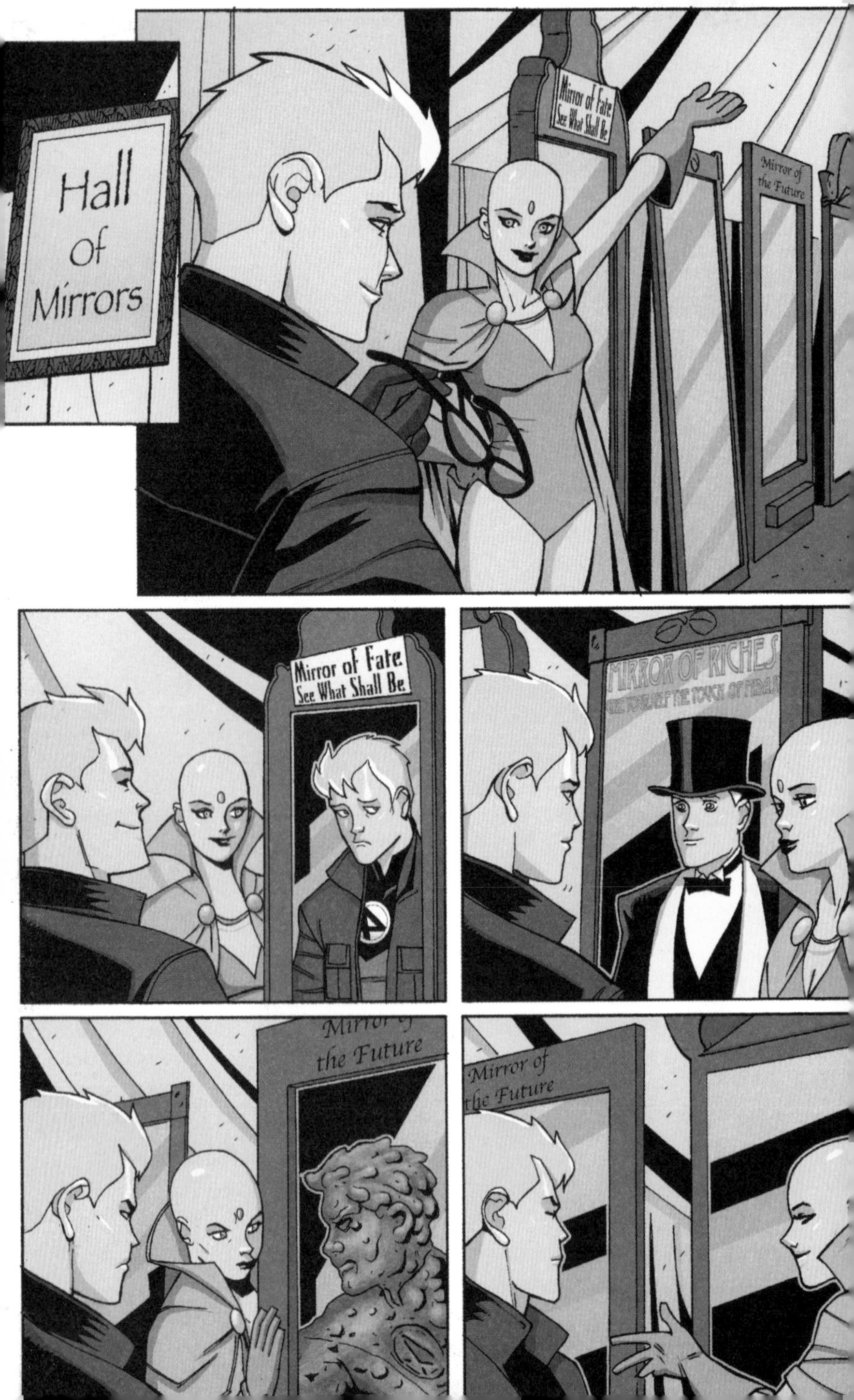
Hall of Mirrors
Mirror of Fate
See What Shall Be
Mirror of the Future
Mirror of Fate
See What Shall Be.
MIRROR OF RICHES
Mirror of the Future
Mirror of the Future

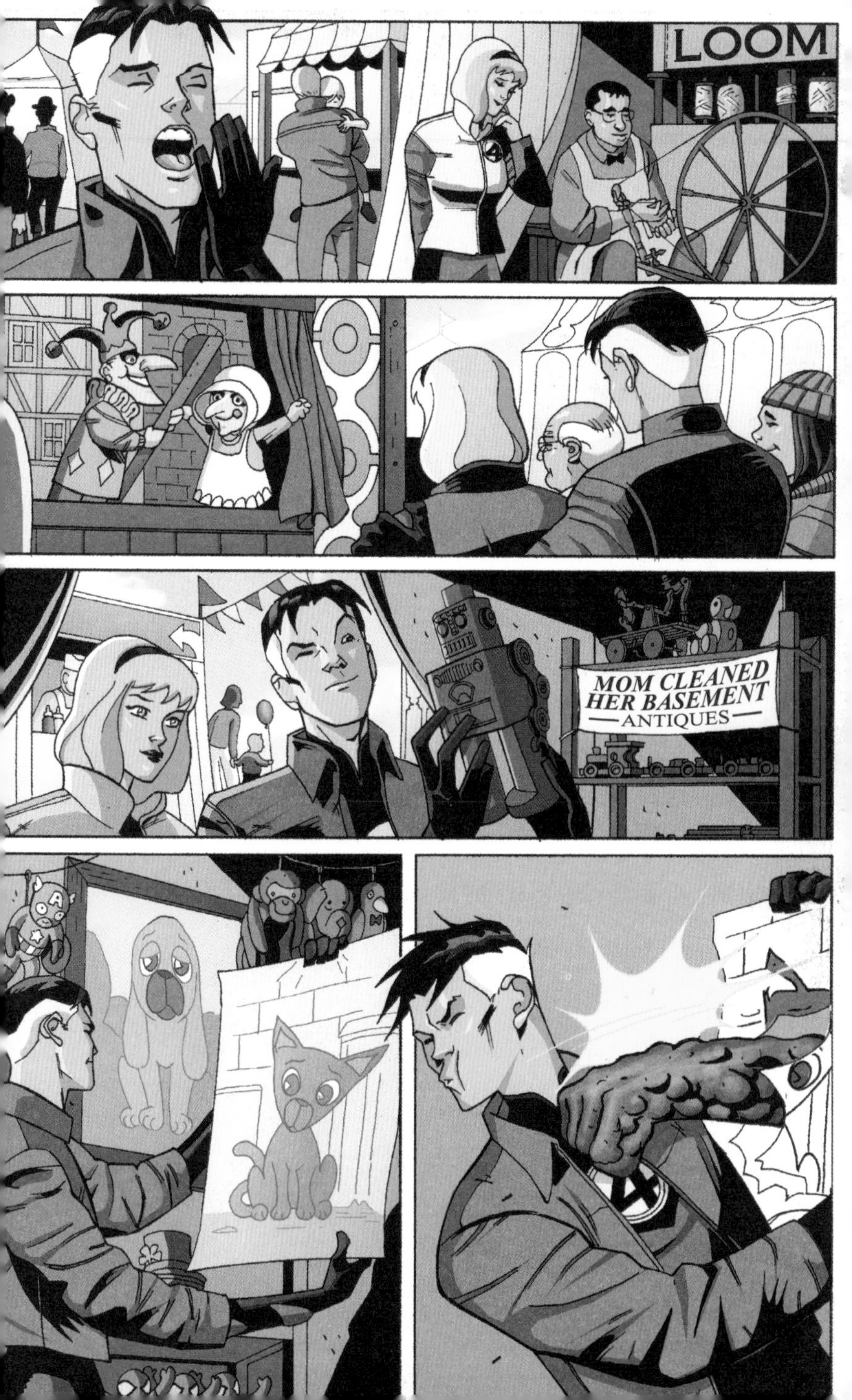
LOOM
MOM CLEANED
HER BASEMENT
ANTIQUES

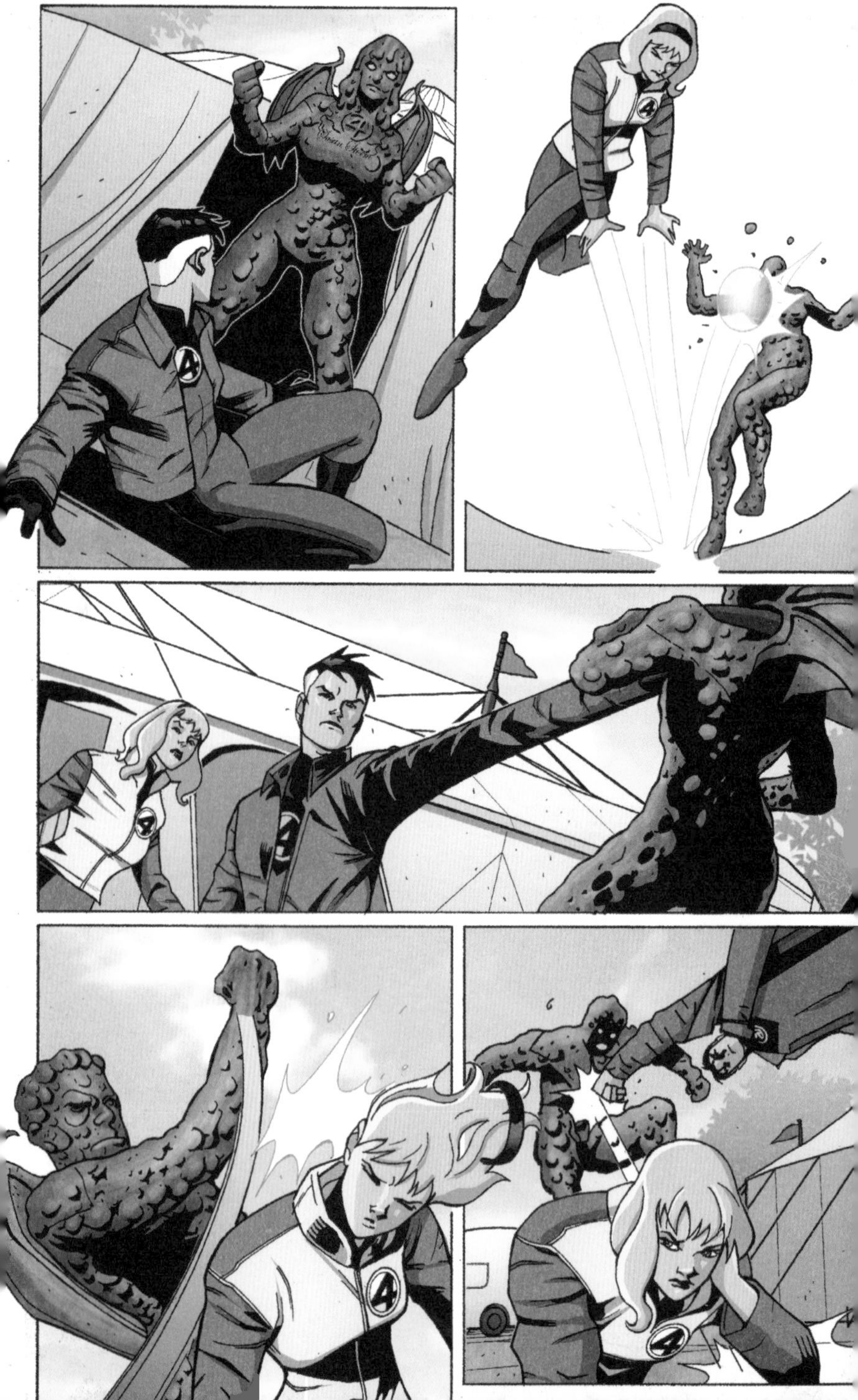

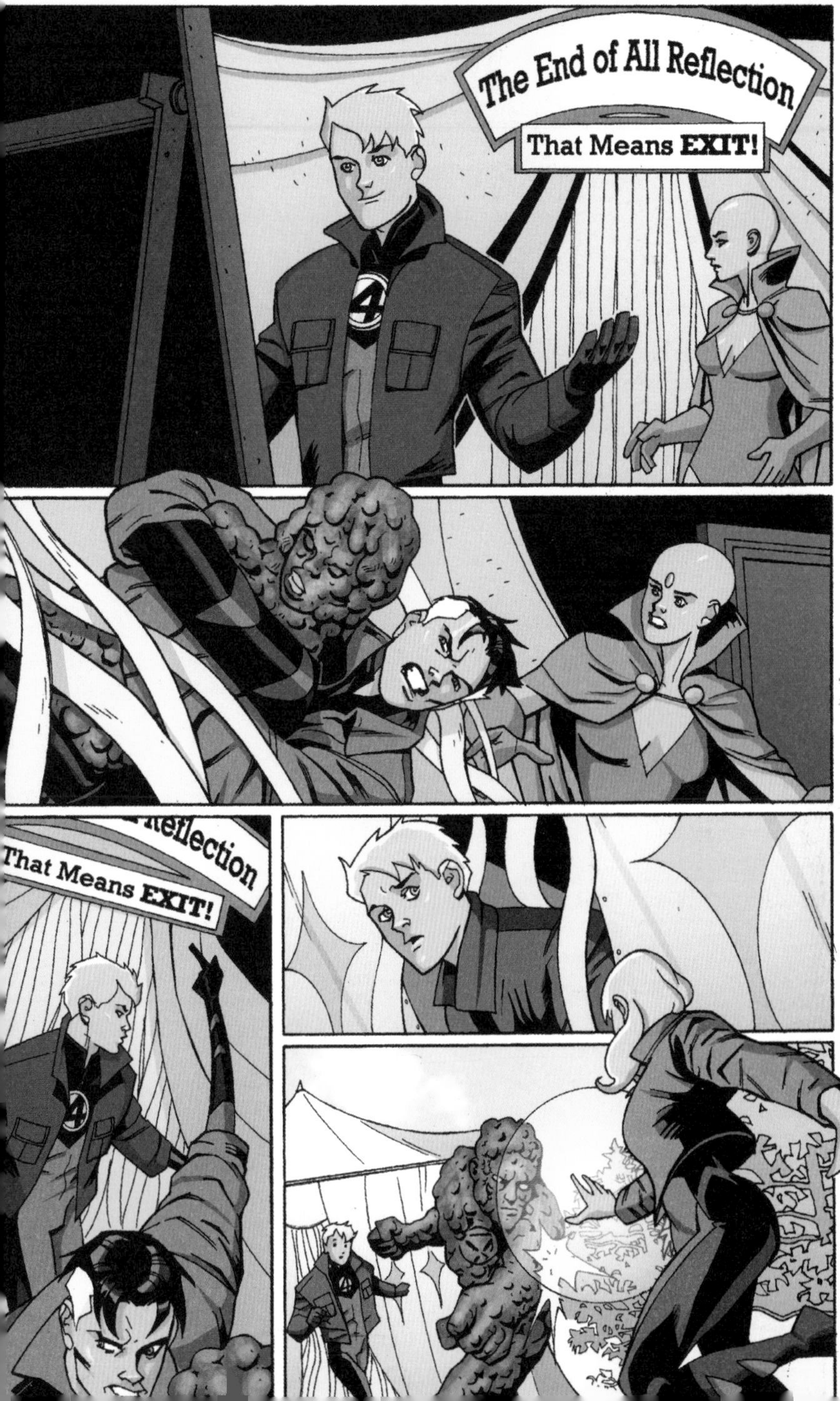

The End of All Reflection
That Means EXIT!
That Means EXIT!

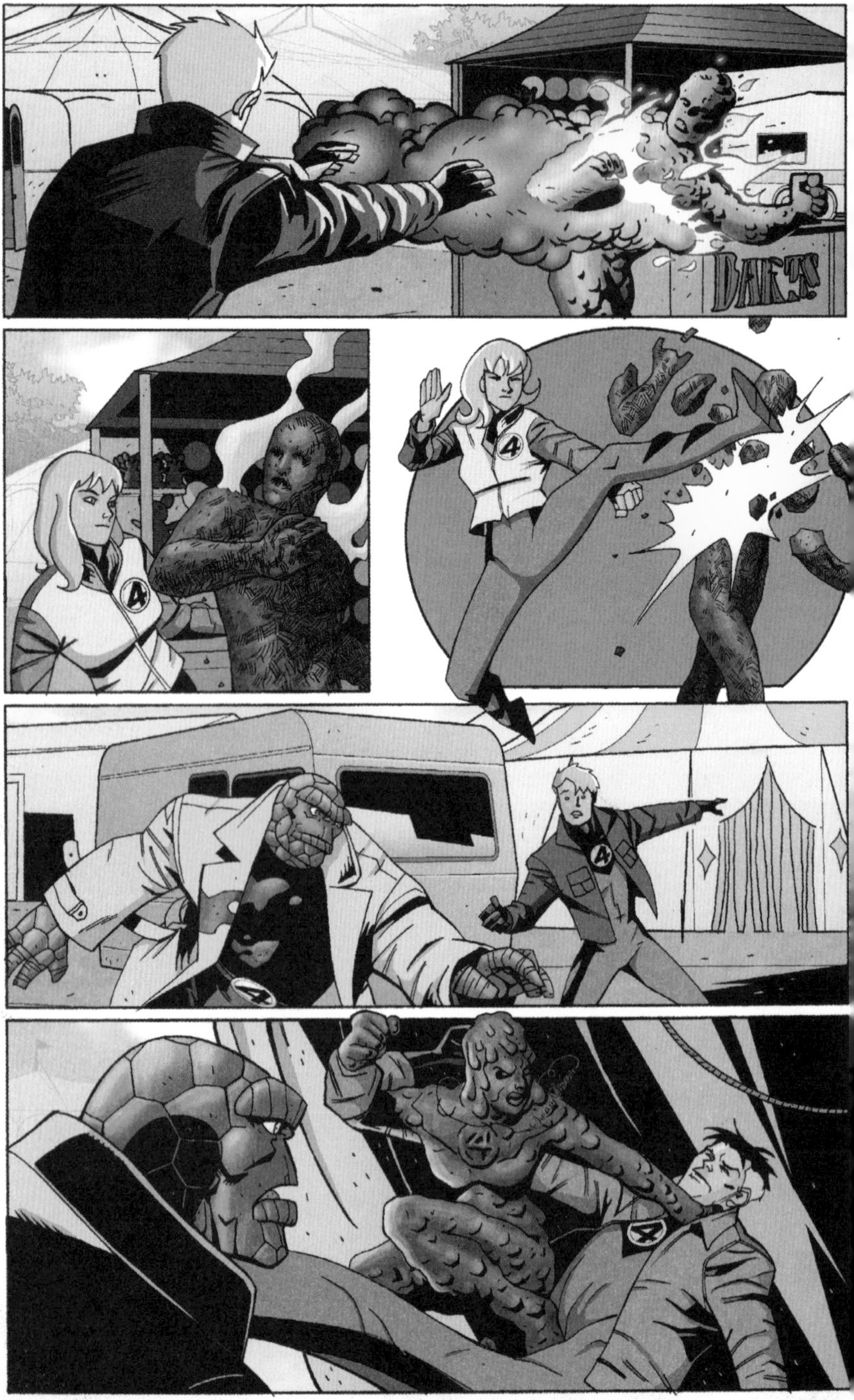
DARTS!

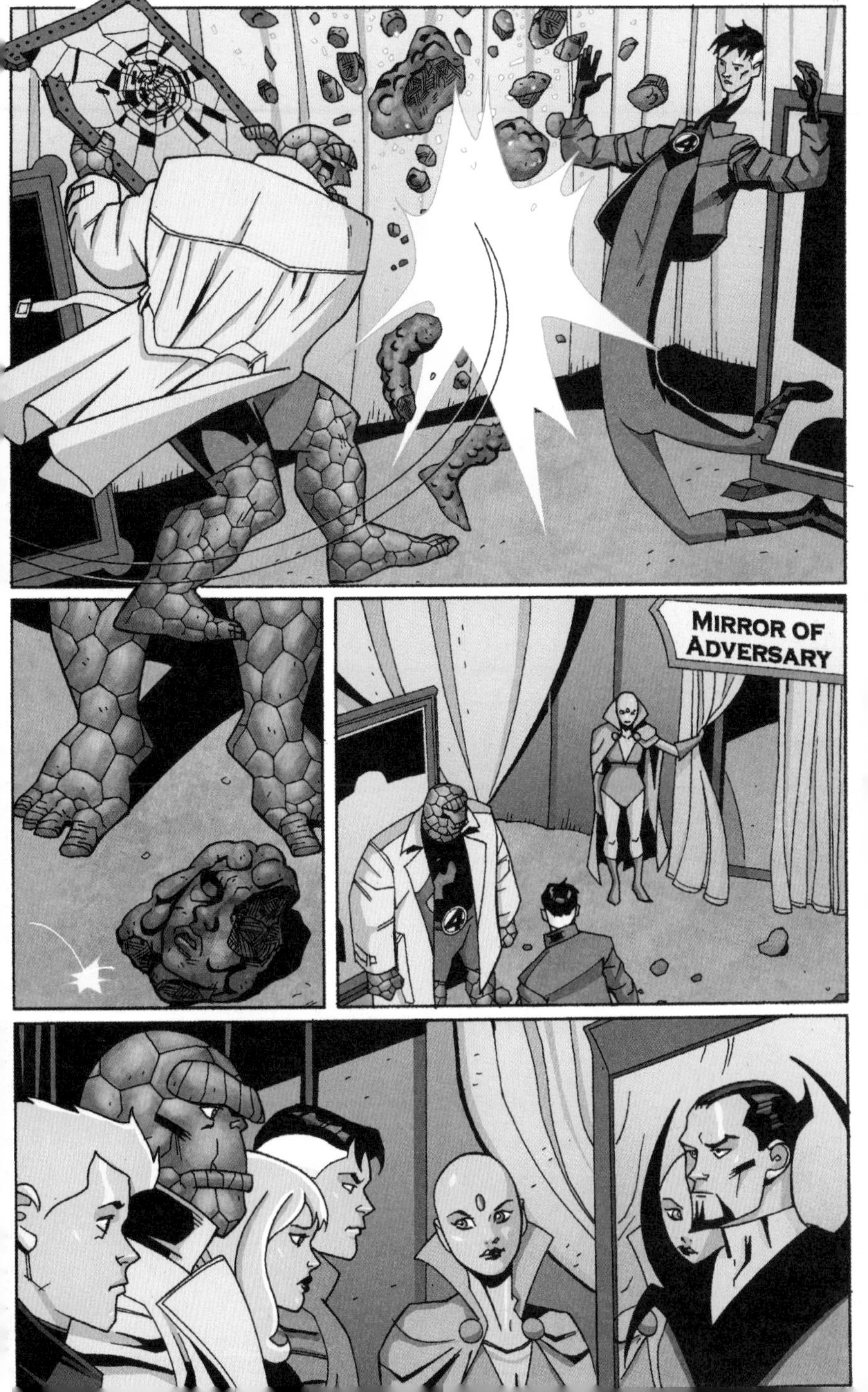
MIRROR OF ADVERSARY

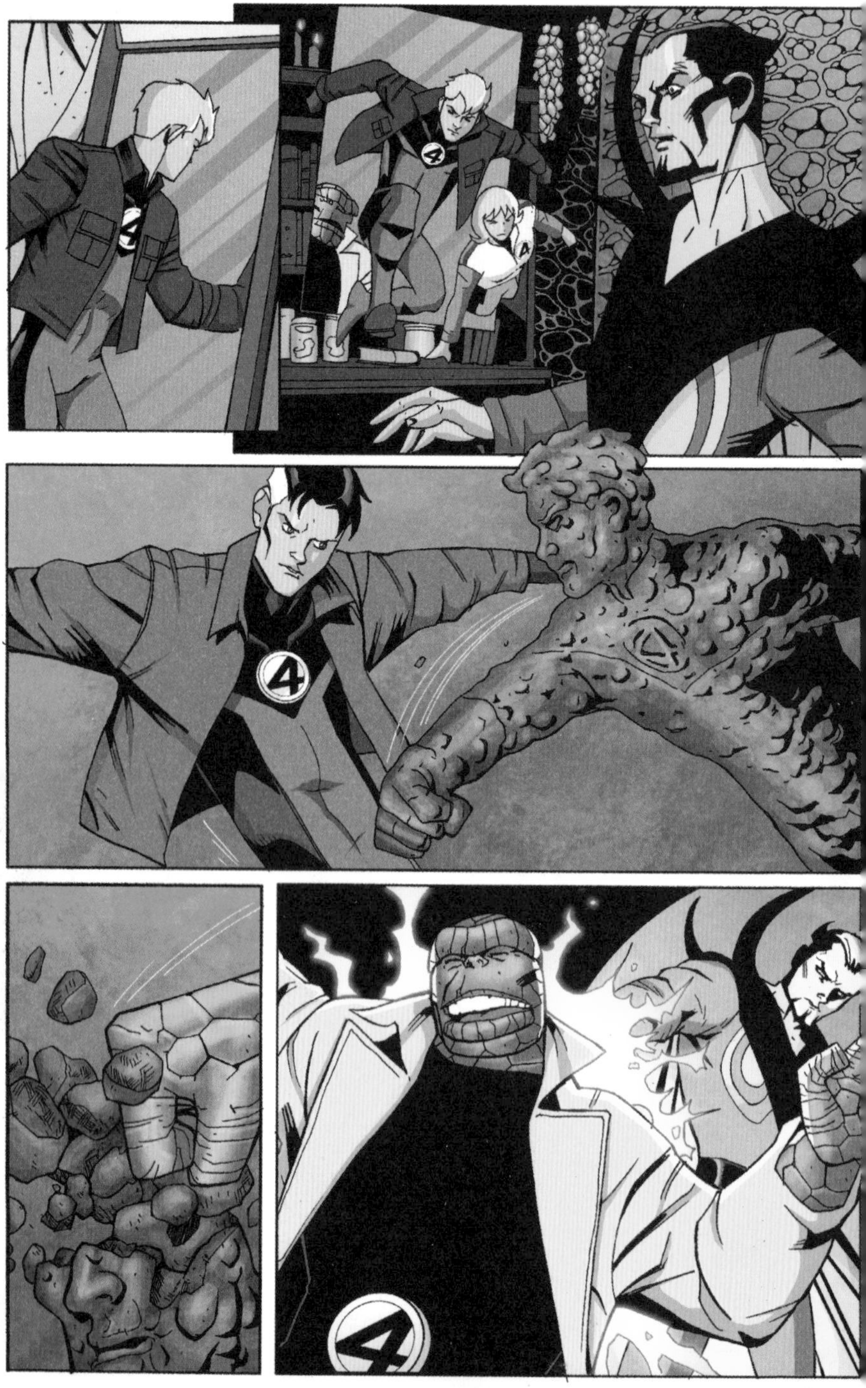

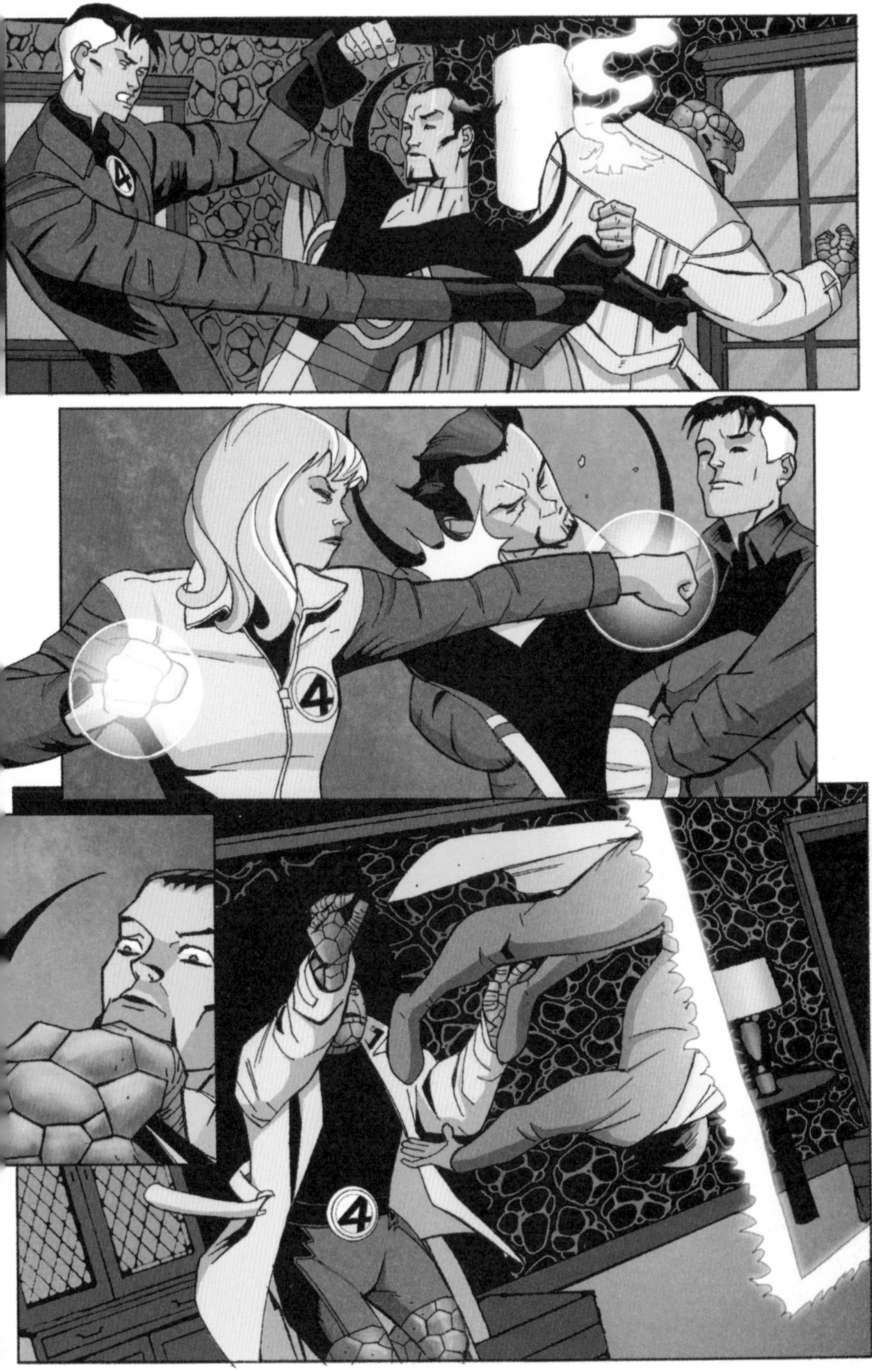

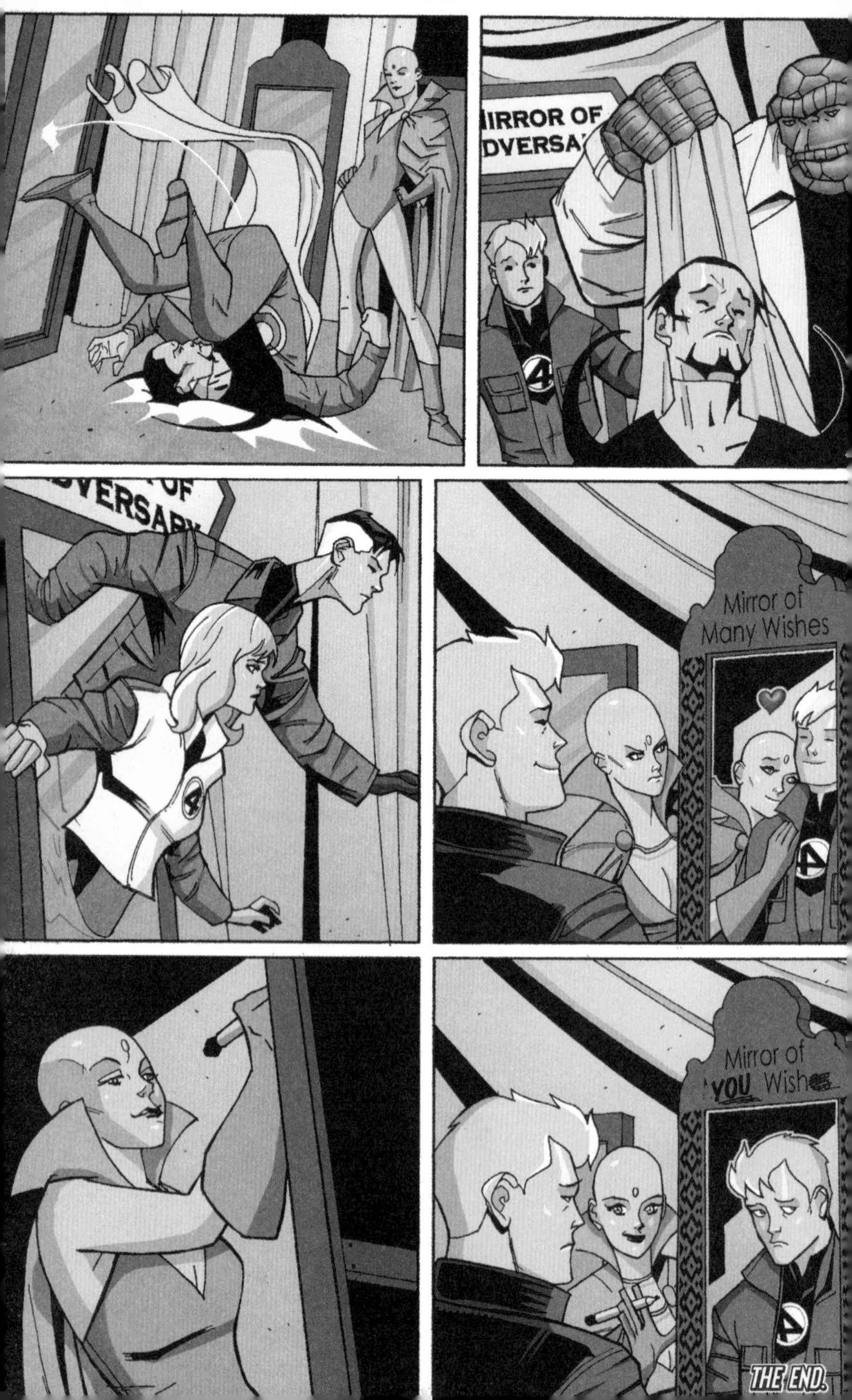

IRROR OF
DVERSA
VERSAR OF
Mirror of Many Wishes
Mirror of YOU Wishes
THE END.

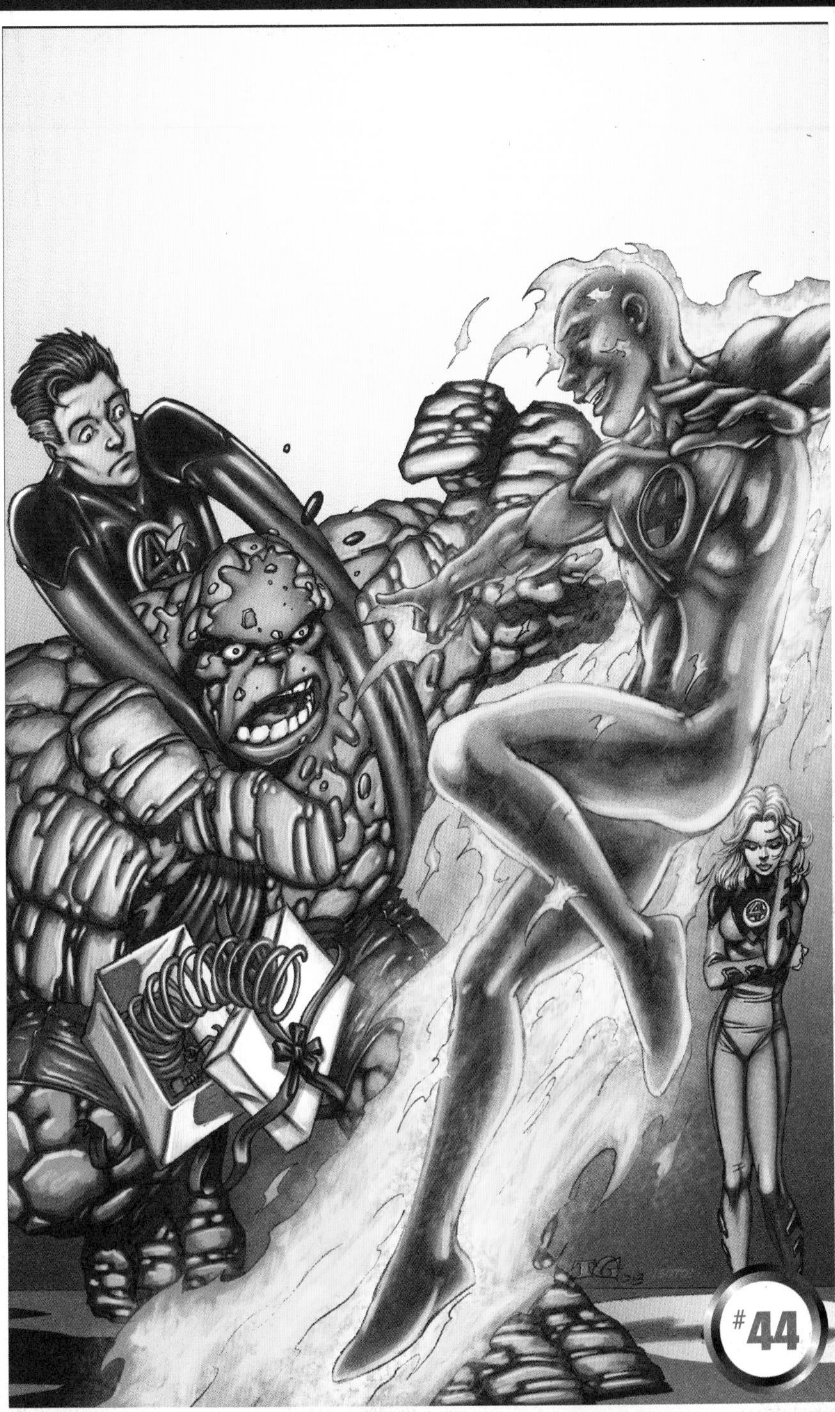
#44

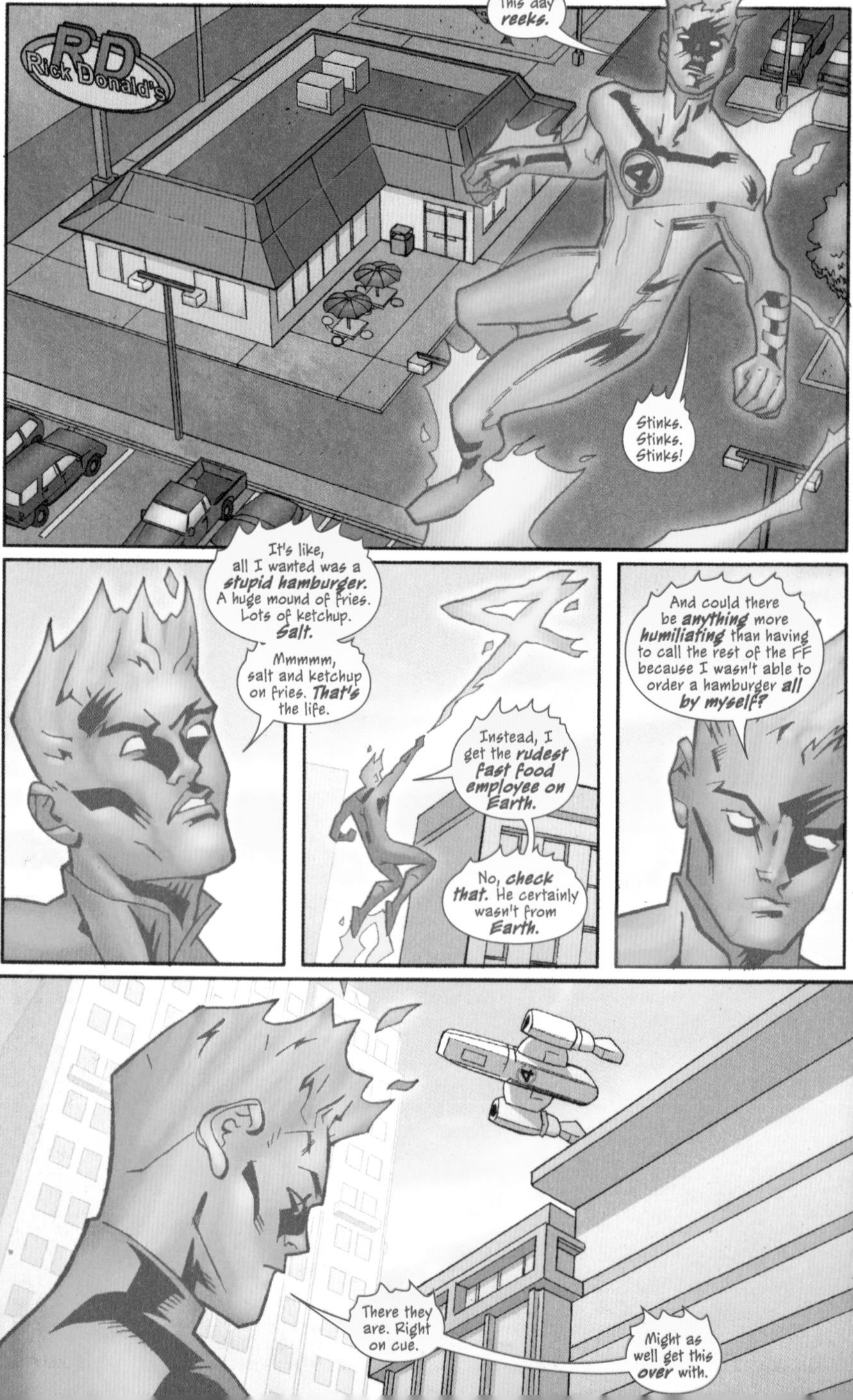
Rick Donald's
RD
This day reeks.
Stinks. Stinks. Stinks!
It's like, all I wanted was a stupid hamburger. A huge mound of fries. Lots of ketchup. Salt.
Mmmmm, salt and ketchup on fries. That's the life.
Instead, I get the rudest fast food employee on Earth.
No, check that. He certainly wasn't from Earth.
And could there be anything more humiliating than having to call the rest of the FF because I wasn't able to order a hamburger all by myself?
There they are. Right on cue.
Might as well get this over with.

WOULD YOU LIKE LIVING DARKNESS WITH THAT?

PAUL TOBIN – WRITER DAVID HAHN – ARTIST SOTOCOLOR'S A. DALHOUSE – COLORIST BLAMBOT'S NATE PIEKOS – LETTERER GRUMMETT & SOTOMAYOR – COVER
RALPH MACCHIO – CONSULTING NATHAN COSBY – EDITOR JOE QUESADA – EDITOR IN CHIEF DAN BUCKLEY – PUBLISHER

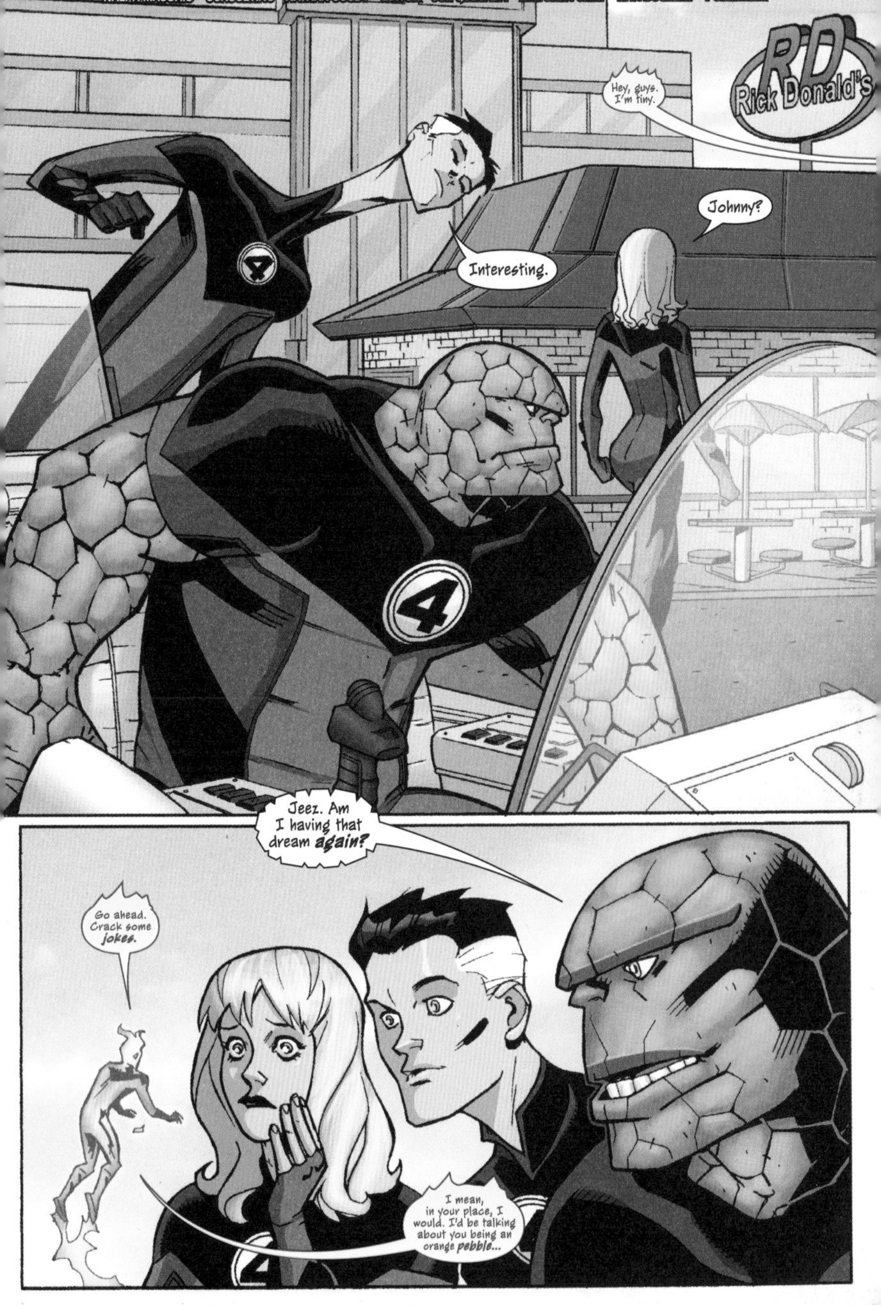
RD
Rick Donald's
Hey, guys. I'm tiny.
Johnny?
Interesting.
Jeez. Am I having that dream *again?*
Go ahead. Crack some *jokes.*
I mean, in your place, I would. I'd be talking about you being an orange *pebble*...

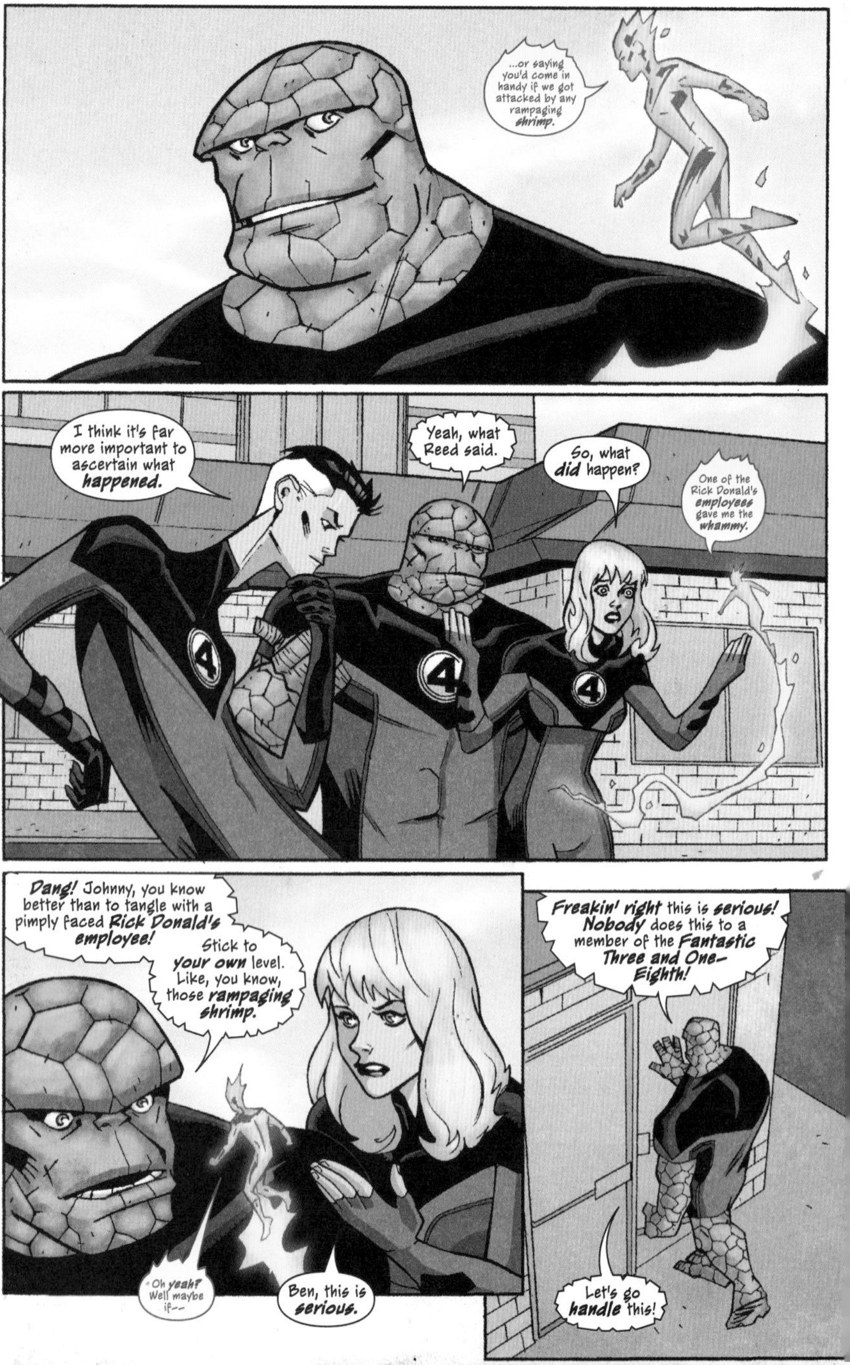
...or saying you'd come in handy if we got attacked by any rampaging shrimp.
I think it's far more important to ascertain what happened.
Yeah, what Reed said.
So, what did happen?
One of the Rick Donald's employees gave me the whammy.
Dang! Johnny, you know better than to tangle with a pimply faced Rick Donald's employee!
Stick to your own level. Like, you know, those rampaging shrimp.
Oh yeah? Well maybe if--
Ben, this is serious.
Freakin' right this is serious! Nobody does this to a member of the Fantastic Three and One-Eighth!
Let's go handle this!

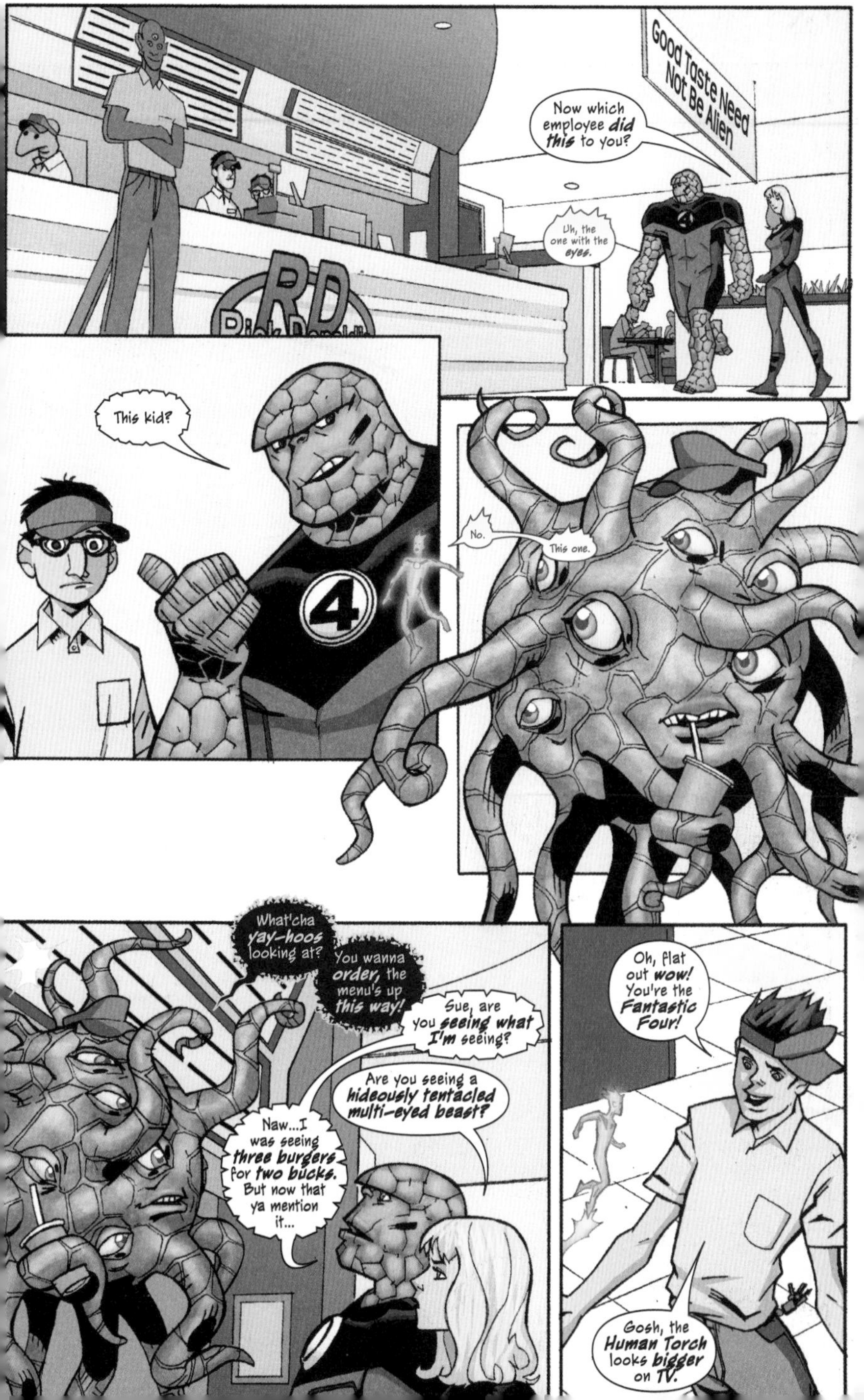
Good Taste Need Not Be Alien
Now which employee did this to you?
Uh, the one with the eyes.
RD
This kid?
No.
This one.
What'cha yay-hoos looking at?
You wanna order, the menu's up this way!
Sue, are you seeing what I'm seeing?
Are you seeing a hideously tentacled multi-eyed beast?
Naw...I was seeing three burgers for two bucks. But now that ya mention it...
Oh, flat out wow! You're the Fantastic Four!
Gosh, the Human Torch looks bigger on TV.

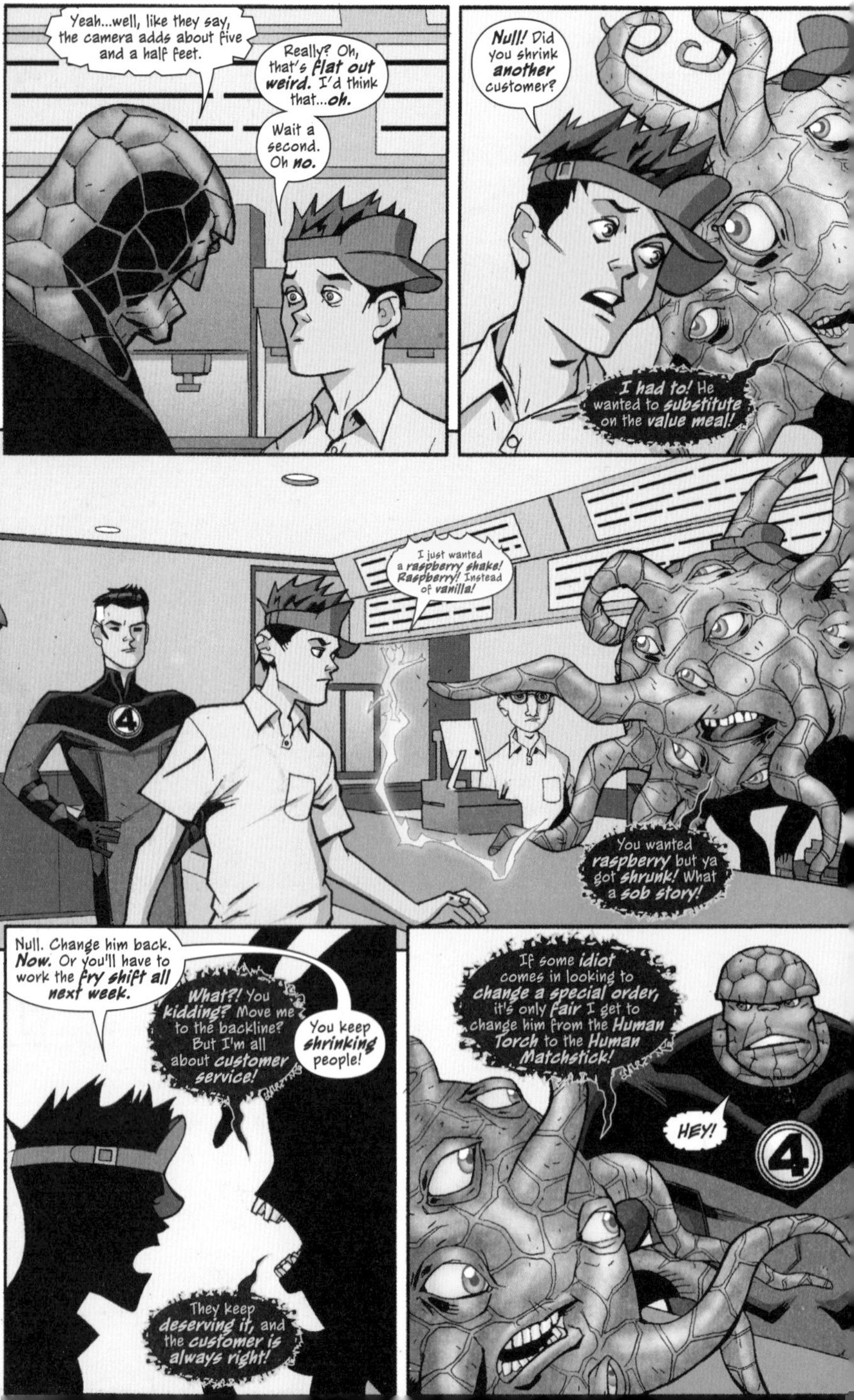
Yeah...well, like they say, the camera adds about five and a half feet.
Really? Oh, that's flat out weird. I'd think that...oh.
Wait a second. Oh no.
Null! Did you shrink another customer?
I had to! He wanted to substitute on the value meal!
I just wanted a raspberry shake! Raspberry! Instead of vanilla!
You wanted raspberry but ya got shrunk! What a sob story!
Null. Change him back. Now. Or you'll have to work the fry shift all next week.
What?! You kidding? Move me to the backline? But I'm all about customer service!
You keep shrinking people!
They keep deserving it, and the customer is always right!
If some idiot comes in looking to change a special order, it's only fair I get to change him from the Human Torch to the Human Matchstick!
HEY!

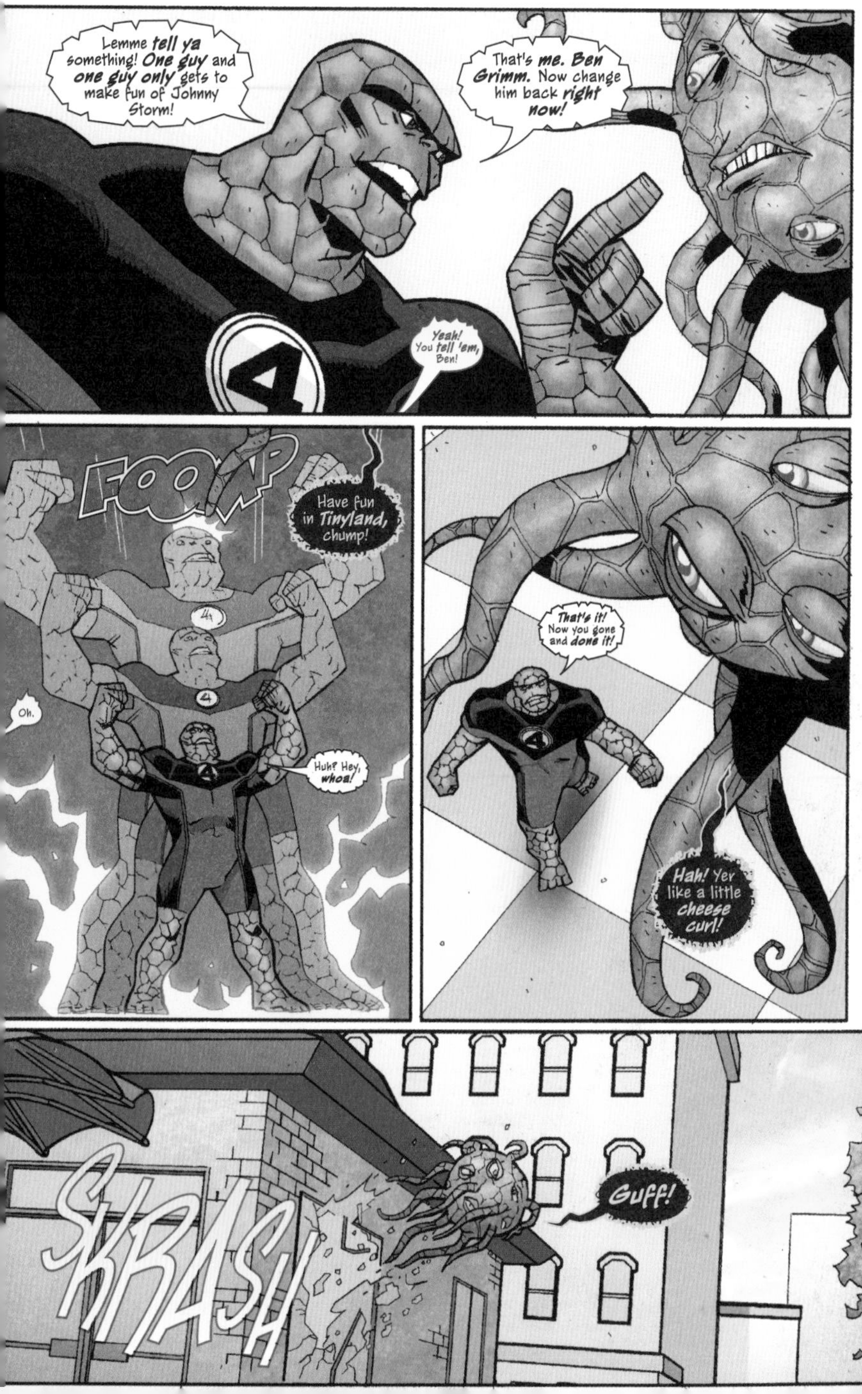
Lemme tell ya something! One guy and one guy only gets to make fun of Johnny Storm!
That's me. Ben Grimm. Now change him back right now!
Yeah! You tell 'em, Ben!
FOOMP
Have fun in Tinyland, chump!
Oh.
Huh? Hey, whoa!
That's it! Now you gone and done it!
Hah! Yer like a little cheese curl!
SKRASH
Guff!

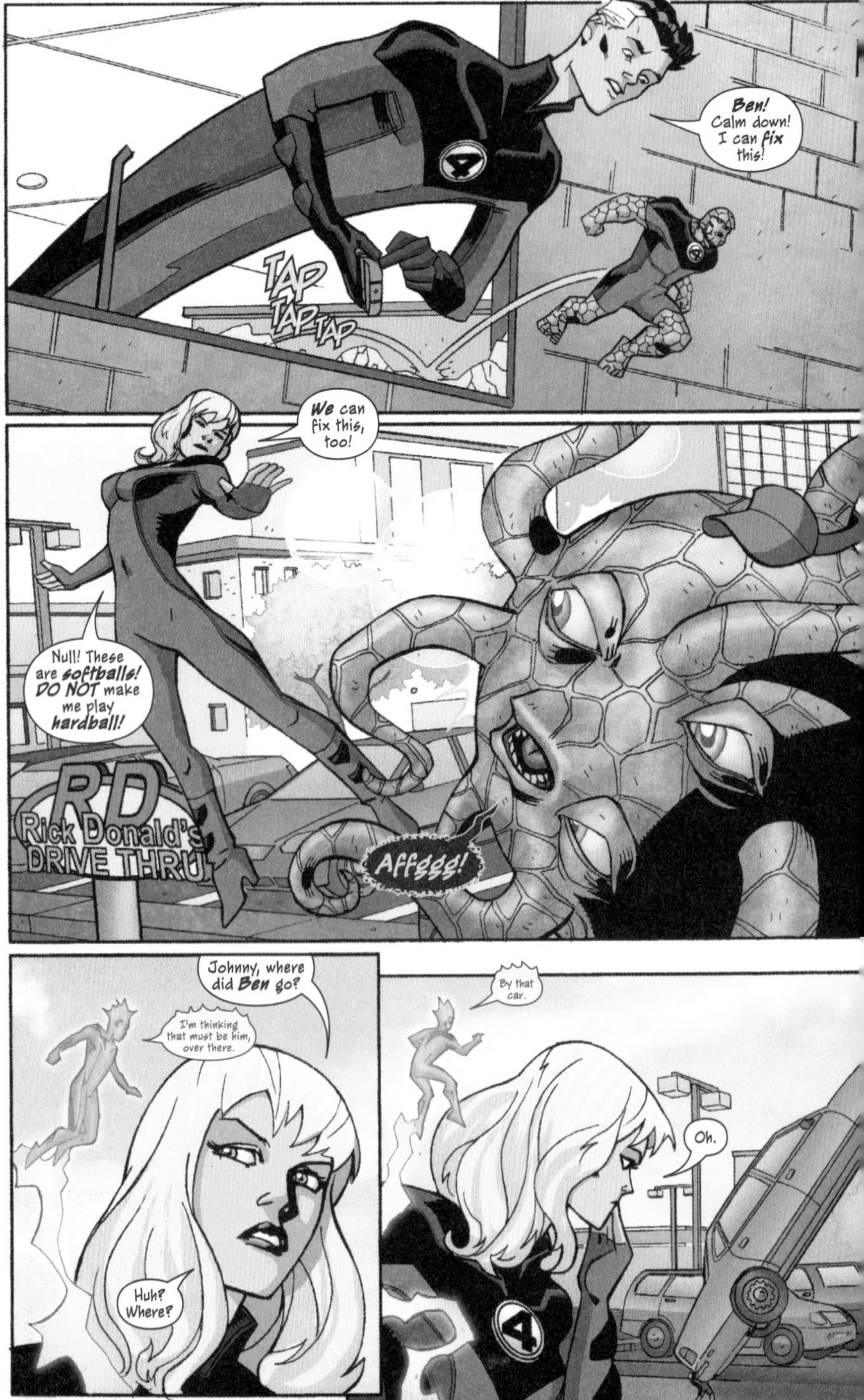
Ben! Calm down! I can fix this!
TAP TAP TAP
We can fix this, too!
Null! These are softballs! DO NOT make me play hardball!
RD
Rick Donald's DRIVE THRU
Affggg!
Johnny, where did Ben go?
I'm thinking that must be him, over there.
Huh? Where?
By that car.
Oh.

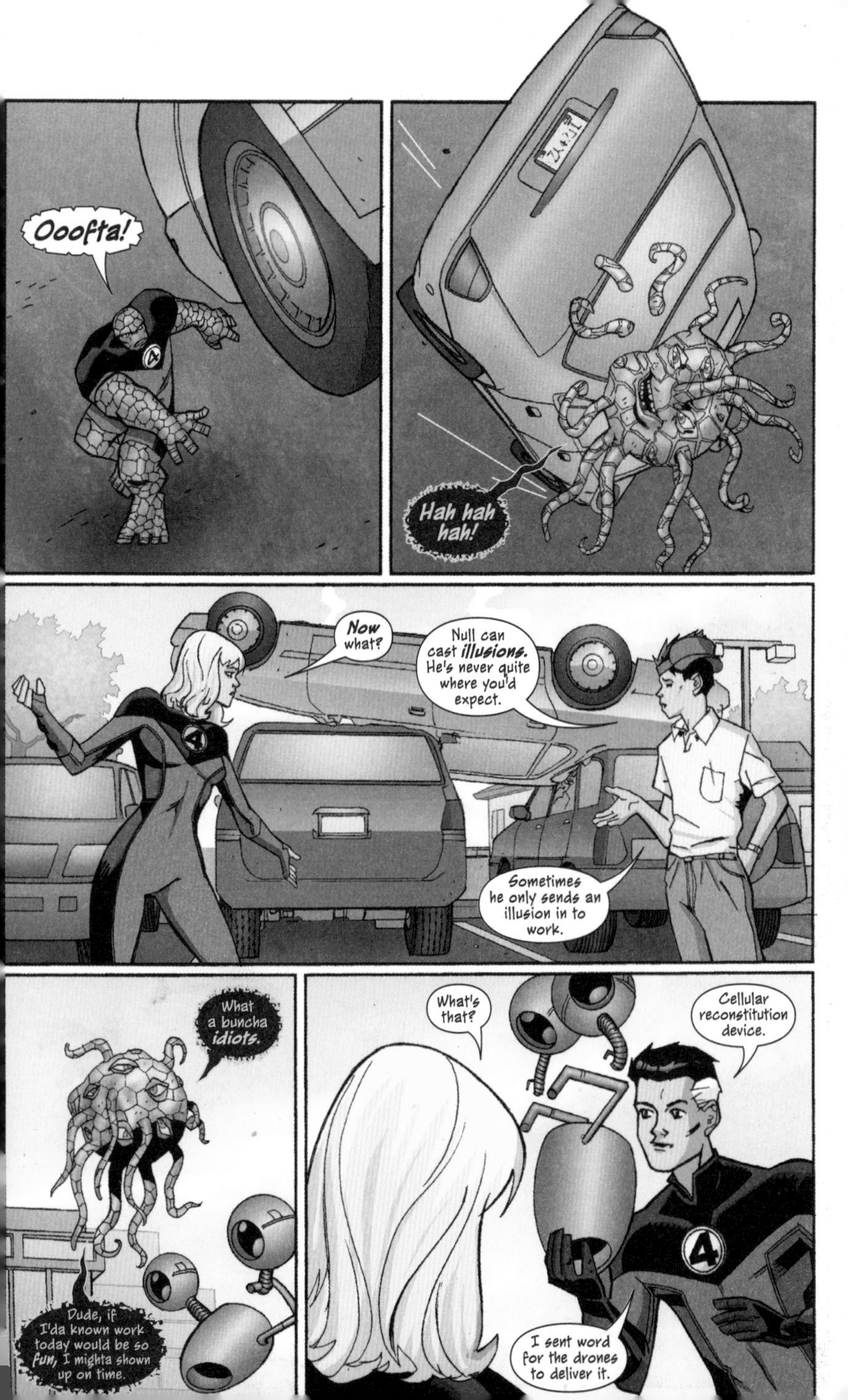

Ooofta!
Hah hah hah!
Now what?
Null can cast illusions. He's never quite where you'd expect.
Sometimes he only sends an illusion in to work.
What a buncha idiots.
Dude, if I'da known work today would be so fun, I mighta shown up on time.
What's that?
Cellular reconstitution device.
I sent word for the drones to deliver it.

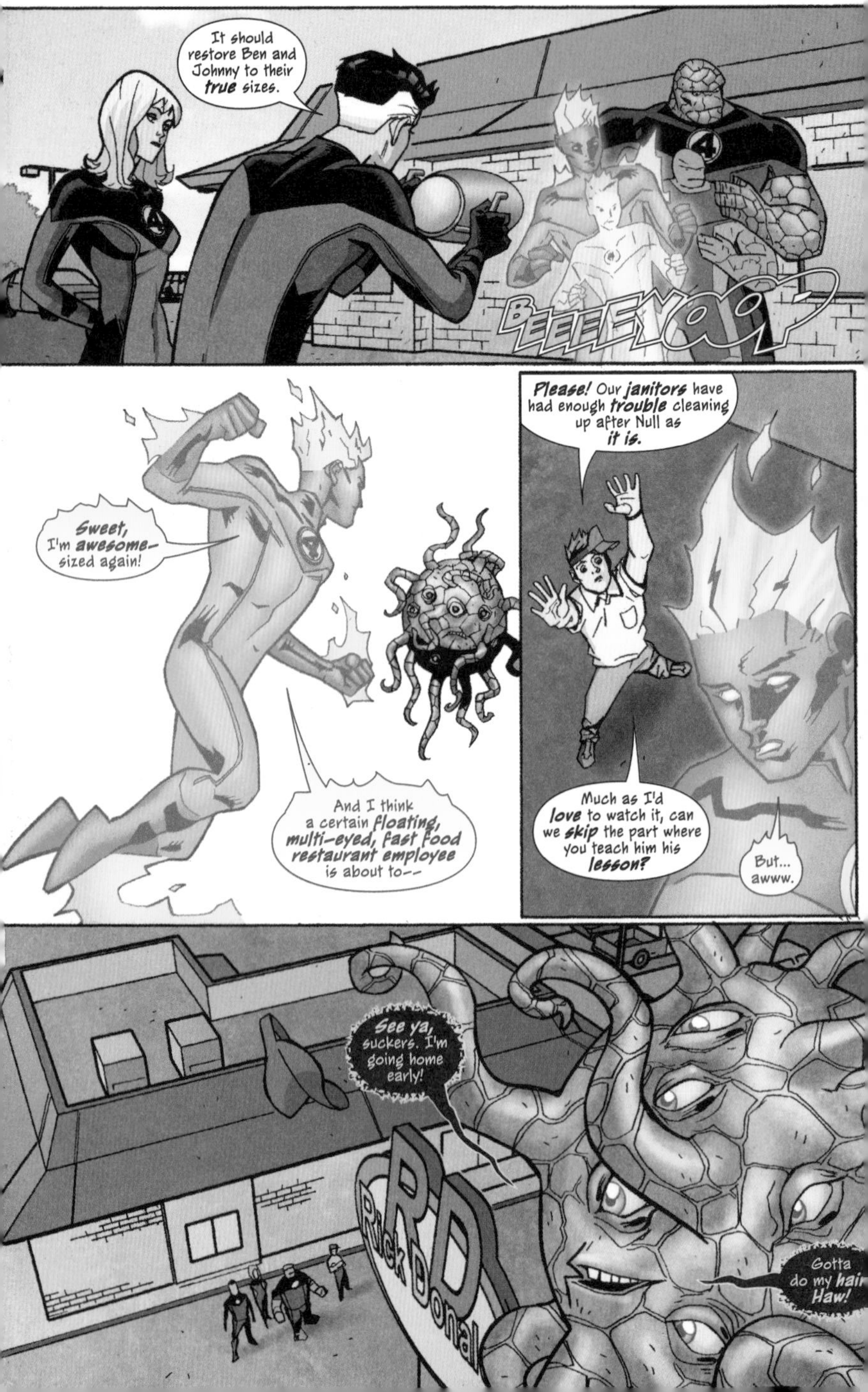
It should restore Ben and Johnny to their *true* sizes.
Sweet, I'm *awesome*-sized again!
And I think a certain *floating, multi-eyed, fast food restaurant employee* is about to--
Please! Our *janitors* have had enough *trouble* cleaning up after Null as *it is.*
Much as I'd *love* to watch it, can we *skip* the part where you teach him his *lesson?*
But... awww.
See ya, suckers. I'm going home early!
RD
Rick Donal
Gotta do my hai
Haw!

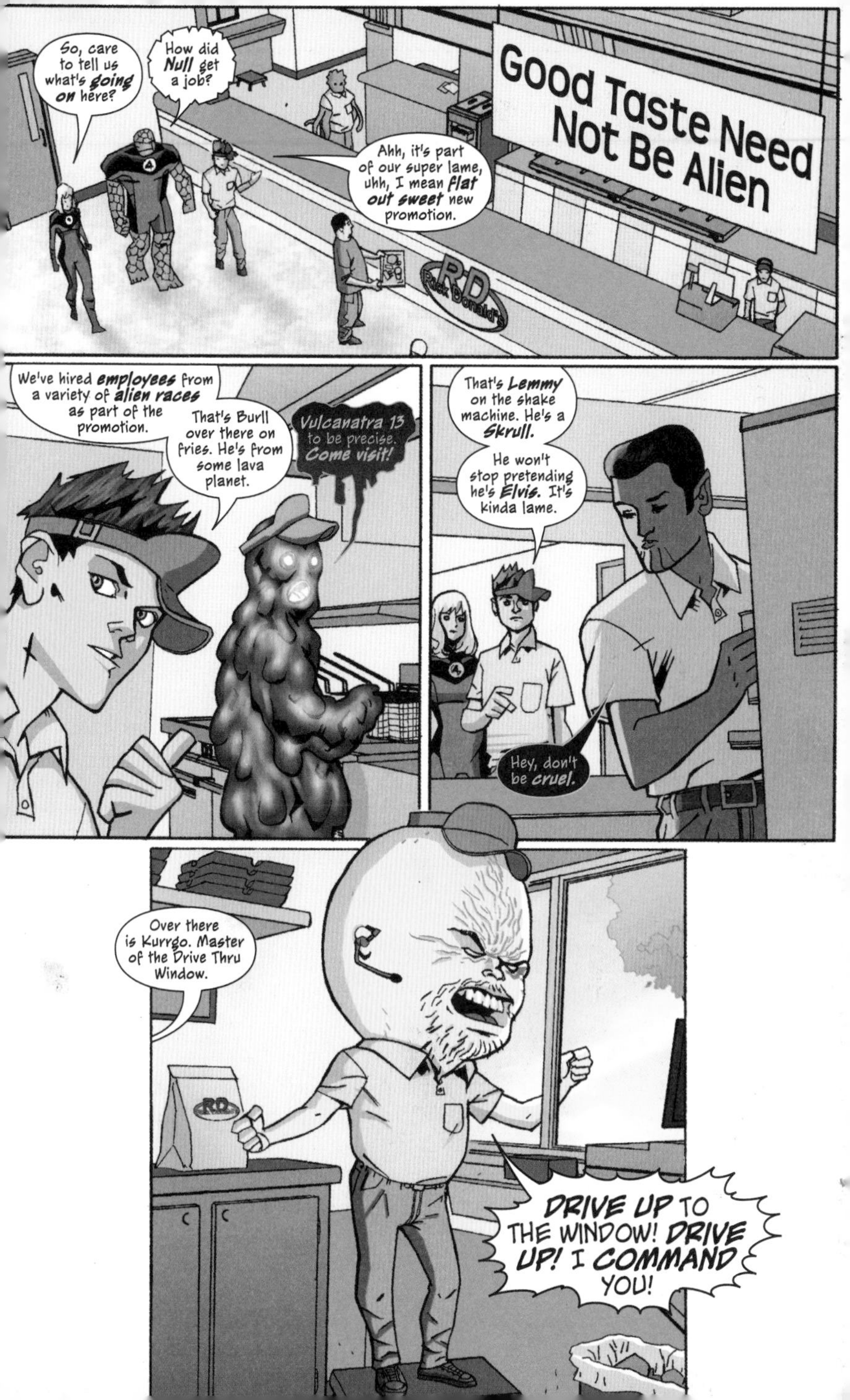
So, care to tell us what's going on here?
How did Null get a job?
Good Taste Need Not Be Alien
Ahh, it's part of our super lame, uhh, I mean flat out sweet new promotion.
RD Rick Donald's
We've hired employees from a variety of alien races as part of the promotion.
That's Burll over there on fries. He's from some lava planet.
Vulcanatra 13 to be precise. Come visit!
That's Lemmy on the shake machine. He's a Skrull.
He won't stop pretending he's Elvis. It's kinda lame.
Hey, don't be cruel.
Over there is Kurrgo. Master of the Drive Thru Window.
RD
DRIVE UP TO THE WINDOW! DRIVE UP! I COMMAND YOU!

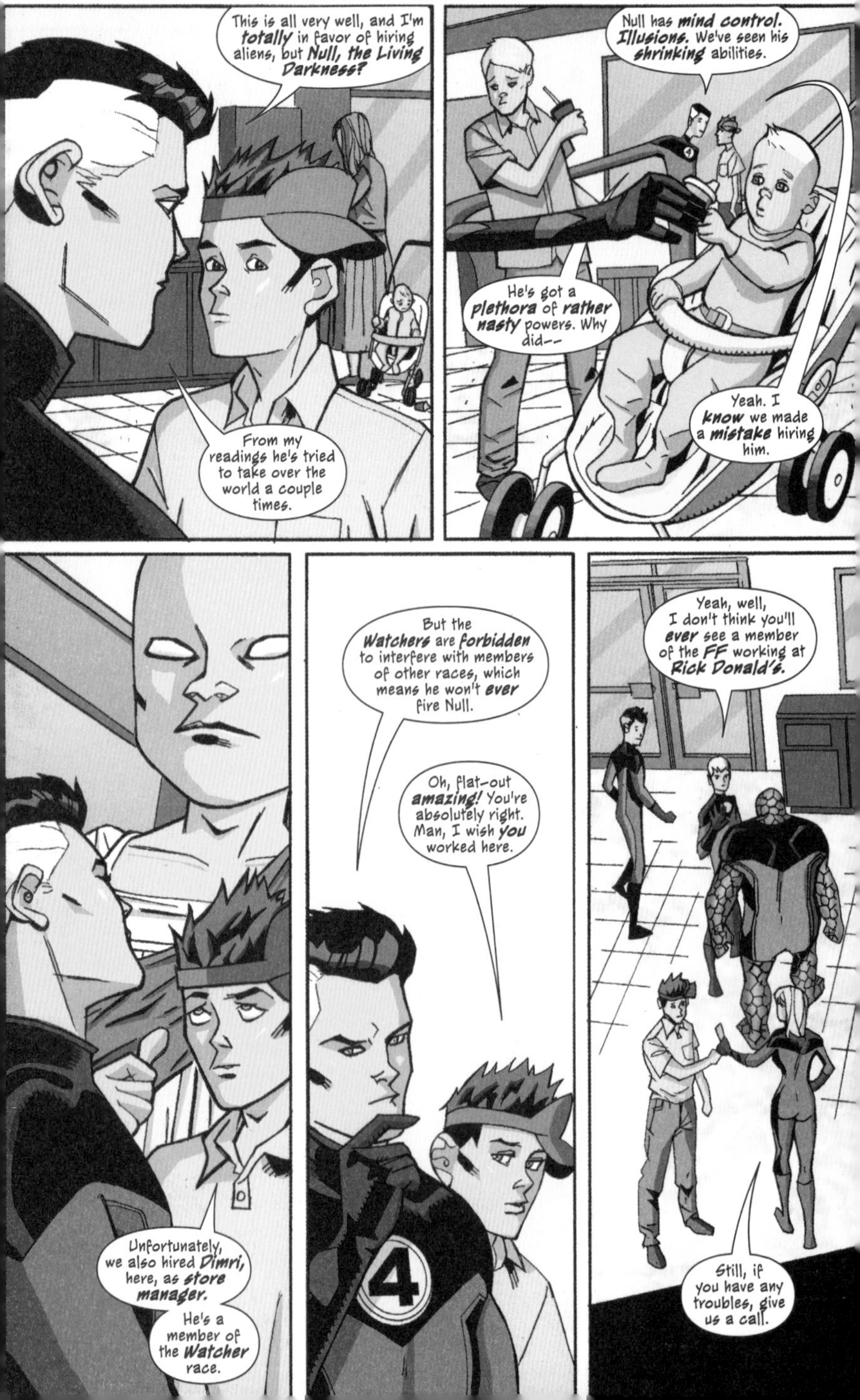
This is all very well, and I'm totally in favor of hiring aliens, but Null, the Living Darkness?
From my readings he's tried to take over the world a couple times.
Null has mind control. Illusions. We've seen his shrinking abilities.
He's got a plethora of rather nasty powers. Why did--
Yeah. I know we made a mistake hiring him.
Unfortunately, we also hired Dimri, here, as store manager.
He's a member of the Watcher race.
But the Watchers are forbidden to interfere with members of other races, which means he won't ever fire Null.
Oh, flat-out amazing! You're absolutely right. Man, I wish you worked here.
Yeah, well, I don't think you'll ever see a member of the FF working at Rick Donald's.
Still, if you have any troubles, give us a call.

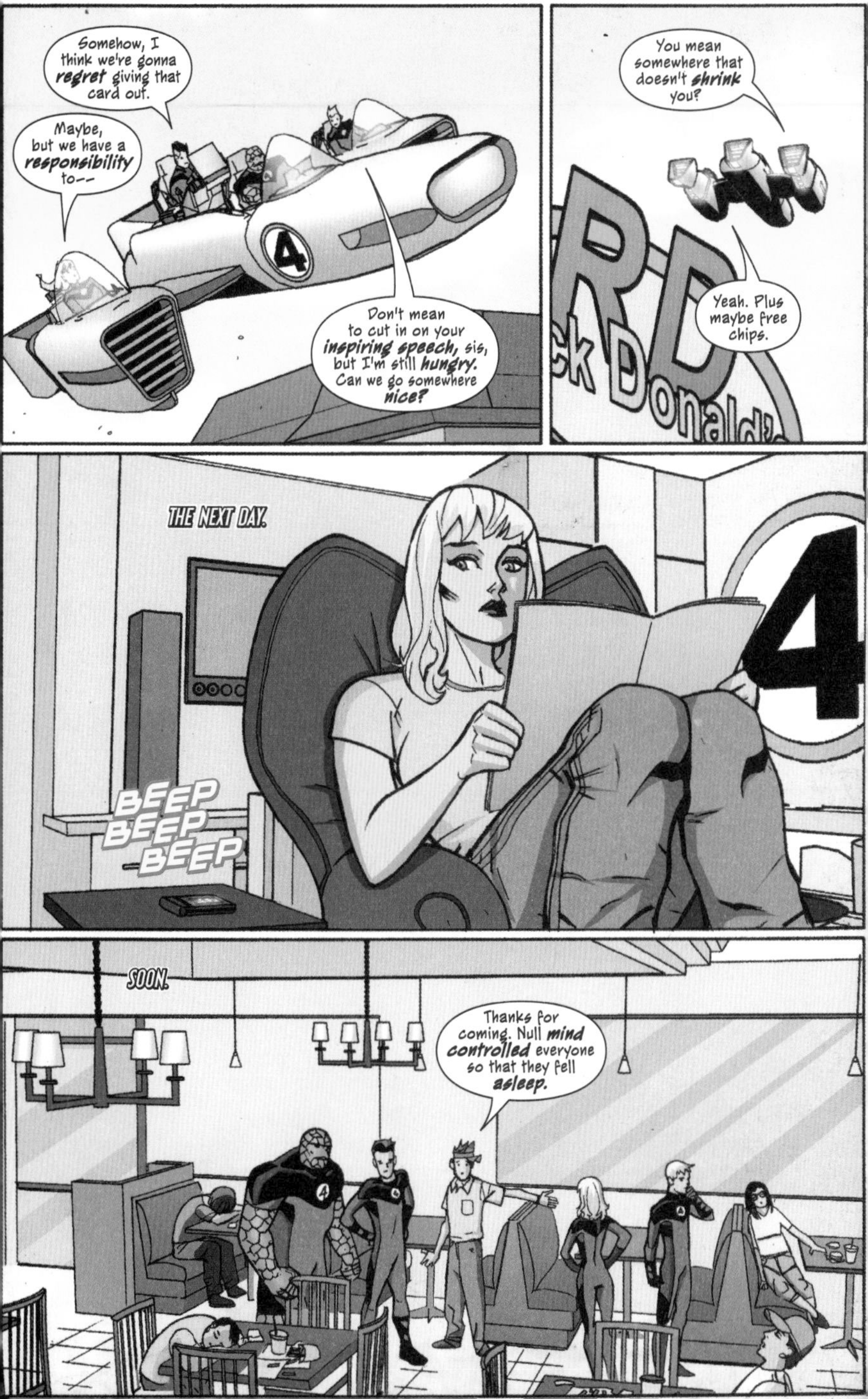
Somehow, I think we're gonna regret giving that card out.
Maybe, but we have a responsibility to--
Don't mean to cut in on your inspiring speech, sis, but I'm still hungry. Can we go somewhere nice?
You mean somewhere that doesn't shrink you?
Yeah. Plus maybe free chips.
ck Donald's
THE NEXT DAY.
BEEP BEEP BEEP
SOON.
Thanks for coming. Null mind controlled everyone so that they fell asleep.

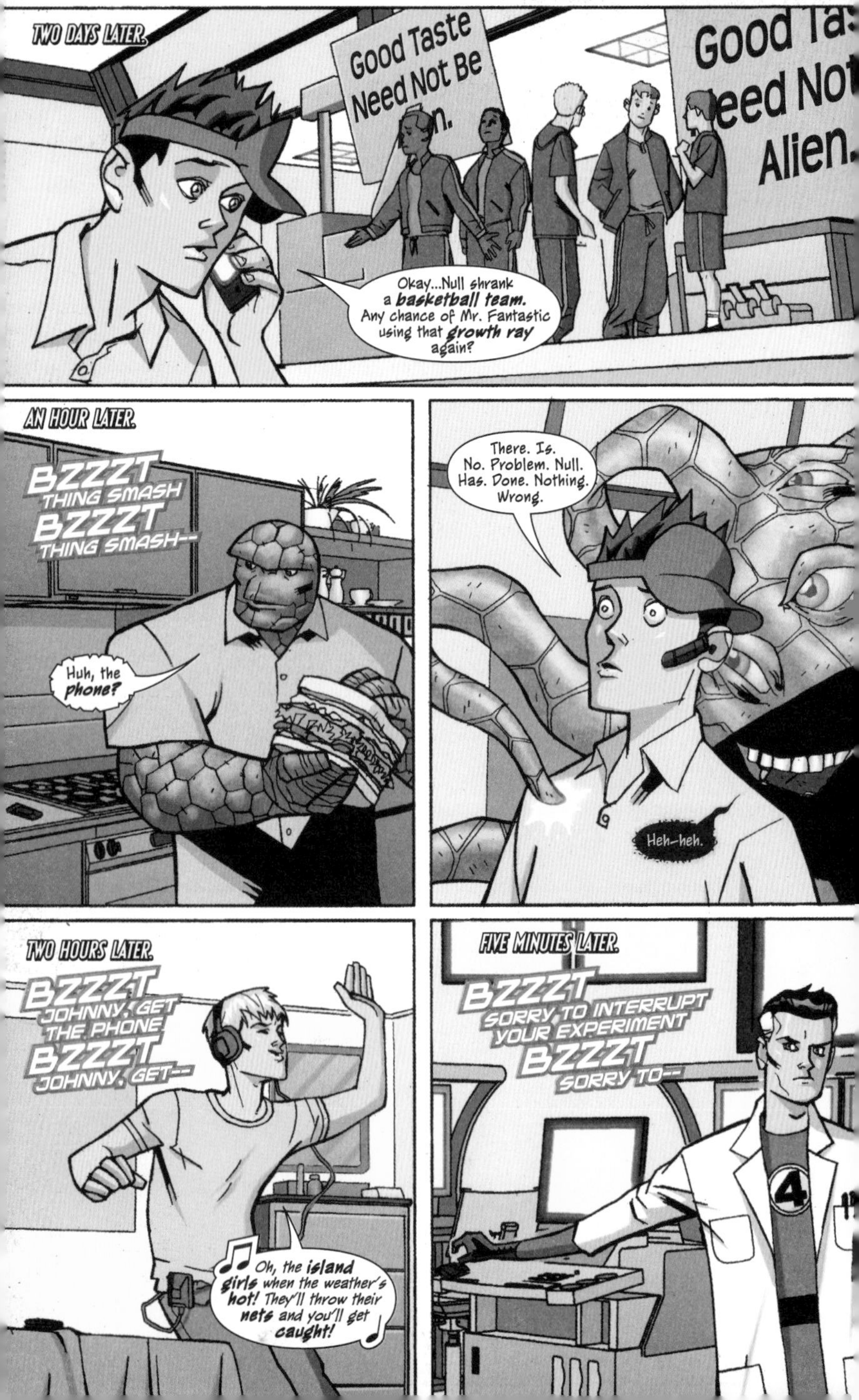
TWO DAYS LATER.
Good Taste Need Not Be ...n.
Good Ta... ...eed Not Alien.
Okay...Null shrank a basketball team. Any chance of Mr. Fantastic using that growth ray again?
AN HOUR LATER.
BZZZT THING SMASH BZZZT THING SMASH--
Huh, the phone?
There. Is. No. Problem. Null. Has. Done. Nothing. Wrong.
Heh-heh.
TWO HOURS LATER.
BZZZT JOHNNY, GET THE PHONE. BZZZT JOHNNY, GET--
Oh, the island girls when the weather's hot! They'll throw their nets and you'll get caught!
FIVE MINUTES LATER.
BZZZT SORRY TO INTERRUPT YOUR EXPERIMENT BZZZT SORRY TO--

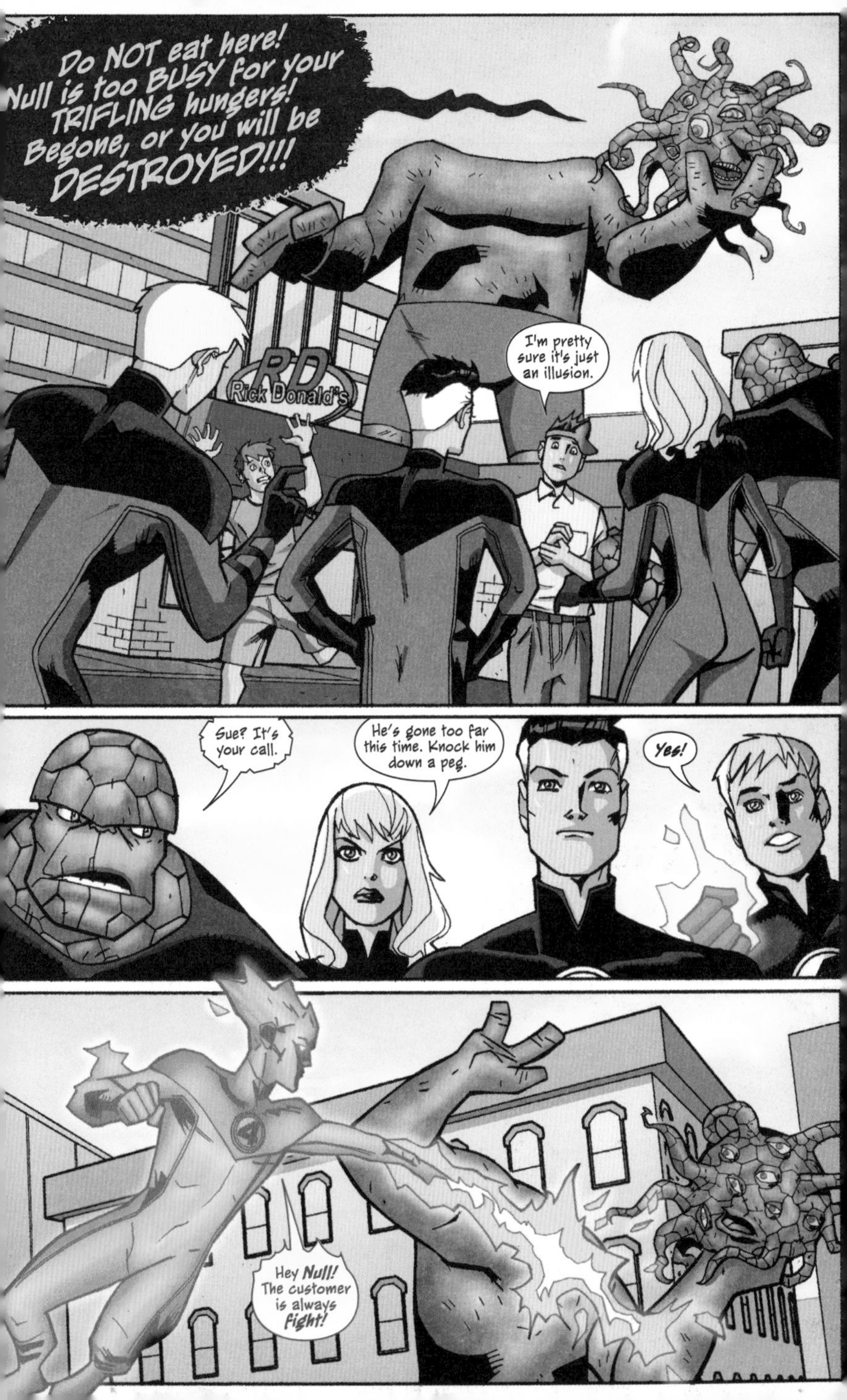
Do NOT eat here! Null is too BUSY for your TRIFLING hungers! Begone, or you will be DESTROYED!!!
RD Rick Donald's
I'm pretty sure it's just an illusion.
Sue? It's your call.
He's gone too far this time. Knock him down a peg.
Yes!
Hey Null! The customer is always fight!

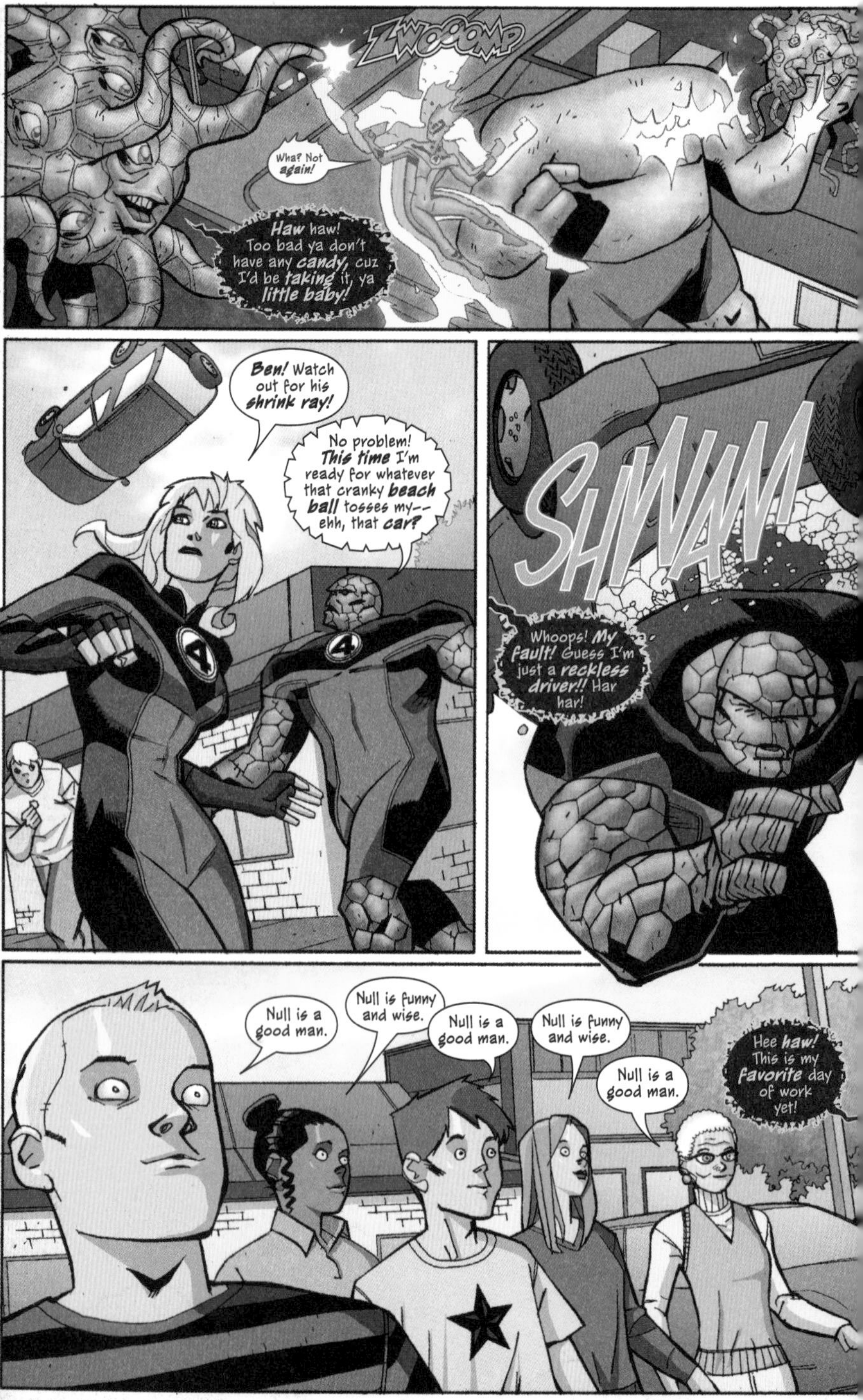
ZWOOOMP
Wha? Not again!
Haw haw! Too bad ya don't have any candy, cuz I'd be taking it, ya little baby!
Ben! Watch out for his shrink ray!
No problem! This time I'm ready for whatever that cranky beach ball tosses my-- ehh, that car?
SHWAM
Whoops! My fault! Guess I'm just a reckless driver!! Har har!
Null is a good man.
Null is funny and wise.
Null is a good man.
Null is funny and wise.
Null is a good man.
Hee haw! This is my favorite day of work yet!

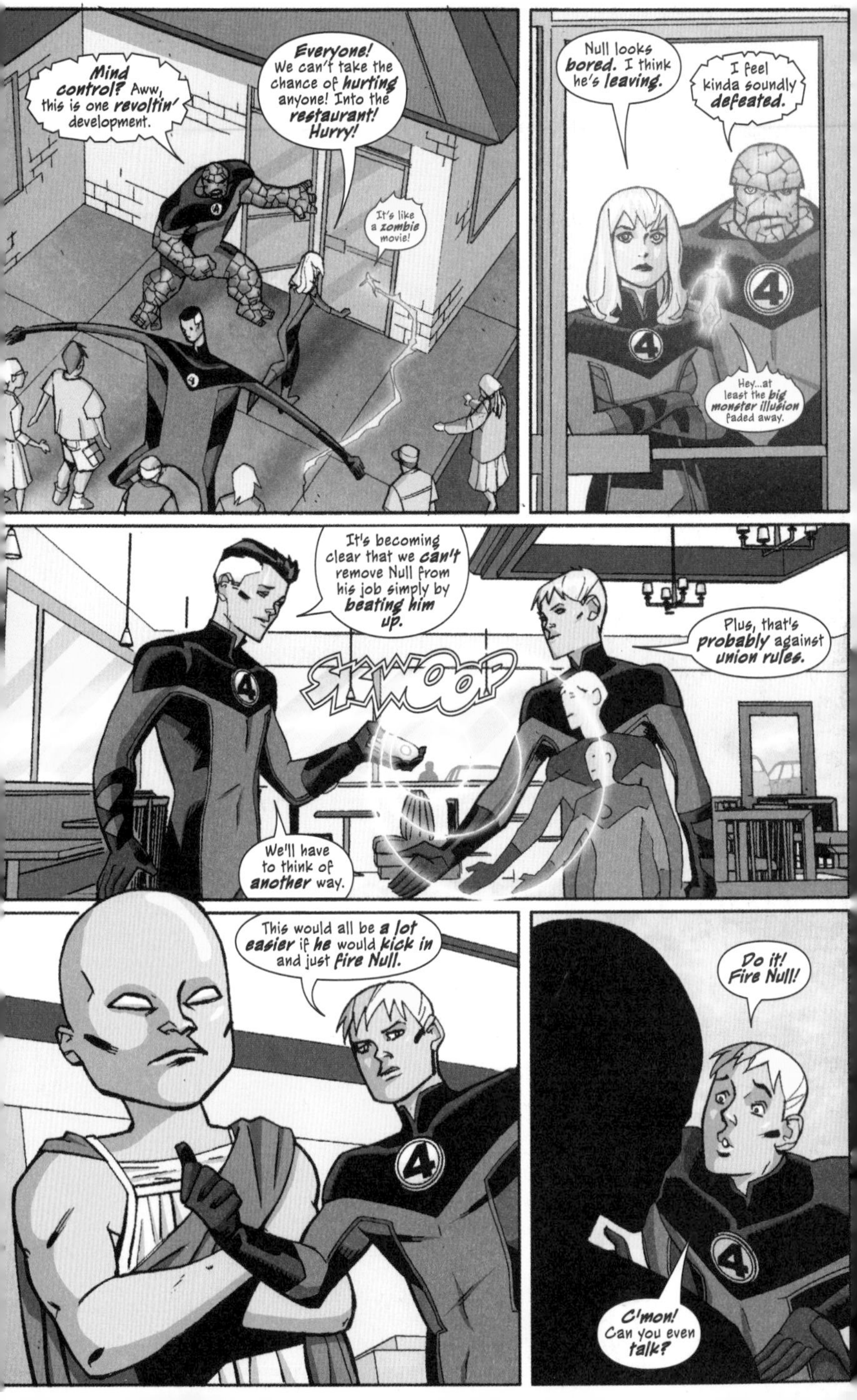

Mind control? Aww, this is one revoltin' development.
Everyone! We can't take the chance of hurting anyone! Into the restaurant! Hurry!
It's like a zombie movie!
Null looks bored. I think he's leaving.
I feel kinda soundly defeated.
Hey...at least the big monster illusion faded away.
It's becoming clear that we can't remove Null from his job simply by beating him up.
Plus, that's probably against union rules.
SKWOOP
We'll have to think of another way.
This would all be a lot easier if he would kick in and just fire Null.
Do it! Fire Null!
C'mon! Can you even talk?

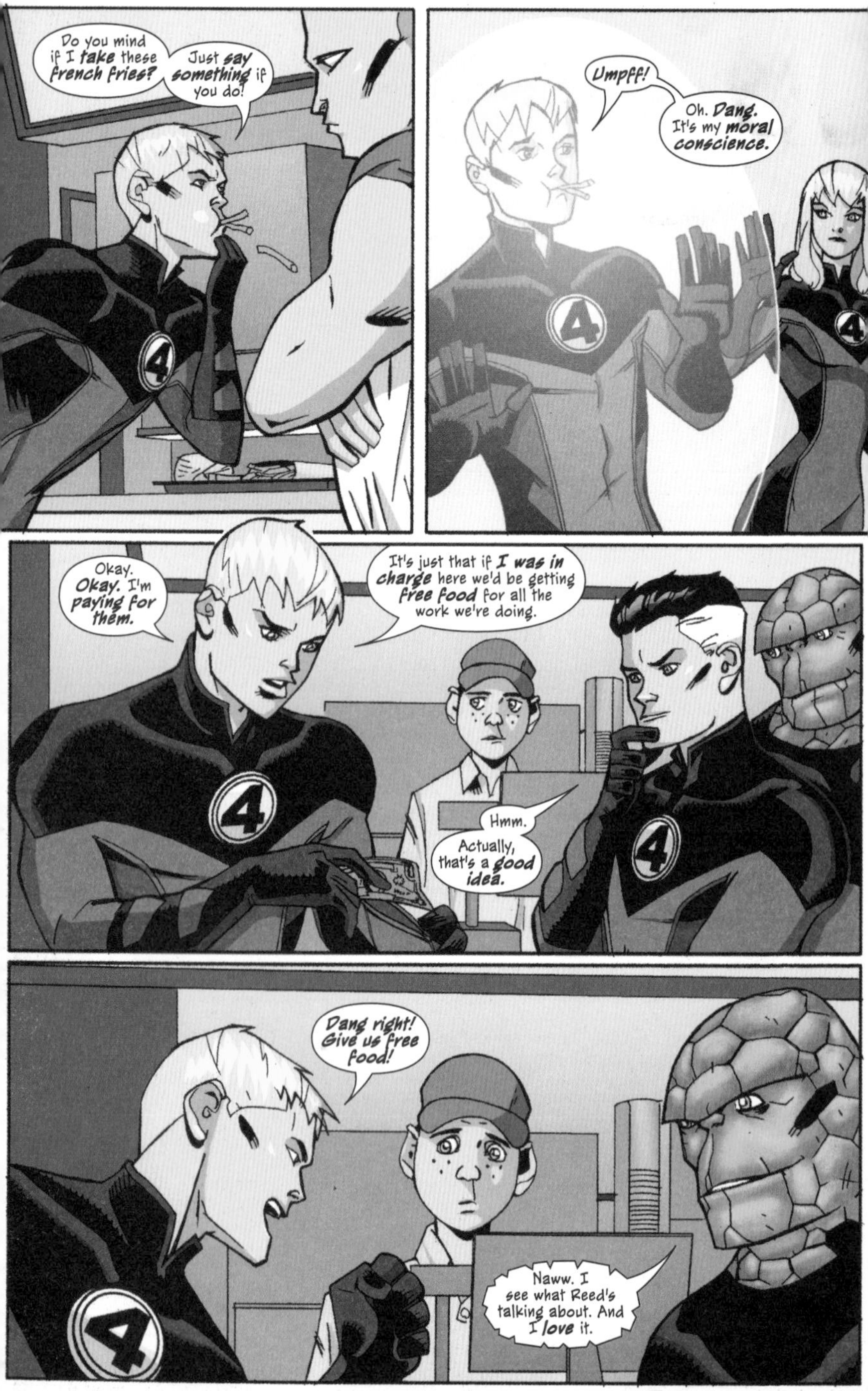
Do you mind if I take these french fries?
Just say something if you do!
Umpff!
Oh. Dang. It's my moral conscience.
Okay. Okay. I'm paying for them.
It's just that if I was in charge here we'd be getting free food for all the work we're doing.
Hmm.
Actually, that's a good idea.
Dang right! Give us free food!
Naww. I see what Reed's talking about. And I love it.

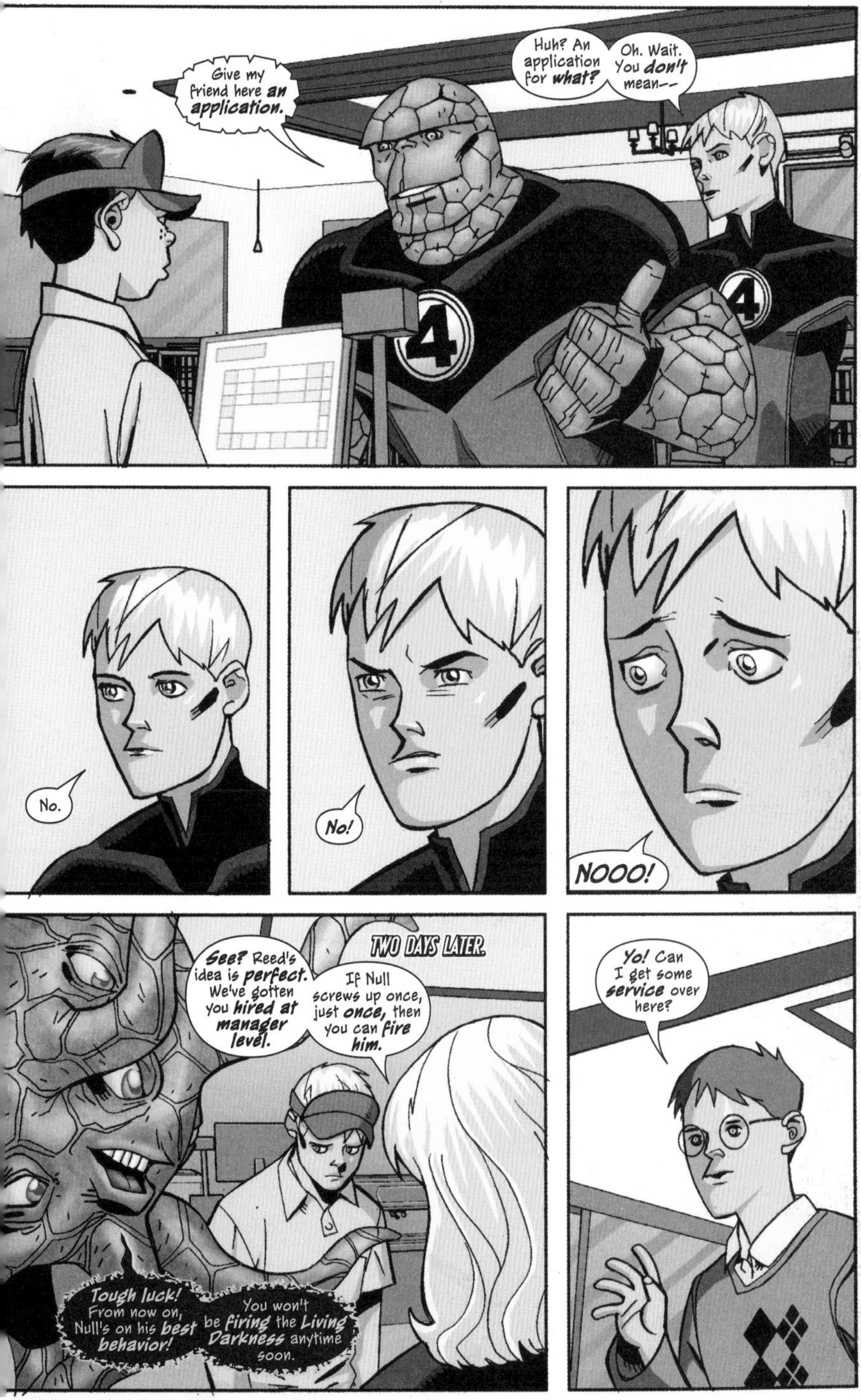
Give my friend here an application.
Huh? An application for what?
Oh. Wait. You don't mean--
No.
No!
NOOO!
See? Reed's idea is perfect. We've gotten you hired at manager level.
TWO DAYS LATER.
If Null screws up once, just once, then you can fire him.
Tough luck! From now on, Null's on his best behavior!
You won't be firing the Living Darkness anytime soon.
Yo! Can I get some service over here?

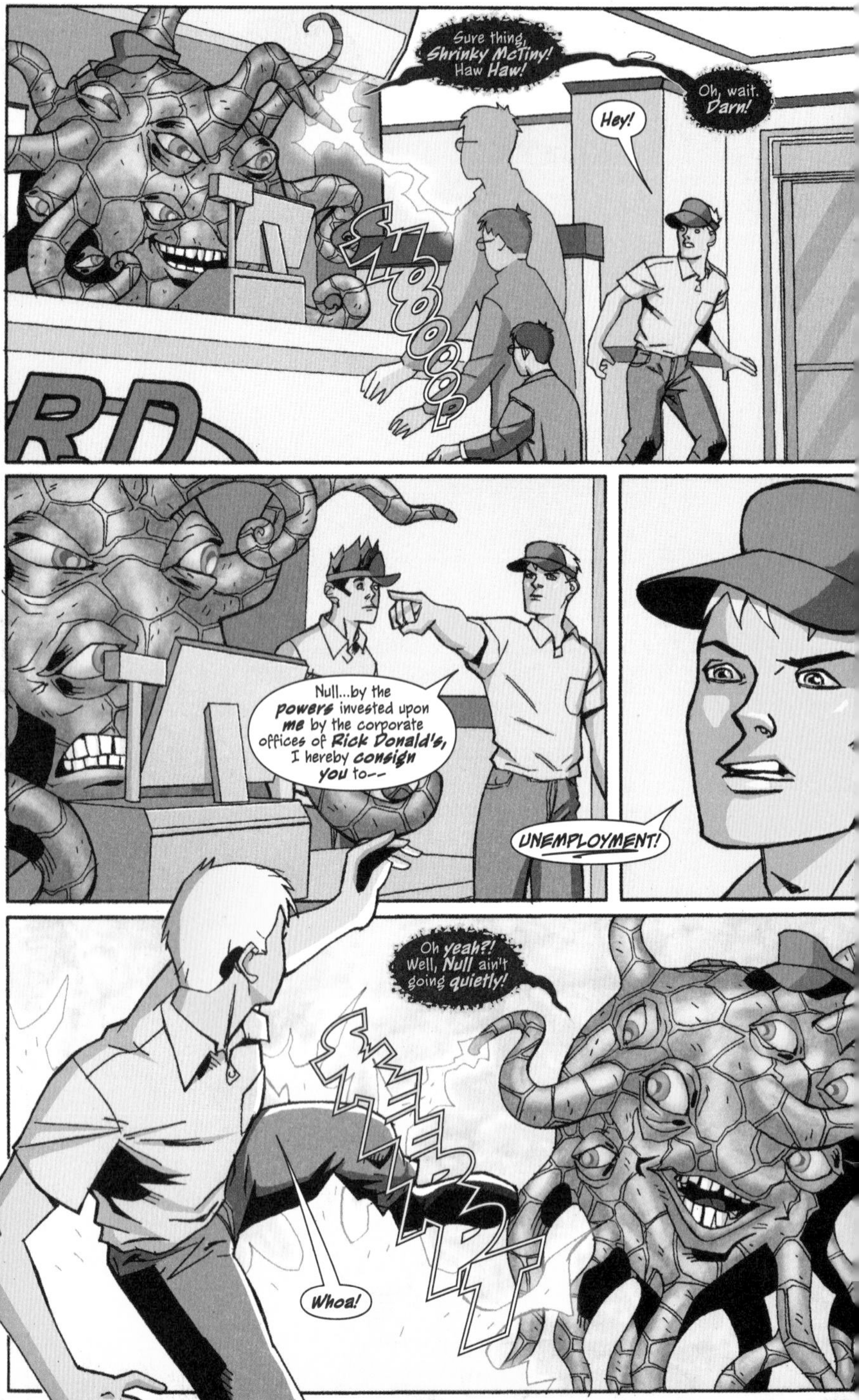

Sure thing, Shrinky McTiny! Haw Haw!
SHHOOOOOP
Hey!
Oh, wait. Darn!
Null...by the powers invested upon me by the corporate offices of Rick Donald's, I hereby consign you to--
UNEMPLOYMENT!
Oh yeah?! Well, Null ain't going quietly!
Whoa!

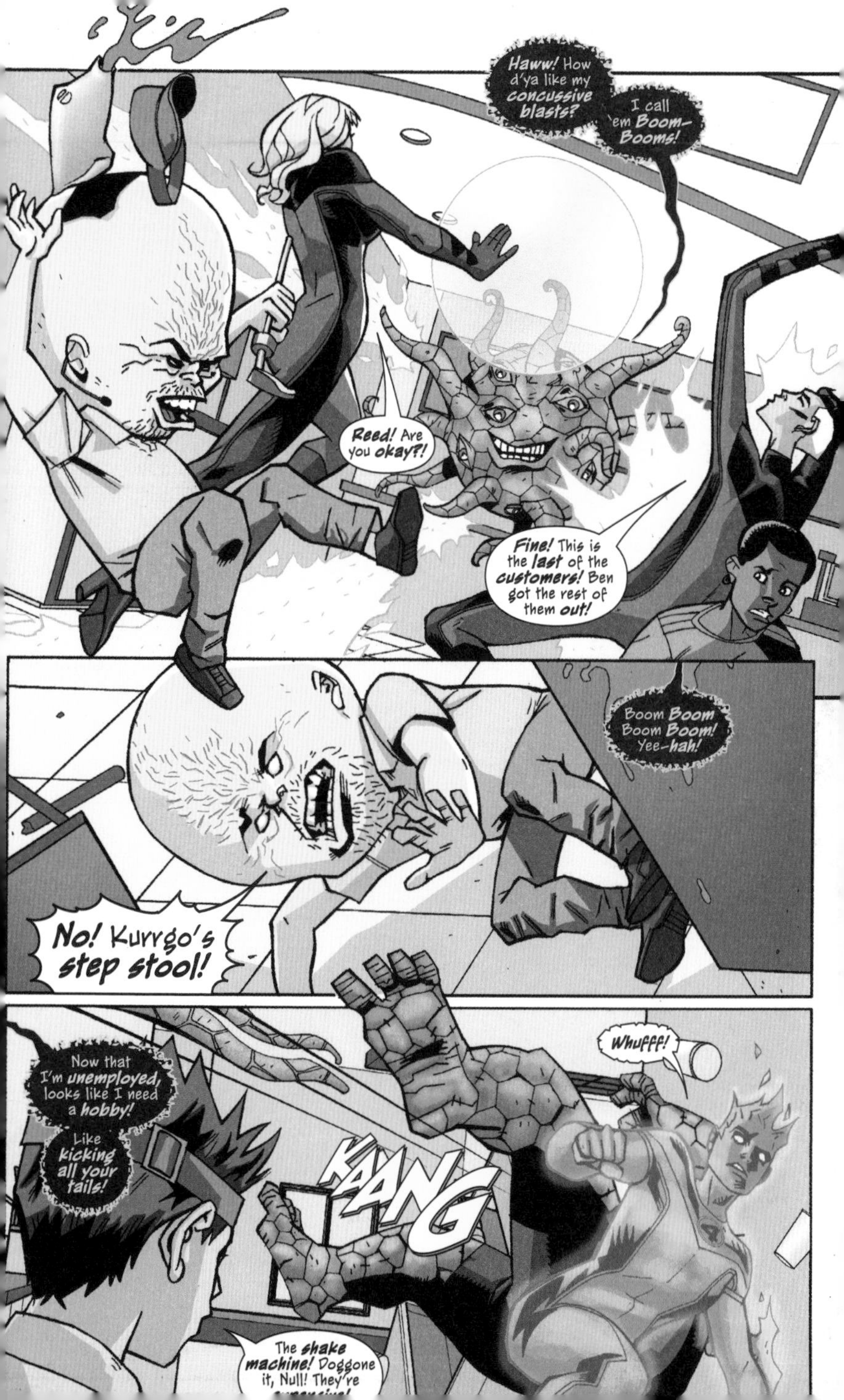
Haww! How d'ya like my concussive blasts?
I call 'em Boom-Booms!
Reed! Are you okay?!
Fine! This is the last of the customers! Ben got the rest of them out!
Boom Boom Boom Boom! Yee-hah!
No! Kurrgo's step stool!
Now that I'm unemployed, looks like I need a hobby!
Like kicking all your tails!
Whufff!
KAANG
The shake machine! Doggone it, Null! They're

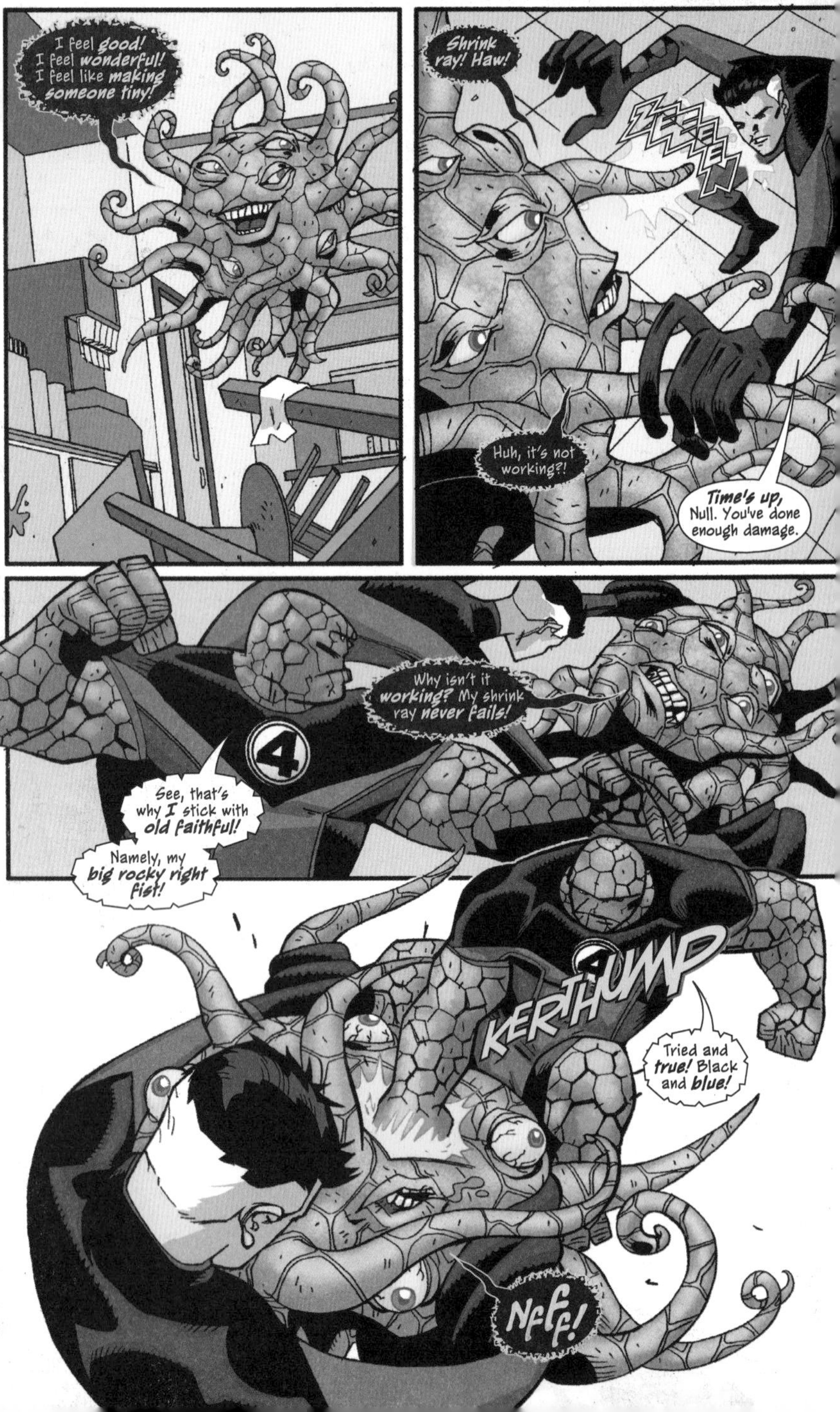
I feel good! I feel wonderful! I feel like making someone tiny!
Shrink ray! Haw!
ZEEEEEN
Huh, it's not working?!
Time's up, Null. You've done enough damage.
Why isn't it working? My shrink ray never fails!
See, that's why I stick with old faithful!
Namely, my big rocky right fist!
KERTHUMP
Tried and true! Black and blue!
Nfff!

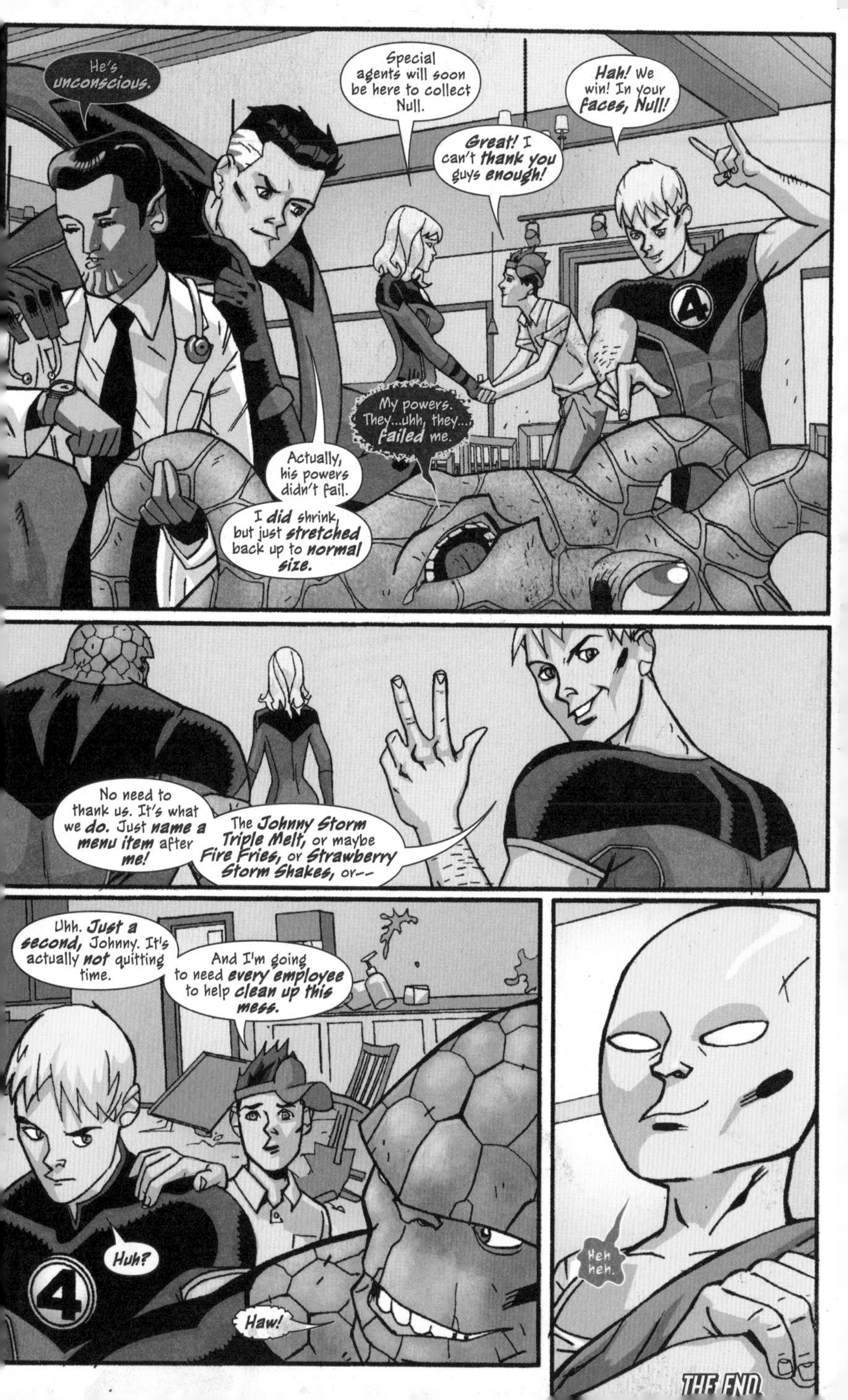
He's unconscious.
Special agents will soon be here to collect Null.
Hah! We win! In your faces, Null!
Great! I can't thank you guys enough!
My powers. They...uhh, they... failed me.
Actually, his powers didn't fail.
I did shrink, but just stretched back up to normal size.
No need to thank us. It's what we do. Just name a menu item after me!
The Johnny Storm Triple Melt, or maybe Fire Fries, or Strawberry Storm Shakes, or--
Uhh. Just a second, Johnny. It's actually not quitting time.
And I'm going to need every employee to help clean up this mess.
Huh?
Haw!
Heh heh.
THE END